THE
PLACE
OF
SHINING
LIGHT

Also by Nazneen Sheikh

Ice Bangles

Chopin People

Heartbreak High

Camels Can Make You Homesick and Other Stories

Tea and Pomegranates:
A Memoir of Food, Family and Kashmir

Moon over Marrakech:
A Memoir of Loving Too Deeply in a Foreign Land

THE
PLACE
OF
SHINING
LIGHT

NAZNEEN SHEIKH

ANANSI

Published in Canada in 2015 by House of Anansi Press Inc.

House of Anansi Press
110 Spadina Avenue, Suite 801
Toronto, ON, M5V 2K4
Tel. 416-363-4343
Fax 416-363-1017
www.houseofanansi.com

House of Anansi Press is committed to protecting our natural environment.
As part of our efforts, the interior of this book is printed on paper that contains
100% post-consumer recycled fibres, is acid-free, and is processed chlorine-free.

19 18 17 16 15   1 2 3 4 5

Library and Archives Canada Cataloguing in Publication

Sheikh, Nazneen, author
The place of shining light / Nazneen Sheikh.

Issued in print and electronic formats.
ISBN 978-1-4870-0014-1 (pbk.).—ISBN 978-1-4870-0015-8 (html)

I. Title.

PS8587.H379P53 2015C813'.54 C2015-902051-4
C2015-902052-2

Book design: Alysia Shewchuk

*We acknowledge for their financial support of our publishing program
the Canada Council for the Arts, the Ontario Arts Council, and the Government of
Canada through the Canada Book Fund.*

Printed and bound in Canada

MIX
Paper from
responsible sources
FSC® C004071

For Laara, Zorana, Lotus, and Ciaran

THE
PLACE
OF
SHINING
LIGHT

ONE

THE HALF-TRUCK MOVED WITH great speed along the rutted road through eastern Afghanistan. The route from the Bamiyan valley to Torkham, Pakistan, was not exactly a joyride. But the driver did not have to bother about slowing down for potholes; the seventy-kilogram package he was transporting had withstood war and destruction for almost five thousand years.

Adeel, the man seated next to the driver, kept a semi-automatic rifle at his feet and had a revolver tucked into a holster under his waistcoat. His face was gentle and his physique deceptively slight. He chain-smoked steadily while staring out the window. Two hours earlier he had undergone a unique yet troubling experience that had left him feeling disoriented.

Adeel was a passionate man often ashamed of the intensity of his responses and the bewildering array of emotions evoked in him by various circumstances. He had spent fifteen years in the army and his last assignment, three years

1

ago, had been with the Pakistani patrol team on the Siachen Glacier. The glacier, seventy-eight kilometres in length and eighteen thousand feet above sea level, was called the "highest battleground on earth." The area was hotly contested by India and Pakistan, as though an extra foot of snow and ice on either side could alter the nature of the conflict. The boundaries of the glacier separated India from Central Asia and Pakistan from China. Adeel was a seasoned mountain climber and a marksman of exceptional skills and he had learned to endure cold and silence well. The stillness of his mountaintop aerie had taught him that his skills of observation could be polished like the facets of a gem. The high-powered lenses of the binoculars he used to survey the ridges of the glacier sometimes played tricks on his mind. A fold of snow could easily become the figure of a man, though an actual man never did appear. Watching the unchanging vastness day after day also gave rise to boredom, and Adeel would allow his mind to wander. Even the hope that an animal might suddenly appear on the glacier—an animal he would shoot, splattering its crimson blood across the white snow—seemed to fade and wither away with time.

At the end of his mountain assignment, Adeel obtained a mysterious discharge from the army and embarked on equally mysterious missions that were presented to him by people he hardly knew but who seemed to have a dossier of his multiple skills. He had been singled out for his athletic abilities and reliability, and was often approached with assignments along these lines. If his brain had been examined during one of these briefings, it would have displayed a seemingly endless grid of interconnected responses. While the details were still being explained, he had already mentally executed the task.

Adeel was on a new assignment now and his responsibility was to faithfully complete his task. He had been handed a vehicle with a driver and two sturdy, brutish-looking men who had been chosen for their physical strength. A bread loaf-sized bundle of banknotes had been tossed at him along with three sets of fake identification papers. Adeel didn't say a word; he simply nodded at his employer and walked away. But nothing in his life had prepared him for the emotions he experienced nine hours later in a torch-lit cave on the cliffs of Bamiyan. The four-foot-high stone statue facing him — a stunning example of Buddhist art that had been placed here by the fourth-century cave dwellers of the region — turned his life upside down.

Adeel crawled toward the statue, moved by the serenity that radiated from the stone. The lidless eyes, curving lips, and sculpted stone folds of the robe exuded a hypnotic power. Tears pricked his eyes, his chest constricted, and he wondered if he was having a heart attack. The two men crawling behind him almost collided with him when he stopped moving. Adeel brushed his eyes with one hand and with the other he withdrew a pencil-thin flashlight from his pocket. He clicked it on and aimed it at the head of the statue, moving it downward very slowly. The dust-laden form appeared to be in perfect condition. He moved toward it, pulled off the black scarf wound around his neck, and rubbed it on the face of the sculpture. The sheen of pale and unspoiled marble resembled human skin; his hand moved of its own volition and his fingers cradled the face, stroking it gently.

Outside, a full moon lit the gentle valley of Bamiyan, where two rivers irrigated the land. The destruction wrought six years earlier by Afghan zealots on two gigantic Buddhist sculptures embedded in a cliff wall was followed by excavations for a copper mine in the vicinity. But this historic site formed no part of Adeel's world. Although he knew that there were museums in Pakistan that at least pretended reverence for historical monuments, an ideologically divisive Muslim diaspora meant that he was expected to pay greater homage to artifacts representing Islamic spirituality.

The statue was placed on its side on a heavy woollen blanket and rolled toward the mouth of the cave and onto a wooden wheelbarrow by the two burly men and pushed down the tortuous incline of the cliff face. The primitive wheels of the cart splintered on the rock-strewn path and it stopped as though in protest at this act of outlandish thievery. The cart itself was then lifted and carried down the hill. The statue was wrapped in two padded quilts and placed in the back of the truck. Adeel had been warned about dodging the ragtag group of Afghan government patrolmen, who cheerfully violated their vigilant stance whenever a roll of banknotes was slipped deftly from palm to palm.

Adeel and the men drove out of Bamiyan and headed toward Kabul, hoping to reach the outskirts of the city before dawn. He knew that the night drive through the Afghan interior would pose few challenges, but the capital would be a different matter. A basket of stiff chapattis and a container full of greasy mutton, cooked with potatoes, had been placed in the truck so that food stops would be unnecessary. However, the two men at the back had savaged the entire supply earlier and now complained because they wanted the hot tea that customarily accompanied meals. They churlishly used the quilt-covered package as a resting place for their dirt-laden feet. Adeel looked at them contemptuously and informed them that there would be no stops on the way. He had already confiscated two hashish cigarettes from the driver when the man had foolishly offered one. Sitting in the passenger seat, Adeel methodically drew walnuts out of a bag at his feet and cracked them with his teeth, ate the meat of the nut, and hurled the shells out the window of the moving truck.

For the first time in his life, Adeel was filled with apprehension about his task. The sculpture—always referred to as the "package" by the man who had employed him—had unleashed a series of dangerous questions in his mind, questions that addressed the faith in which he was raised. For a Muslim, devotion was absolute, while the manifestation of faith was a prescribed set of edicts that, for Adeel, had evolved into a series of robotic exercises. On the odd occasions when Adeel entered a mosque, or touched the venerated Koran, or stroked the small amulet his mother had placed around his neck, an incomprehensible vacuum filled his mind. He gave a perfunctory respect to all of these symbols of his faith, but the stone Buddha had done something that none of them was able to do: it had filled him with tranquility, made him feel as if he'd been touched by an infinite universe that was beyond even the scope of his imagination. And Adeel had surrendered to the sensation. He felt as though he was standing at the edge of a pool where strife sank, like a pebble, to the bottom and disappeared forever.

Although, the more disciplined and practical aspect of his nature fought against this surrender, his soul had spontaneously embraced it. Who were these ancient people, he thought, who could create such wondrous art and then disappear without a trace? The Afghan guide who'd led them to the cave mentioned that the Buddhists preceded the invaders who, between the eighth and twelfth centuries, destroyed temples and statues, including the fort of Bamiyan. After the invasions Buddhism declined in the region, and Islam spread throughout all of Afghanistan.

Adeel closed his eyes and tried to force these thoughts from his mind. If he was to complete the theft with which he'd been tasked, he had to empty his mind of all doubts in the few hours it would take to reach Kabul. He needed the large sum of cash offered by the antiquities dealer in Pakistan in order to settle an old family debt. Adeel's widowed mother had been eased out of her comfortable room in the modest family home that had been built by his father and forced into a small, airless room by the spiteful wife of his older brother. Even her kitchen privileges were viewed with disdain by his insensitive sister-in-law. Adeel felt that his weak-willed brother, who had permitted his domineering wife to take such liberties, had dishonoured his mother, and he wanted to build an addition to the house where his mother would have her own living and eating space. The money from smuggling the statue would enable him to begin construction.

As Adeel stared out at the dark night, the winding road illuminated by the truck's headlights, he fought the impulse to order the driver to stop so that he could go around to the back and gaze at the face of the sculpture again. The two burly men who guarded it hailed from the Pakhtunkhwa region of Pakistan, and one of them had spat on the floor, declaring the statue unclean and from the *"farangi."* Adeel toyed with the idea of placing a well-aimed blow at the man's chin to drop him to his knees before deciding to ignore his ignorant gesture. He regarded both men as oxen, dumb brutes who had one purpose, and that was to be beasts of burden. However, they were also fighters who could disarm an assailant without the use of weapons. Adeel knew any display of emotion in front of them could disrupt the chain of command.

For Adeel, the sculpture was a talisman, and proof that war and destruction could never completely erase history. He remembered the village school he'd attended as a teenager, where he was beaten savagely for stealing a book belonging to the history teacher. He had simply meant to go through it at his leisure and then slip it back into the schoolmaster's desk. But he was caught when a boy in his class reported the theft to the teacher. The book was pulled out of Adeel's worn school satchel and the blows of a thin reed cane rained down on his neck and shoulders. When he returned home from school his mother wept as she applied a balm to the red welts, while Adeel completely dismissed the subject of history and abandoned the luxury of intellectual curiosity. He matriculated successfully from the school without reading by consigning lectures to memory.

His father's sudden death had forced Adeel to abandon college and join the army. Adeel blossomed in the military and won approval for his intelligence and his ability to accept discipline and the rigours of physical training. By a stroke of luck he won a place at the military academy and graduated with honours as a second lieutenant. The commanding officer of the unit, Major Zamir, kept a close eye on Adeel and singled him out as an example for the men in his unit. Not wanting to win the disfavour of his friends, Adeel diplomatically kept his distance from his superior. The major was a maverick. He was often seen at the officers' mess hall with his face buried in a book. He was known as a dreamer who occasionally disregarded military protocol. Adeel often felt that Major Zamir belonged to another time, when men wore flowing capes and rode their horses like the wind.

Years later, it was Zamir who arranged for Adeel to be part of the Siachen Glacier patrol unit. At the time, Adeel had noticed with a pang of sorrow the web of fine lines surrounding Zamir's eyes, the hardening of his fine features, and his smoker's cough. The man seemed to have lost his soul somewhere along his dazzling career path. What sacrifice had life exacted from him? Adeel had thanked him for his new position, saluted him, and walked away without realizing that the next time they met would be under vastly different circumstances.

THE FIRST BLUSH of dawn rose over Kabul as the half-truck entered the city. Plonked onto a dusty plain, the city revealed all the ravages of civil unrest—the destruction of property along with defensive barricades, sandbags, and barbed wire. Military vehicles were present, along with trucks bearing NATO symbols. Although the residents of Kabul slept peacefully, elsewhere in the rough sprawl of Afghanistan, bombs exploded, rifles were discharged, and fires raged, burning people and vehicles with relentless frequency.

Adeel, used to sublimating both environments and actions to his will, knew he could easily be out of his depth in Afghanistan. A random barrier or checkpoint could materialize around any bend, creating unmanageable problems. Sleep-deprived, yet with the alertness of a hunter, Adeel knew he had to guide the driver quickly to the road that led out of the city, where a rendezvous had been arranged. They were to meet a man named Gul-Nawaz at a teashop with a green door. Gul-Nawaz had arranged for the local guide, who had led them to the cave, and payment had to be made for his services. The smuggling operation worked through a network of agents who always had to be kept happy. Any slip-up meant that the next border crossing, at Torkham, would not take place.

THE TWO MEN in the back of the truck banged on the panel separating them from Adeel and the driver. Adeel knew they would have to stop, but he told the driver to head in the direction of the highway leading out of town. It took them another twenty minutes to reach the small mud and stucco teashop with the green door. When the driver halted the truck in front of it, the two men in the back jumped out immediately, turning their backs to urinate at the side of the road. Adeel climbed into the back to check on the quilt-wrapped package. Then he returned to the front to pull out the small nylon bag lying under his seat. He counted forty notes and stuffed them in his pocket, zipped the bag, and pushed it back under the seat.

When Adeel banged on the green door, there was no sound from inside. He banged again, heard movement and the sound of a metal bolt sliding back.

When the door opened, a man stood before Adeel, rubbing sleep from his eyes. Behind him were rows of shelves lined with enamel teapots.

"Wait. I have to light the fire," he mumbled and retreated back into the shop.

Adeel followed him. Inside, he pulled the roll of money from his pocket and held it out. "This is for Gul-Nawaz. We need tea. You must hurry."

Gas hissed out of a canister and the Afghan set a kettle of water on the tiny stove. He ignored Adeel, lined up six enamel teapots, and spooned green tea leaves into each one.

"Are you Gul-Nawaz?" Adeel asked.

"Who wants to know?"

"The money is for him. Where is he?" Adeel said sharply and stuffed the roll of notes back into his pocket.

"Don't be frightened," the man said.

Adeel did not respond. He stood silently until he heard the water hissing to a boil. The man swung around, brandishing two teapots in his hands. Adeel leaned forward and took them from him.

"Wait," said the man, lifting a cracked saucer with small crystals of crude sugar.

"No. We are Pakistanis," Adeel said. "Drop the sugar in the teapot."

"And I am Afghan," replied the man, "and you have come to steal in my country."

Adeel's guards entered the room. The Afghan handed them two small bowls, and they grabbed the teapots and stepped back out into the street. Adeel took a third teapot and bowl and headed out to find the driver. The man was kneeling by the side of the road saying his prayers. Adeel placed the teapot and bowl on the hood of the truck and went back into the shop.

"I must leave the money and go at once," Adeel said, ignoring the teapot that was being held out to him.

"Drink your tea. Your journey is long," replied the man.

Adeel took the bowl and swallowed the boiling tea, singeing his tongue.

"How much money do you have for me?" asked the man, holding out his hand.

"Enough," replied Adeel, pulling out the wad of Afghanis and handing them to the man.

Gul-Nawaz counted the notes.

"The man in Torkham waits for you. You must listen to him and move quickly."

"What is his name?" asked Adeel.

"He has your photograph; he will find you."

"Here, this is for the tea." Adeel extended another bill in Afghan currency.

"Even thieves are guests in my country," replied Gul-Nawaz before walking away, ignoring the money.

THE DRIVE TO Torkham was picturesque, as the men travelled through the Kabul gorge, dry plains, and barren mountains. A caravan of lumbering buses, minivans, and even private taxis prompted reckless overtaking exercises. Toll barriers appeared, and buses carrying heavier than allowable loads were penalized. The largely empty half-truck with a quilt-wrapped bundle did not draw any unwarranted attention. As the border into Pakistan and the Khyber Pass inched closer, the flow of people, vehicles, and consumer items cheerfully contradicted the notion that hostilities existed between Pakistan and Afghanistan. The faces, clothing, and attitudes of the people in the frontier town were completely integrated.

For Adeel, who was carefully revising a new plan of action in his mind, the sights and scenes outside the slow-moving truck were of very little interest. His limbs were rigid and tension sat like a band around his lower head and neck. In less than an hour, his life was going to change. He was going to become a fugitive.

The faces of his mother and Major Zamir flitted through his mind. They had both commanded his respect, and he had given it willingly. His mother's fierce love for him would never erode, but if she knew what he was about to do, grief would bludgeon her and, in all probability, she would perish. He had to find a way to reassure her and explain that he would be absent from her life for a while. Zamir, if the news reached him, would be disappointed too, perhaps even angry. He had passed on an invisible mantle of honour to his protegé and would not take Adeel's act of theft lightly.

At the Torkham border, two men in uniform approached the truck. Adeel pulled a brown envelope out of the glove compartment. The envelope contained his national identity card and crisp American fifty-dollar bills; border guards had a preference for U.S. currency. Adeel took off his dark glasses and gazed at the man who'd approached his window. He faced the smirking guard calmly and extended the envelope. The man lifted the edge with the tip of one finger, and then said something to his partner, who was checking the driver's identity card.

The other guard immediately walked around the front of the truck, peered inside the cab, and said, "We thought you would come much later."

"I did not make any stops on the journey," replied Adeel curtly.

He watched as the brown envelope was passed from one man to the other, and curiosity instantly replaced greed in the expressions on their faces. They knew richer and more powerful people had arranged this, and the deal, whatever it was, had to be bigger than the ten fifty-dollar bills in the envelope. Adeel was amused as he saw the guards toy with the idea of making another side deal and then reject the thought: they had to know he was armed, and the steely glare he levelled in their direction was making them uneasy. Their instructions were to let the truck cross the border and to look the other way when a Pakistani truck moved toward it.

The last step was crucial. Adeel and his package had to

change vehicles beyond the border, since vehicles from one country could not enter the other unless they belonged to a foreign aid agency or had a commercial import licence. Once they were safely inside Pakistan, the package would be transferred quickly from one vehicle to another. Wrapped in its heavy cotton quilt, the statue would be protected from prying eyes.

Adeel extended his hand out of the window for his fake ID card to be returned, then nodded to the driver, who started the truck and released the clutch.

The Torkham bazaar was filled with roadside food shops and crowds of people, some carrying bundles on their heads. Adeel felt a rush of adrenaline when he saw a mottled brown truck ahead. The man standing beside it gestured furiously at them. Adeel's driver turned the steering wheel and pulled up parallel to the brown truck.

The two burly men lifted the package from the back, staggering under the weight. For a moment it seemed that the statue might fall, but they managed to straighten up and place it in the back of the brown truck, where Adeel and the driver were now waiting. As the driver put the key in the ignition, Adeel instructed him to stop. He would drive the truck through the Khyber Pass to the city of Peshawar. That was where he would pay off the two muscle men.

The driver of the truck seemed puzzled. "It is not like a car," he said.

"I can drive anything, and I am tired of just sitting here," Adeel said.

"There is a lot of traffic," the driver said, putting his hand on Adeel's forearm. "People try to overtake you and force you off the road."

The driver mistakenly put his hand on Adeel's forearm, who reflexively tensed his biceps muscle before carefully removing the hand from his arm. He had silently indicated his strength to the driver. He then climbed out of the truck, and walked around to the driver's side. Reluctantly, the driver moved over and took his place in the passenger's seat. After he slammed the door shut, Adeel started the truck and smoothly put it into gear. Then he smiled.

"I was in the army. I have a lot of experience driving trucks," Adeel lied.

"Ah! So we are in good hands," the driver said, sounding relieved.

Adeel smoked as he drove, and the driver obligingly lit his cigarettes along the way. Adeel was preparing himself for his first daring act. He was familiar with Peshawar, which teemed with military officials who used the city's magnificent fort as their headquarters. There were also large Afghan housing settlements, the inner bazaars and the pristine, cordoned-off cantonment where the governor of the province resided. When he reached the city, Adeel decided he would make a stop for food and tea. His aim was to find a stall somewhere along the road that was close to the highway leading out of Peshawar. Other than the money that lay in the nylon duffel bag under his seat and his fake ID, Adeel carried an unregistered mobile phone in his pocket and the revolver concealed in an underarm holster. He leaned over and placed the rifle at his side.

The city of Peshawar was noisy; the snarl of engines, the screech of mural-embellished rickshaws, and the sound of police whistles split the air. There were hordes of people riding placidly on scooters and motorcycles through the toxic diesel fumes and the grimy dust. It was a city where a native Pathan was undistinguishable from an Afghan, since both wore the same cap and dress. Here and there a delicate bundle of fabric rode pillion on bicycles next to women with half-covered faces, or sometimes a tiny child sandwiched between two adults. Adeel caught a glimpse of the large, fearful eyes of a woman as he drove past. In that fleeting second his mother's face swam before his eyes and he felt as though a knife had been plunged into his heart. His reflexive discipline asserted itself and he regained his composure, banishing the thought from his mind as quickly as it had entered.

After half an hour of dodging and weaving through traffic he saw a kebab shop with an outdoor charcoal brazier. Although it was mid-morning, the clay ovens spat up piles of steamy naans, and iron skewers threaded with meat and vegetables lined the grill. Groups of men were clustered around, waiting in anticipation.

Adeel parked the truck close to the stand and turned to the driver. "Take the two at the back and get some food. Feed them and then let them have tea as well. I will be back in twenty minutes." Adeel held out a five-thousand-rupee note.

The driver's eyes lit up at the large sum of money. He could order a couple of kilos of meat with that. He grabbed the note, jumped out of the truck, and went to get the men out of the back. All three dashed over to the barbecue stand and elbowed their way past the people ahead of them. Adeel reversed the truck and made a U-turn, narrowly escaping a collision with a car that blew its horn furiously at the unexpected manouevre. His hands felt clammy on the large steering wheel as he sped ahead. It would take the men at least an hour to get through the money and the food—an hour before they realized he was not returning.

TWO

THE CELLPHONE VIBRATED ON the table. Khalid ignored
it. He loathed the telephone and considered it a harbinger
of evil. Good news never came on the phone.

Where was Faisal? he wondered. The phone normally
rested in his nephew's pocket and he answered it efficiently,
erecting a barrier between Khalid and the world.

As he gazed at the red-brick structure being erected on
his estate, a smile lit Khalid's face. This was going to be the
family burial tomb. He had arranged to have verses of the
Koran carved into the stone borders of the multi-arched
structure. The tomb was being built on a small hillock so
that Khalid could contemplate it from the top floor of the
massive pavilion that housed his living quarters.

Khalid had purchased ten acres of rolling hills outside
the city of Islamabad and, over the past five years, had added
structures to his estate in order to house his collection of art.
Very few people in the country knew that his estate existed.
Khalid lived with his small family and the men he employed,

allowing only his extended family and a few antiquities dealers to visit. However, once or twice a year Khalid threw a
party and hired caterers from town who transformed his
open-air patio into a Mughal pavilion. Lights were strung
up to illuminate the pavilions that dotted the estate, rose
petals were strewn on the marble laneways, and all of the
fountains were turned on. Along with the caterers, a clutch
of musicians and dancing girls were hired for the evening.
During the party, Khalid transformed into a boisterous
and genial host. But in the past two years, due to financial
considerations, the party had shrunk; the guest list now
comprised only his family members from Lahore.

Khalid rubbed his aching shoulder and drew his fine
pashmina shawl around him. The remains of his uneaten
breakfast lay in front of him on an ornate tray that was at
least five hundred years old. Nestled between the teapot and
the teacup was the black phone that continued to vibrate.

Khalid, who'd had strange dreams the night before,
looked down at the phone. A sense of dread gripped him.
He resisted the urge to send the tray flying off the table or
hurl the phone against the wall, and, instead, did something
he had not done in years — he answered the phone.

The conversation lasted for forty seconds.

Suddenly, Faisal appeared at his shoulder, "I am sorry,
Chachu," he blurted, noting the phone in Khalid's hand.

Khalid ignored him and made three rapid calls. He spoke
quickly but with authority. He then turned and handed the
phone to Faisal.

"I want you to tell me immediately if a call comes from
Peshawar." He rose from the cane chair and marched toward
a large octagonal building.

The building was Khalid's Allah museum — a place he

had recently begun visiting for longer periods of time. The ground floor housed massive glass-and-wood cabinets that displayed large Korans he had acquired from Iran, Turkey, and some Middle Eastern kingdoms. The gold-leaf calligraphic script glinted as though the gold had been hammered and reduced to ink that very day. In between the cases, rare and ancient carpets hung from the ceiling. The collection itself was priceless and had been assiduously collected over many years.

An outside staircase led to the second floor, where there was a room that had an altar close to one wall. The altar was in fact a miniature *Ka'ba*, the revered stone in the city of Mecca that Muslims circled during their annual pilgrimage. Before the altar was a prayer rug with a large metal bowl containing water, where Khalid would prostrate himself and pray in loud ringing tones.

Despite being a swashbuckling sort who hobnobbed with the Taliban in Afghanistan in search of antiquities and made a fortune in Japan and New York selling those antiquities, Khalid was a troubled man. His younger son, Hassan, who had very little interest in his business, had broken his heart. Hassan had spent a vast sum of his father's money setting up an expensive car dealership, only to lose the total investment in six months. To add insult to injury, Hassan had also secretly contracted a second marriage. Khalid's refusal to accept the new wife — or to even allow her to be received in his home — further alienated father and son. Khalid continued to support his son financially only because Hassan had given him two grandchildren from his first marriage.

Hassan played the role of the dilettante son of a wealthy man to perfection. Sometimes he wandered through the estate acting like a devoted father, playing with his two toddlers; at other times he left to run mysterious errands in town. He texted for hours with the young woman whom he had beguiled into a civil marriage, or he sat before his computer jabbing at the keyboard. He kept a wary distance from his father.

Khalid's entire life had centred on his dream of building a private museum to house his antiquities, and he'd mistakenly thought his son would manage his dream for posterity. The construction of the family burial tomb reflected the pervasive sense of sadness that had flooded Khalid over the past few months.

The news on the telephone had come as a blow to Khalid, and he sought refuge in his spiritual sanctuary, weeping away his dark rage. He had trusted his ISI contact—a brigadier he had known for years—when the man recommended Adeel. Now he was convinced that the brigadier's many assurances regarding Adeel's skills and loyalty had been false. It had taken Khalid close to six months, through a shadowy network of people both in Afghanistan and Pakistan, to acquire the stone sculpture, and he had a guaranteed buyer in hand—at three times the statue's value. The Pakistani buyer had an insatiable appetite for antiquities and enormous wealth at his disposal.

Now, instead of hunting for antiquities, Khalid was going to have to hunt for Adeel.

After two hours, Khalid rose from his prayer rug and walked over to the large room in the next building that he used for business.

Art dealers from all over Pakistan offered Khalid their collections in this garish room, which was heavily carpeted and furnished with faded velvet couches. On the walls, and within two glass-fronted cabinets, priceless objects lay in splendour. The displays were Khalid's way of letting the dealers know that they would have to come up with something that could equal his current collection if they expected him to buy. Today, the room was empty except for Faisal, who handed Khalid his BlackBerry as soon as he entered the room.

"Brigadier sahib, I am looking for a solution," said Khalid to the man on the other end of the phone.

"We will find him," came the brigadier's confident reply.

"Was he the right man for the job?" asked Khalid.

"Absolutely," the brigadier replied. "He has worked for me for years, ever since we pulled him out of the military. He is a machine, not a man. He follows orders."

"It shouldn't be difficult to find him. The truck is brown in colour. I will have to replace it if it cannot be found," added Khalid.

The cost of the shabby yet sturdy truck did not concern Khalid as much as the next phone call he had to make, to the city of Shiraz in Iran.

"Don't worry. ISI has no problem locating people in Pakistan," the brigadier said. "I will be in touch soon with good news."

Khalid knew all about ISI's capabilities. Pakistan's highly controversial intelligence was staffed mostly by military men, and was often accused of running a shadowy empire that ushered in heads of state and liaised directly with foreign governments. Khalid had courted the brigadier, for years, plying him with cases of Johnny Walker Black and even a silver water ewer that predated the sixteenth-century Mughal era by five decades. Khalid had also shared some of his earlier smuggling antics with the brigadier, who had been suitably impressed and had even murmured that

Khalid could have had a good career with ISI.

"We play chess, my dear Khalid. Pakistan is like a stupid, reckless child, but there are avenues for great opportunity as well," the brigadier had once told him.

Khalid recalled the start of his career in antiquities: His father would drive a tonga on the Mall Road in the city of Lahore, carrying a few artifacts from the Gandhara period. The young Khalid would sit in the ramshackle horse-drawn buggy and wait while his father approached the front door of some great Punjabi home where he knew there was interest in art. Khalid could not believe how dirty terracotta pieces of pottery or stone figurines could result in his father returning with a handful of hundred-rupee notes. Sometimes his father seemed almost sad when a particular artifact was sold. That was when Khalid had the first inkling of his father's passion. Khalid's father had advised him, when he was still a child, that he should never become attached to an artifact, but instead sell it and endeavour to secure the highest price. The money his father earned supported Khalid's siblings and mother and put food on the table. For his father, Pakistan was only a modest land of opportunity; the objects he sold there did not fetch the high prices claimed in other countries.

When Khalid grew up, he opened a showroom in Bangkok from which he could ship his artifacts all over the world. Pakistan was a young country then, and there was no great importance paid to antiquities being smuggled abroad. Over the years, Khalid sold art in London, New York, Paris, and Tokyo—and amassed a fortune. Eventually, he returned to Pakistan, bought his ten acres in the rolling countryside, built his compound, and leisurely began serving his international clients as well as some second-generation Pakistani clients of his father's era. He arranged the marriages of his two children and sent his elder son to Bangkok to handle the showroom there, but he kept Hassan by his side in Pakistan.

Khalid forced his mind back to the present. He had another call to make, and it would be a difficult one. He had a bill to settle and would have to delay payment, which was not how he liked to conduct his business. Khalid paid promptly for his purchases. Yet since Hassan had squandered about two million U.S. dollars on his car dealership, Khalid's reserves were currently short.

There was a fair amount of disturbance on the phone line, and Khalid tried three times before being successfully connected.

"How are you, my friend? I am sorry I have been delayed in calling you but there are good reasons for this," Khalid said loudly.

"Salaam, Khalid," said Reza Mohsinzadegh, whose voice was not at all effusive.

"Reza, I need a little more time to transfer the payment."

"That will not be possible, Khalid, we have an agreement," said Reza. Although he spoke in English, his Iranian accent became heavier with ire.

"I am waiting for a payment myself and there has been an unforeseen delay. Reza, please, we have been doing business for many years."

"You must respect my wishes." Reza's voice rose.

"I always do. But I want you to be reasonable. It is a large payment and I need some time, that is all." Khalid hated the wheedling tone he had to adopt.

Reza was a senior official in the Ministry of Culture and Islamic Guidance in Iran, and he was not averse to making cultural artifacts disappear. Khalid had stumbled upon him at a gallery in London where some rare Persian manuscripts

22

were being exhibited. Khalid pursued his friendship, entertaining him lavishly in an expensive restaurant where Reza ordered champagne while Khalid discussed his great love for Persian history and antiquities. Khalid deliberately courted and tempted Reza, whom he knew instinctively wanted to make more than his government salary. That night, Reza mentioned that some rare folios of Persian manuscripts had come his way through unusual circumstances and had not yet been added to the museum's inventory. Knowing their value, Khalid took the bait. Over a period of ten years, Reza contacted Khalid about various artifacts and Khalid arranged their transportation into Pakistan. In his lighter moments, and in safe company, Khalid would chuckle and boast that his bribes to the Pakistan customs officials in Karachi were in the millions.

On this day, though, Reza Mohsinzadegh was in no mood to exchange pleasantries. He wanted his payment.

"My dear Khalid, do I have to inform your government about this last purchase?"

"I don't think that would be good for your health, Reza," Khalid said sternly.

"My hands are tied. As for my health, a good masseuse can untangle the knots this conversation has created!"

"I know just the spot. Bangkok is famous for masseuses. Your health will be restored in more ways than one. Let me arrange a week there for you," said Khalid.

"Khalid, I will give you forty-eight hours." Reza spoke briskly. "After that, there will be no further contact between us. Instead, our governments will talk."

The line went dead.

Khalid silently handed the phone to Faisal and, with the other hand, waved him away. He closed his eyes and leaned back on the couch. He thought very carefully about Reza's ultimatum. Was the man prepared to lose his job in Tehran over a delay in payment? Perhaps he had made enough money from Khalid. Maybe his retirement villa in Shiraz had finally been completed. The last shipment of antiquities that Khalid had bought had come into Pakistan through a diplomatic courier, and Reza had taken many risks. It was always money, Khalid thought. Someone was putting pressure on Reza and he had to buy his way out. People had to be paid. Khalid knew that better than anyone.

Hassan appeared in the doorway, wearing a long white *kurta* with a high Chinese collar over blue jeans. Khalid gazed at his son's impossibly beautiful face and grief lanced his heart.

"What is it?" he said softly.

"I bought a new computer today," Hassan announced from the doorway, not stepping in.

"A computer?"

"Yes, a laptop. I can help you with your emails," Hassan replied hesitantly.

"I do my business with a handshake," Khalid said brusquely.

"It's all your fault!" Hassan burst out.

"What is my fault? You squandering my money? Not continuing with your education? Abusing your wife and marrying a prostitute illegally?" Khalid shot back.

"I never had a father."

"I never had a father either because he worked day and night, but at least I learned from him."

"I hate the things you collect."

"I buy history, Hassan. It is the only thing that tells us who we are," replied Khalid.

"I prefer animals."

"What kind of animals?" Khalid asked, bewildered.

"Horses, buffalos, and camels. We can race them and make a lot of money," Hassan replied.

"Get out!" Khalid shouted.

As Hassan spun around and darted away, Khalid lit a cigarette with trembling fingers and tried to regain his composure. Reaching his son was next to impossible. Sharing his present dilemma with him was unthinkable. Only Faisal, his devoted nephew and assistant, could be relied upon. Faisal was the son Khalid deserved. He could never inherit anything from Khalid, yet the young man stayed by his side, learning everything he could about the world of antiquities. Faisal entered the room quietly. His devotion brought tears to Khalid's eyes; all he could do was clasp Faisal's shoulder and embrace him.

Knowing that Khalid was upset, Faisal said, "*Chachu*, you are my father and my teacher, and it is an honour to be by your side."

Khalid knew that these were the words he would never hear from Hassan.

"Faisal, I have two obstacles to overcome. I need solutions immediately."

"Please do not worry. Just tell me what you need to do first," said Faisal.

"The ISI agent turned out to be a thief and has disappeared with the statue. We need to find him ourselves."

"We have a senior contact with the police in Peshawar," replied Faisal, reaching for the phone.

"No." Khalid removed the phone from his grasp. "We have to work independently. The police cannot be involved."

Faisal stood up. "Then I will go myself and take two people with me."

"I need you with me, Faisal. I need you to contact the carpet dealer."

Faisal was stunned. The man Khalid referred to was the greatly feared leader of a Taliban group who was seldom seen in public. Khalid had befriended the man in Afghanistan after one of Khalid's gem traders was kidnapped and the "carpet dealer" rescued him. Khalid flew to Kabul to thank the man in person and reward him with a very large sum of money. As the two men sat cross-legged on a faded rug, Khalid convinced the bearded Afghan with the hard eyes to come to Peshawar to trade. Khalid made a casual request for some carpets to get his business started and overpaid generously to buy the dealer's eternal goodwill. The man shifted his base to Peshawar and became prosperous. The carpet business was a convenient cover for his work with the Taliban.

Khalid opened a little notebook and read out a number for Faisal, who dialed the phone and handed it back to Khalid. The telephone rang for a long time. Eventually, it was picked up, but no one spoke.

"Sher Khan, this is Khalid. I need your help, brother."

"Wait, I will call you back."

The line disconnected and Khalid waited. After a minute, the phone rang from a blocked number.

"*Salaam alaikum*, Khalid sahib." Sher Khan's voice was unmistakeable.

"*Wa-Alaikum-Salaam*. I need an Afghan lion to hunt a jackal for me."

"You want him alive?"

"Yes. He has taken something that belongs to me," said Khalid.

"Khalid sahib, it is always better to kill the jackal."

"That is not how I do business, Sher Khan. He will never find a job again and that will kill him for us."

Details were exchanged, and Sher Khan assured him that a tracking team would depart immediately. Khalid thanked him profusely.

KHALID HEADED FOR his personal living quarters, where his wife, Safia, had turned one of his exhibit halls into a bedroom flanked by a sumptuous marble bathroom. A velvet canopy hung above their antique, hammered-silver bed. Their sitting room had a matching set of pure silver armchairs and a chaise upholstered in brocade. The walls displayed stunning works by famed Pakistani artists. Around the room, glass étagères housed exquisite sculptures and silver filigree work from Kashmir. The entire suite shimmered with an ethereal light. A door through the sitting room led to the dining room, and beyond this to his wife's kitchen. The kitchen had a large glass window that looked out onto rolling hills. Here Safia cooked all the family meals herself, sorted her fresh produce from the markets, and placed packages in her deep freezer. This was her chosen world. Khalid could have placed an army of kitchen staff at her disposal but she refused. She cooked for Khalid, Hassan, and the rest of the family — even guests never ruffled her feathers. She could prepare an array of dishes at short notice.

As Khalid entered the kitchen, Safia looked up from the carrots she was slicing.

"Are you ready for lunch?" Her curly brown hair rippled down to her waist.

Khalid shook his head.

"What is it?"

"My shoulder is hurting again," Khalid said.

Safia set the knife down and rinsed her hands at the sink. She returned to her husband and placed her hands on his shoulders.

"Come with me. I will massage some ointment into your shoulder."

Khalid followed her to their suite. Just under five feet tall, Safia had retained her girlish appeal; it often appeared that she skipped rather than walked. Khalid loved his wife deeply, fully aware that all of the wealth he placed at her disposal was of very little interest to her. Her simplicity and domesticity was how she expressed herself. She loved her children fiercely and habitually sheltered Hassan from Khalid's wrath. But she loved her husband too, and possessed a thorough understanding of his temperament. Khalid suspected that she knew it was more than an aching shoulder that had brought him to her kitchen at midday. They seldom met at lunch, but always had dinner together unless he was entertaining for business. Half of Khalid's business world was known to her and the other half concealed. Safia had grown to love the art that Khalid collected and, followed by a retinue of housekeeping staff, she organized mammoth dusting exercises a couple of times a week.

After taking off his shirt, Khalid sat bare-chested on the edge of the bed. Safia knelt behind him, applied the ointment with light fingers, and then massaged his shoulder. Her hair, which slipped over his shoulder, was lightly scented with a fragrance he could not place. The tenderness of his wife's ministrations made Khalid close his eyes and savour this blessing in his life. When he opened his eyes a few minutes later, his gaze rested on the antique Persian glass perfume bottles adorning Safia's ornate dressing table.

Reza Mohsinzadegh's thin-lipped, pallid face floated in Khalid's mind. He stiffened involuntarily.

"What are you hiding from me, Khalid?" Safia whispered.

"I have a bill to pay, Safia, and it is large," he said, then rose from the bed and slipped his shirt back over his head.

"Do you need money?"

"I have money, but there has been a delay in its arrival. I will get it," he said, and smiled at her.

"I can give you what you need." Safia replied, sitting back on the bed.

"Oh, so you have a secret bank account now." Khalid winked at her.

"No, I have my Mughal jewellery. It belonged to a queen, but I am content to be myself. Sell it," Safia said.

"Please do not talk about the jewellery I have given to you. You will wear it forever," Khalid replied.

"You have given me so much, Khalid. I want to help if you are in trouble."

"I do not need your help, Safia," he replied, then walked out of the bedroom.

The sun blinded him as he walked across a large terrace that led to a flight of stairs. Reza had to be reminded of a few hard facts. Khalid returned to his office and called Shiraz again.

"Khalid, I am in a meeting," Reza said curtly.

"You will have a bank credit in a week, Reza. That is the best I can do. Listen to your Persian nightingales and wait," Khalid said before disconnecting the call.

A few minutes later, Khalid stood before the intricately carved door of his Mughal pavilion. One of his workmen flipped through a heavy ring of keys until he found the right one and opened the door. Khalid stepped inside and motioned to a stack of paintings that leaned against a wall. He sat in a chair and asked the man to turn each one over for him to see. The works by Pakistan's legendary trio of master artists — Naqsh, Sadequain, and Gulgee — still enthralled him. Khalid felt as if he were at a poker table, holding three aces.

THREE

GHALIB — BENT OVER the billiard table. He glanced over the cue at his fourteen-year-old protegé and noticed how his worn T-shirt outlined the contours of his rib cage. He looked down the length of the table and slammed the cue into the cluster of balls. The game was over. He had lost again. Ghalib straightened up, handed the cue to the next teenager who stepped forward, and walked out of the large playroom and onto the unpaved ground. The wall sconces embedded into the stucco walls of his ancestral village home, deep in the heart of the Punjab, lit the night air. He gazed toward the main wooden gate and nodded at the armed guard who immediately shot up from his reclined position. Ghalib's two cars were parked farther down the driveway under a vast tree. In the distance a huge generator, sitting on a trailer behind a tractor, hummed furiously. Here, in the village, was where Ghalib felt most comfortable. It was 1 a.m and although the night stretched ahead of him, it was in fact only the start of his day.

Ghalib wore a blue-plaid cotton sarong and a white undershirt, but his feet were encased in soft leather slippers. At seventy-three, his belly had distended and his balding head retained only a ring of grey hair. He wore spectacles and his gait was ponderous thanks to the stiffness that plagued him in one hip. His melodious voice and expressive face still retained all the evidence of a superbly handsome man. Although his life had once been as redolent as the champa tree, Ghalib was now covered with a deviant stench; these days, he lived only to fulfil his sensorial pleasures.

Ghalib had not worked for more than five years in his entire life. He lived on his inherited wealth, which took the form of agricultural land. His only noteworthy pursuits were his poetry and paintings. His most costly addiction was the acquisition of art. His other addictions did not cost him a penny.

Ghalib's latest act of lunacy was a run for Parliament in his home constituency's upcoming elections. Ghalib embellished his existence with lofty dreams of putting this political feather in his cap. He actually believed that if he delivered his hard-pressed and disenfranchised villagers' vote bank to his political party, he would be rewarded with a weighty cultural portfolio. No one in Ghalib's immediate circle had the courage to tell him that he had not lifted a finger to improve the conditions of the villagers by either building more schools or setting up a medical clinic. His reputation in the village was based solely on philandering and the assumption of a thoroughly courtly air.

Ghalib was typical of Pakistan's landed gentry, who controlled the destinies of people whose lives bore a striking similarity to the indentured serfs of an earlier era. He maintained two country estates and a large town home staffed by villagers who continued to see him as a benign patriarch. His largely invented family history was part and parcel of Punjabi culture. Punjab was a sprawling province responsible for most of the agricultural revenue of the nation. Provincial folklore and mythmaking were equally fertile. In the salons of his country home, large, framed portraits of his turbaned and bearded ancestors, eyes glowing, hung in dubious splendour.

As the largely ignored son of a dazzling father, who rejected Ghalib's mother for a foreign wife, Ghalib had no endearing father-and-son tales on which to fall back. He was educated at good schools, picked up an undergraduate degree from Oxford, sat for the civil service exam, and added an American diploma to his resumé. He then married a slender, luminous-eyed woman from a noted family, produced two beautiful children, published poetry, and painted sporadically. After the untimely death of his young wife, he spiralled into severe clinical depression, from which he emerged after a few years, and constructed his town-and-country life. He became a master consumer with appetites that were carelessly concealed. Of late he had become more reclusive, abandoning his society friends but holding court at night with art dealers, pimps, singing girls from Lahore's red-light district, and a host of teenagers from his village. His generosity knew no bounds as he fed and watered his motley entourage by ordering copious meals from his gentlemen's club.

Ghalib was served by a personal valet who dressed him to the point of kneeling down and slipping on his socks. His house boasted a moody chef; a lascivious, burly head butler, who was a fount of gossip; a good-looking, tall chauffeur with an erect carriage; and a comely maid who was not averse to offering sexual favours to her employer or his guests. There was also a gaggle of gardeners, handymen, carpenters, and a group of cleaning boys who did rotational visits from the villages. Members of his staff travelled with him back and forth from town to country along with his easels, paints, and canvasses. Being a nocturnal creature, Ghalib travelled late at night with a pistol under the driver's seat and a prepared meal served to him by his valet in the moving car. Life was good for Ghalib and despite his largely fictional ailments, he was built to endure.

Ghalib's art collection was substantial and worthy of any museum. The paintings had been skilfully amassed, and interspersed among the masterpieces were his own works: large canvasses bearing the vision of a Punjabi artist besotted by large trees and women with almond-shaped eyes and mounds of pubic hair. His work was largely second-rate, with an odd exception or two in which Ghalib had taken some risks and pulled off a wonderful painting. Had he starved in a garret, his work would have more likely achieved its potential.

As Ghalib entered his interlocking suite of rooms in the manor house, near-silent footsteps followed in his tracks. It was an old game. Ghalib skirted the pantry, which housed double freezers and a supply of snacks. There were biscuits, chocolates, potato chips, cans of diet soft drinks, and fruit heaped in baskets. He lingered briefly to collect a few items, including a handful of chocolate bars for the person in pursuit.

The boy, Saqib, stood framed in the doorway of Ghalib's bedroom. Tall and slender, he remained motionless, yet there was a studied air of insolence about him. Whenever Ghalib singled out one boy in the village, that boy's social posture was immediatebly transformed: "I am the chosen one," the new favourite's attitude said. Saqib knew that the events in this room would unfurl as they had countless times before. Ghalib's reclining figure was as deceptive as the sketches of nude women on the wall above his bed. The temperature was high on this June night, but Ghalib's bedroom was kept comfortable by the air conditioner hung high on the stucco wall. The only evidence of heat shone through Ghalib's eyes, which were hidden behind his spectacles. The teen's body language spoke volumes: part braced and attentive, part fraught with anxiety.

"Come here," Ghalib commanded in English. He was paying for the boy's education at a privileged school in the village.

"Press me, boy, press me," Ghalib commanded.

Saqib walked briskly over to him and hovered near his legs. He started massaging Ghalib from the ankles upward, his strokes firm but slow. He gathered the mounds of calves in both hands and pressed down. Ghalib sighed, removed his glasses, and placed them on the pillow beside him.

"Are you studying hard?" asked Ghalib in a languorous voice.

"Yes. I am the first in my class," Saqib replied.

"Well done!" Ghalib's arm shot up, holding out a chocolate bar.

Saqib leaned forward, gripped the bar with his teeth, and jerked his head away. Ghalib immediately rolled onto his back and burst out laughing. Saqib pulled the chocolate bar from his mouth and tore the wrapper off.

"None for me?" asked Ghalib, sitting up against the pillows.

Saqib continued to eat, without looking at Ghalib, until the last chunk of chocolate disappeared in his mouth. He then rubbed his mouth with the back of his hand and looked up.

"Your teeth will rot," Ghalib said, adopting the air of a stern headmaster.

"Rot?" Saqib did not know the word.

"I am rotting; the flame is fading." Ghalib pointed his index finger right at Saqib's face. "You will bring life to me!"

Saqib did not understand all of the English words, but he understood "you." Silently, he removed his T-shirt.

IN THE MORNING, the billowing fold of Ghalib's belly spilled over the bed; the boy—almost skeletal, all bony arms and legs—lay curled up by his side. They could have been a grandfather and grandson sleeping side by side. The bedroom door always remained locked until mid-afternoon. No one dared to knock.

By the time Ghalib pressed the bell by his night table to order his breakfast, the boy had vanished, leaving the crumpled wrappers of many chocolate bars at the foot of the bed. He worked his way with gusto through a glass of *lassi*, fried *parathas*, and an omelette, and then summoned his valet to draw his bath. It was three in the afternoon and Ghalib knew he had visitors waiting.

Ghalib had to finalize his decision to sell a parcel of land and had summoned the estate's overseer to handle the transaction. He dressed slowly in his room, slipping into a starched white *shalwar kameez* and a pair of highly polished shoes. Ghalib strolled toward the shade of the large tree in the front patio, where chairs and a circular table had been arranged. His stout estate manager, dressed in pristine white clothing with a white muslin turban wound around his head, sat on one of the chairs. Ghalid's valet had placed his three telephones on the table. The manager leapt up when he saw Ghalib and clasped his outstretched hand in a double-handed shake, bowing his head slightly. Ghalib ordered tea for the manager, then lifted one of the phones and scrolled through his missed calls. When he saw Khalid's number his pulse jumped. He was certain that his latest acquisition had arrived and Khalid wanted to discuss transportation and payment. Ignoring the manager, Ghalib walked away and called Khalid immediately.

"Hello, Khalid! Deliver it yourself and come for a few days. I shall throw a party for you," said Ghalib.

"Do you have the payment in hand?" said Khalid.

"I am making arrangements as we speak," Ghalib lied.

There was silence for a few seconds and then Khalid spoke.

"There is a small delay. I may even need the payment before delivery this time."

Ghalib laughed. "Hold the items I have sent to you to be sold as the deposit. The mangoes are ripening in the orchards and are waiting to be eaten. Bring Safia with you."

"We shall see. I have a busy evening. I have some visitors here," Khalid said before ending the call.

Ghalib was concerned. Khalid had not been his usual affable self. The call was brief. No pleasantries had been exchanged. And it was the first time Khalid had asked about his payment or demanded money in advance. Was Khalid trying to raise the price of the sculpture at the last minute? Khalid knew very well that Ghalib would never let the sculpture go. Perhaps he had another buyer and demanding payment before delivery was simply a ploy. He looked over at the estate manager, who was sipping his tea placidly.

"I need the money for the land immediately," Ghalib told him.

"Well, sir, that is what I have come to discuss. It is a great mistake to sell that parcel of land. The farm account is not that healthy at the moment. We need to see how strong the yield is this year," he replied.

"You were given instructions two weeks ago," Ghalib said. His voice had taken on a distinctly cold tone.

"Yes, but I thought I should give you correct advice as your estate manager."

Ghalib looked at him with loathing and tried to control his rising tide of anger.

"I need the sale to be executed immediately and the money transferred into my personal account. Not the farm bank account." Ghalib rose from his chair and walked away without looking back.

Ghalib was used to leveraging bank loans when his crops did not yield enough profit. He was also used to bartering with Khalid and some of the other art dealers with whom he did business. He sat on a magnificent fortune, but the bills for his art purchases were shocking—they often robbed him of operating cash and the funds required for the salaries of his domestic staff. The maintenance of his three large homes also suffered. Over the years, unwashed carpets, stained upholstery, and dust-laden display cabinets had reduced his homes to a state of splendid squalor. But Ghalib was oblivious to it all. He had stopped entertaining and lived largely out of his gargantuan bedrooms. And while he would often rearrange his art and sculptures, he almost never replenished his household linens.

Ghalib walked toward a huge side garden, which flanked a course for miniature golf. Next to that stood the unfinished home he was building for his married son. Behind the house was a small mosque, also incomplete. The magnificent turquoise tiles designed and ordered by Ghalib from the city of Multan covered only half of the building. Ghalib walked to the front patio, where he found fifteen men seated in a circle. The volunteers of the political party for which he was supposed to be campaigning had also come to see him today.

Straightening his posture, Ghalib strolled toward them as they looked up at him uneasily. The men had been asked to bring votes for Ghalib's candidacy come election time. They now wanted to know what benefits their support would bring. They mentioned the need for schools, the lack of electricity, and their need to access water to irrigate their small parcels of farming land. They even hinted at their wish for administrative positions at the grassroots level.

Ghalib doled out promises, convincing even himself that, if elected, he would make good on them and fulfil all of the group's requests. But in the back of his mind, Ghalib's thoughts turned to Khalid. The memory of their brief phone conversation sat in the pit of his stomach like an undigested meal.

FOUR

FROM A SAFE DISTANCE, Adeel watched as the truck was disguised. Two men had already sprayed a coat of metallic blue paint over the entire body. The large shed in which they worked was an auto repair shop that also did some bodywork. The men in the tattered clothes who worked there were Peshawar's master artists. Using stencils, they festooned the truck with garish flowers and prancing animals. When they were done, the formerly brown truck would be unrecognizable, and would blend seamlessly with all of the other gaily decorated vehicles moving through Pakistan. Adeel had paid the shop owner an extravagant amount to perform the service. To accommodate Adeel further, the owner had also supplied a new licence plate and fake registration.

As Adeel waited for the paint to dry, he changed his clothing and left the shed to go visit the local bazaar. The black scarf wound around his neck was woven into a loose turban, and dark glasses shaded his eyes. His beige trousers and leather jacket had been replaced by a billowing *shalwar kameez* and was topped off by a wool waistcoat.

The dirt-infested and malodorous bazaar greeted him at end of the alley. Adeel walked up to a small store and purchased a phone card. Then he hunted for a telephone booth; he found one within a short distance.

He dialed his mother's number.

"Ami-ji. Don't talk. Just listen. I have to be very quick."

"Adeel, Adeel my son." His mother's voice burbled with joy.

"I am doing a very special job. I cannot come to see you and may be gone for a long time. Wait for me and I will send for you. Never repeat this conversation to anyone."

"Are you safe, my son?"

"Yes, I am. Please forgive me but I must go right away."

"Adeel, I love you," said his mother, and Adeel knew there were tears rolling down her face.

"People may come to you asking about me. You are to tell them nothing. Do not believe anything they tell you about me. "

"Are you wearing your *taveez*?"

"It never comes off my neck."

"Then nothing will happen. I will wait as I always do."

As Adeel hung up the phone, his fingers reached for the amulet his mother had given him when he was sixteen. The fine leather cord had softened over the years and now had the texture of silken thread. At the centre of the amulet was a piece of agate etched with an Arabic prayer. When Adeel stroked the prayer stone with his thumb, he did not think of God but of his beautiful mother's face. After his father had died, Adeel had dedicated himself to caring for her. He knew his mother was a woman of great courage and fortitude. She would miss him terribly, but she would wait, and keep his secrets.

Adeel's next mission was to locate a bank, so he hailed a taxi and asked the driver to take him to another section of the city. Twenty minutes later he stood before the automatic teller machine of the Habib Bank and withdrew as much cash as he could. He then searched for the post office, bought a padded envelope, and put another card and the money into it, along with a note to his mother telling her to use the cash whenever she needed it. Adeel walked toward the main road. He found a motorcycle rickshaw and headed back to the garage.

In the shed's dank and gloomy interior, the toxic fumes of the cheap spray paint still lingered in the air, while the truck stood like a bird of paradise in the middle of the room. The garage owner greeted Adeel with a broad smile, then shouted over his shoulder, drawing out of the shadows a man holding a large ball wrapped in leaves. He parted the leaves to reveal a glistening round of Peshawar's famous cottage cheese, made from rich buffalo milk. Eaten sparingly, it was a supply of protein that would last for days.

An hour later, Adeel headed north out of Peshawar in the painted truck, travelling at high speed through small towns and across long, barren stretches of road. He mentally noted the changes of climate and topography, convinced that a destination where he could find temporary shelter would present itself. He knew he needed to avoid settled communities at all costs, but beyond that, he had no idea where he was going to spend the night.

Adeel headed toward the province of Hazara, an area of soaring mountains, deep gorges, pine-clad forests, and a sparse, largely ignored population. In the back of the truck, along with the sculpture and the cheese, were additional food supplies he had picked up at the bazaar: oranges, bags of walnuts and dried apricots, hard, dried rusks of bread, and a bag of cucumbers. He would not pick up any meat until he reached a cooler climate. He knew how to light a fire, and could roast a sliver of meat on the tip of the combat knife he carried with him.

Adeel had hidden his long-range rifle under the seat, but his revolver was concealed under his waistcoat. He was moving through a territory that was not as inundated with violence as the rest of the country. However, there had been an incident of sectarian violence the previous year when a busload of men was slaughtered simply because they were Shia. The police and military were unable to keep the zealots or the underworld bosses in line.

Adeel despaired over the slowly eroding face of the true Pakistan. He raged internally at the hordes of bearded and ill-kept men who now roamed through the country, some even occupying seats in government. Most of them had no higher education to boast of, yet they ruled their equally uneducated and underprivileged constituents with an iron hand. These were the men who insisted that the state needed to be ruled by the church, but most of them had learned the Koran by rote, without true comprehension, because it was written in Arabic. These men lumped outmoded cultural taboos together with acts of shocking social injustice and declared them religious edicts. It was perplexing to Adeel how they managed to hold 187 million people hostage to their ideas.

Adeel thought about his childhood and his family. His father, a minor employee in the railways, had been a handsome man with a clean-shaven face, partial to Western-style trousers and well-pressed cotton shirts. His beautiful mother's head had never been bundled in headscarves or shawls. A gauzy *dupatta* lay draped across her chest and shoulders except during prayers, when it was draped lightly over her hair. They had no family car, only a motorcycle. On outings, Adeel and his brother rode sandwiched between their parents. Adeel could remember the sheen of his mother's hair as it whipped though the wind, and the hands she placed around her husband's waist as young Adeel pressed himself into her body. When his father died, Adeel had been sorely tempted to teach his mother how to drive the motocycle. But the changing face of Pakistan had made him cautious; the sight of his mother riding a motorcycle might easily incur the wrath of the community.

Adeel's father had viewed his wife as a comrade-in-arms. He had taught her how to read and write, and would hand her a roll of banknotes whenever he received his salary, trusting that she would manage the family expenses. Adeel grew up knowing that his father's small, worn leather wallet was nearly always empty except for his railway pass and faded wedding photograph. On one rare occasion, he was taken to a country fair by his parents and given a twenty-rupee note by his father.

"Go buy some bangles for your mother," his father had said, winking at him.

Ten-year-old Adeel, unable to locate the bangle stall, bought a hair ornament instead. His father's eyebrows scrunched together in silent displeasure, but his mother promptly fastened the ornament to her long braid.

"Where is the change?" his father had asked.

"It cost twenty rupees," Adeel replied, frightened.

"You have been cheated," his father declared.

Adeel remained silent and stared at his feet.

"The man saw a nervous little boy so he knew it would be easy to cheat you," his father said. "Always stand confidently, and never let anyone know that you are nervous or afraid."

DRIVING STEADILY NORTH on the mountain road, Adeel noticed the temperature change with the elevation just as the first roadside marker, for the town of Balakot, appeared. The small town was located in a region where a devastating earthquake had occurred a few years ago. Large boulders had rolled down the mountain, destroying homes and schools. The death toll was staggering.

The mountain roads were too narrow to pull over on, so Adeel decided to pass Balakot before finding a place to stop. He wouldn't be able to linger in the town, lest any image of his vehicle, or himself, were to remain in some local's memory. His stomach growled but he kept driving. Closer to Balakot, the evidence of the earthquake's destruction initially made the little town seem abandoned. Two local hotels, both with terraces overlooking the busy bazaar, came into view. The tantalizing smell of grilled kebabs rose in the air as he drove past. Adeel decided to continue north toward the Kaghan Valley. A vacation destination for many, the area offered trout fishing and mountaineering. Roadside vendors cooled bottles of soft drinks and watermelons under the water of the springs and small waterfalls that cascaded down the mountains.

Adeel stopped the truck next to a river, where he refilled his depleted water jug. He ignored the vendors and kept his turban low over his forehead. Then, someone behind him spoke.

"Are you going to Kaghan?"

"Yes, beyond it," replied Adeel, not turning to look at the speaker.

"Can you give me a ride?" The voice was female, and Balti-accented.

"No. I am picking up a few people a mile from here." Adeel climbed into the truck and reversed without looking at the woman who was trying to move closer to the window.

Adeel drove fast, avoiding the road that climbed higher to Naran, the magical holiday spot that sat on the peak of the mountain, and heading for the valley below. He knew the road ahead would be full of hairpin turns, so he stopped at a wide bend to eat. Adeel pulled out the cheese and a handful of dried apricots, then rolled up both windows, got out, and locked the truck. He disappeared into the thick shrubbery by the side of the road, where he ate and smoked two cigarettes as he lay on the ground. He removed his dark glasses and washed his face using the water he had collected in the plastic jug. Then he went back to the truck, opened the padlock on the back, and stepped inside. The statue lay there, rolled up and bolstered by wool blankets on either side. He pulled out one of the blankets and found a rough woollen beret. He took off his turban, replaced it with the beret, and draped the blanket around his shoulders. He now resembled the men of the region. His rest stop had taken about forty minutes.

He walked to the front of the truck, toward the driver's-side door. He had taken only a few steps when he stopped in his tracks. A woman had materialized on the road like a ghost. A bundle of twigs wrapped in twine perched on her head, and a cotton bag was slung over one shoulder. Her bare face was surrounded by matted hair, and her lips and cheeks were cracked and chapped red. She had a curious Asian tilt to her eyes, which made Adeel think that her features were perhaps Balti. Her body was slender, despite the faded maroon cotton tunic she had wrapped around herself. She had to be the woman who had asked for a ride. But how had she managed to reach him so quickly? She had an athletic appearance and probably the stamina of the people from the mountain communities.

"Move, I have to open the door," Adeel said curtly, avoiding further eye contact.

"Please, give me a ride. My feet hurt," she said.

"No. Move!" Adeel said, unable now to avoid looking down.

The woman's feet were caked with dried blood and dirt, and rested on a thin plastic sole across which she had tied strips of cloth. His heart sank; he knew she had walked for miles, probably stopping regularly to retie the cloth strips. He steeled himself, eased past her, and climbed into the truck. He bent forward to turn on the ignition. She spoke again.

"Please."

Her entreaty felt like a blade cutting through him. Adeel glanced up, allowing himself a quick look. She must be a local woman who had gone out to collect firewood, he though, yet something was wrong about her appearance. It was not just her features; the style of slinging her bag over only one shoulder was not like the women of this region. Perhaps she was from the Gilgit Valley. He paused, wanting for some inexplicable reason to shed the unease he felt at refusing to assist.

"If you wait by the side of the road the next bus will take you. I cannot," he said gruffly, holding out a five-hundred-rupee note.

She drew closer to the open window and spat furiously on the bill, which Adeel had allowed to slip from his fingers as he was certain she would grab it. The currency sank to the ground. Her nostrils quivered and a tear rolled down the side of her face. Her response paralyzed him for a moment; he slid his foot off the clutch.

"Get in. Take that bundle off your head and do not talk to me."

She got into the truck and sat next to him. Her hand, slim with dirt embedded in the nails, curled on top of the bundle of twigs on her lap. The smell of her unwashed garments and a sense of apprehension engulfed Adeel—by picking her up, he had violated his own personal security rules.

"Where is your home?" he asked casually.

"It is wherever I find shelter."

"Where is your family? You must have a husband."

"My husband threw me away and my family lives far away in Skardu," she replied.

Adeel's thoughts raced furiously. He knew he had to leave her somewhere, but the hairpin bends had already appeared in the road. He would have to wait for some road-side dwelling or food shop to appear so he could drop her off before they reached the Kaghan Valley's main town. Their trip would take at least an hour and a half. Adeel avoided looking at her, but he was sure now that she was a Balti, hailing from a region where a few bloodlines mingled together, including Tibetan. It explained her pale skin and straight black hair.

Her marriage situation was the same as thousands of other women in Pakistan, thought Adeel, yet she had spit on a sum of money that could feed her for a day or put new sandals on her feet.

"I can sleep in the back of the truck," she said, breaking the silence.

Adeel did not respond.

"I am going to drop you off in five minutes," he said coldly.

"I have no place to go."

"So you are like me." The words leapt out of his mouth before he could stop himself.

"I can cook for you," she said.

He glanced at her sideways. In the planes of her sunburned face he thought he saw the face of the marble statue travelling in the back of the truck. Adeel sensed the hazard of his present situation and knew he had to make a decision. She too was in a precarious situation, he reasoned. Perhaps he could use her as camouflage.

Adeel drove faster, as though speed would obliterate the necessity to make a decision.

The signposts for the hamlet of Kaghan began to appear, accompanied by fading billboards advertising trout fishing and whitewater rapids. Even though a sprinkling of tiny hotels had been added in the past few years, foreign tourists visited the area infrequently.

Adeel knew that before he stopped the truck, the woman's face would have to be concealed.

"Do you have something to cover yourself with?" He made a circular motion with his finger close to her face.

She took her hands off the twig bundle and tugged at her throat, pulling a piece of black cloth from her clothing. As she wrapped the scarf around her head, he saw a fringe of silver sequins at one end.

"No! No!" Adeel shouted. "You have to cover your head with something simple, like a *chadder*!"

She lifted her chin and gave him a defiant look. "You are not my husband!"

Adeel slammed on the brakes and the truck shuddered to a halt. He pulled out a cigarette and lit it very slowly. After a long drag he turned to her. Her profile was stern despite the line of sequins spread across her forehead. The bundle of twigs was on her lap again, but her hand was no longer relaxed; it was clenched around some branches. He could see a fine line of veins through her pale skin. He sensed her fear. He was frightened himself, but decided to take a chance.

"Look, I am a man who has to hide for a while. Travelling with me is very dangerous. You need to carry on with your journey. I cannot help you."

She turned toward him, allowing her eyes to search his face.

"I can show you where to hide. We can cross the Babusar Pass into Gilgit."

Adeel closed his eyes; he could see the map in his mind. There would not be enough fuel to make it that far. He'd have to stop in Kaghan. Even though it was June, huge blocks of ice still covered some of the roads. One could only know for sure that a road was open upon reaching it. He wondered if the woman, who claimed that she belonged to no one, might be his greatest ally in his current situation.

"You have to listen to me if you want to stay in the truck. We cannot be seen closely by anyone along the way. Do you understand?"

She smiled. He was dumbfounded. The smile ended in two perfect dimples. Merriment and youth shone from her slanted eyes. Adeel realized she could not be more than twenty-five years old. In spite of the grime that covered her, he felt a sudden attraction. He looked down at his fingers, embarrassed by his thoughts. His cigarette had burned down to the filter and he flung it out of the window, turning away from her to hide his confusion.

"Can I have one?" she asked, gesturing to the pack lying on top of the dashboard.

"You smoke?" He could not help smiling.

"Yes." She smiled back.

"It's not good for you," Adeel said as he lit a cigarette, handed it to her, and started the truck.

Dusk crept in stealthily, as did the first sign for the Kaghan bazaar. Adeel's mission was to find a petrol station. The woman slid down farther on the seat and hid her face; she seemed to have grasped his desire for anonymity. He leaned over and grabbed the bundle of twigs from her lap and shoved them to the floor. When the truck rolled into the only petrol station, Adeel got out while she remained inside the truck, half concealed. There was a line of sturdy Jeeps ahead of them. The Jeeps carried local tourists up a treacherous seven-kilometre incline that ended at the legendary Saif-ul-maluk Lake. Snow-covered mountains ringed the lake. The underground springs and glaciers turned the waters the colour of jade. It was one of the most breathtaking sites in the entire area. Adeel knew the lake well and thought it was highly unlikely that the woman in the truck had ever seen it. When the gas tank was full, he paid from his stack of dwindling currency. His next challenge would be to find them a place for the night.

They drove on for ten minutes before Adeel found a room on the second floor of a shabby wooden hotel. He moved the truck to a back alley so he could get the woman up to the room without drawing too much attention.

"Come with me," Adeel said. "You'll have to walk

quickly. We will stay here for the night and leave at dawn."

She leaned down to collect her bundle of twigs.

"No, leave them."

"How will we light a fire?" she asked.

Adeel didn't answer. "Follow me," he said, as he raced up a dingy stairwell and reached the door of the room. She made a sound behind him.

"Hurry up," he said, and turned the key in the lock.

"I will sleep outside," she replied, refusing to budge.

"No, you cannot be outside and neither can I."

Adeel turned around and grabbed her arm.

She tried to pry off his hand, but she was no match for Adeel, who pulled her inside the room. He pushed her forward and locked the door. The shabby room had an electric heater and a wooden bed with a small table next to it. The woman leaned against the wall and slid down to the floor. Adeel checked the small lavatory. It had a toilet, a cracked water basin, and a small bathing trough with a tap mounted over it. He turned and switched on the heater.

Then he crouched down on the floor in front of the woman, making certain he wasn't too close.

"I am going to go buy some food. You can wash in the bathroom and then you can rest on the bed. But if you leave the room, you will be in trouble and will never ride in the truck again," he explained.

She remained silent, her face buried on her knees. He had no choice but to trust her. He rose, walked to the door, and locked it from the outside.

The main street was lit by the charcoal braziers of food shops. His stomach rumbled, but before he could buy any food, he had another mission to complete. Most of the little shops carried woollen blankets, shawls, caps, and flimsy local sandals. He searched further until he came to a shop that sold sturdier fare. As he hunted through a pile of cheaply made local gym shoes, he tried to imagine the size of her feet, made a wild guess, and bought a pair of shoes and two pairs of woollen socks. He also bought a shawl of coarse brown wool. Finally, he picked up some food and returned to the hotel exhausted.

Upon reaching the room, he placed the packages on the floor and inserted the key in the lock. He pushed the door to open it but felt resistance from inside.

"It's me," he whispered. "Don't push."

When he entered the room she was standing next to the bed. He turned the light on and the naked bulb overhead illuminated the room. Her appearance was astounding. Her straight, coal-black hair—still damp from washing—framed her face. Her hands and feet were clean.

"I brought you some socks and shoes," he said and held the items out to her.

She looked at him warily but did not move. Her eyes were on the food wrapped in newspaper.

"Okay, never mind the shoes. I know we're both hungry,"

Adeel sat on the edge of the sagging mattress and peeled away the paper from the food. She moved closer and sat on the floor. He handed her a long kebab and a hot naan. She waited, and only after he had taken his first bite did she began to eat. For a few minutes, they ate in silence. Finally, he stood up, crumpled the wrapper in his hands, and gestured toward the shoes.

"Try them on. If they do not fit I can change them."

She extended a foot, pulling the shoes closer to her. Then she tried to push her foot into the shoe with the laces still fastened. He knelt down beside her, untied the shoelaces, and handed the shoes back. She thrust her foot into them, but he could not tell if they fit. She removed the shoes quickly and slipped a sock over her bruised foot before trying again. Her eyes widened and she looked at him.

"It is good, but is this a shoe for a man?"

"No. It is for outdoors. Women wear them too," Adeel explained, amazed that he had gauged her foot size correctly.

She closed her eyes for a moment and he felt a rush of pleasure. His emotions were confusing and that unsettled him. Adeel had sublimated his sexuality for the whole of his adult life, including his resistance to an arranged marriage. He'd always thought that if he were going to be attracted to a woman, it would be someone of his own social standing. His mother would not have it any other way. He'd certainly never imagined that he'd be attracted to the likes of this wild creature sitting on the floor in front of him.

"You sleep on the bed. I will sleep on the floor," he told her.

She did not respond. Instead, she lay down on the floor against the wall, her back to him. The shoes were still on her feet.

"You can't sleep with your shoes on," he said.

When she didn't reply, he picked up the woollen shawl and draped it across her body. He slipped out of his own shoes, sank onto the sagging mattress, then immediately got up again to switch off the overhead light.

She sprang up immediately, looking panicked.

"It's all right," Adeel said. "I can sleep with the light on."

He lay down on the bed and turned his back to her.

FIVE

Sher Khan lived in a warren of rooms above two local restaurants in Namak Mandi, a neighbourhood as old as Peshawar itself. Fortunes had been made by the restaurant owners who served the unending line of people that started to form at midday and lasted until late at night. Everyone wanted to taste the speciality: lamb marinated and grilled in salt. Most out-of-town visitors to Peshawar did not leave without sampling the dish. Sher Khan had traded the carpet business he'd once run for the food business; it was safer, and it was a perfect cover for all his activities. Members of the Taliban couldn't be too careful.

On this day, Sher Khan was awake before dawn. He sprang from his bed in the half-light, ready to tackle the assignment at hand: arrange the hunt for Khalid's missing employee and property. He would not let his friend and old benefactor down.

Sher Khan activated the phone he only used for tasks such as this. He dialed a number, disconnected after three rings, and repeated the exercise three times. It wasn't long before a second phone rang. He answered immediately.

"I want three this time, with the car we use. When that is settled, come here immediately." Sher Khan hung up as soon as he was finished talking.

He thought back on his conversation with Khalid. He had detected an element of stress in his friend's voice. Sher Khan was a hunter by temperament and he could smell fear — even across a phone line from another city. Training groups of men for combat had enabled him to weed out the weak, those who might compromise a kill. The ability to snuff out an undeserving life with surprise and immediacy was his area of expertise. A corrupt government — or a disloyal army linked to an arrogant intelligence agency that used the police force as its personal lackeys — had to be reminded once in a while that there were men like Sher Khan willing to do what was necessary to cleanse Pakistan.

This mission, though, was personal. When he found the thief who had troubled his friend, perhaps he would cut off both of his hands. Now, however, was time for prayer. He cleared his thoughts, performed his ablutions, and knelt on an oblong rug woven of the finest silk and wool threads. At the end of the prayer, he made a personal request to Allah, asking only for victory.

Sher Khan walked down a flight of stairs to the store-room of his restaurant. Sacks of flour and large canisters of salt and cooking oil lined the walls. He opened a sack of flour, thrust both hands deep inside the bag, and pulled out a large, clear plastic envelope filled with money. He dropped it casually into an empty jute bag that he looped around his wrist and then went back upstairs to have his breakfast on his front porch. The entire street would be asleep for another two hours.

Sher Khan's teenaged nephew brought him a tray of tea and food. The boy was an orphan who had been adopted by Sher Khan and was being educated at the local *madrassah*. The boy had a fine intelligence, but he preferred working with food, so Sher Khan permitted him to serve breakfast before he headed to school. The boy was like a young hawk that could be trained to soar to glory, he thought. Shortly after the boy's mother had died, the police had shot his father. In retaliation, Sher Khan ordered an assault within twenty-four hours. When the corpses of the four slain police officers were presented to him, he felt the boy had been suitably avenged. The matter was settled.

As he drank his second cup of tea, a police vehicle drove down the street, stopping right in front of Khan's porch. The driver, a man named Nadir, jumped out, climbed the stairs to the porch, and bent low, clasping both of Sher Khan's hands in greeting.

"You will be looking for a man who is driving a truck with this licence plate. I want him captured and brought back with the vehicle," Sher Khan said softly.

The man wore a police uniform stolen from the Frontier Constabulary, a special arm of the military. He leaned forward, silently listening to Sher Khan's instructions. Then he straightened up, took the stacks of currency Sher Khan extended to him, and headed back to the Jeep.

"Contact me only on the special phone, Nadir," Sher Khan called after him.

Nadir, who was a prized member of the Taliban, lifted his hand in a farewell gesture without turning around. The police vehicle and the uniforms had been stolen months ago to assist in specific assignments. Everything was in God's hands, but Nadir had a particular facility in making even God bend to his will. Nadir was in exile from Afghanistan, and he believed that *jihad* was an avenging sword that established the place of God's warriors. Nadir had personally killed more than eighty people using bombs, grenades, and automatic rifles. He would offer himself for a suicide mission in the blink of an eye. Sher Khan knew that the assignment to capture a common thief likely did not inspire Nadir; nevertheless, his loyalty remained unquestioned.

IN THE GENTRIFIED village of Barako with its fake farms, Khalid rifled through the morning papers that Faisal had brought in from town. A schoolgirl who had been shot in the picturesque Swat Valley had gobbled up every line of newsprint. Pakistan continued to make the news in the far corners of the world. Khalid could smell something rotten in the shooting. It was a fix; he was sure of it. How could an assassin at such close range miss killing the girl? The nation had been targeted, he reasoned, and the schoolgirl had been carefully chosen as a vehicle to destabilize the region. Election fever had overtaken the country. Politicians roamed the countryside making false promises, and a nervous president kept increasing the size of his personal security team. The Taliban chose their targets with impunity. Khalid knew their tactics well. They had helped him bring mounds of lapis and many sculptures out of Afghanistan. Khalid had learned to arm himself whenever he walked with them, and even rested in their hiding places as a show of fake camaraderie. The money Khalid paid them went directly to arms dealers, who sold them the weaponry and materials for their bombs. These men had ended the Russian occupation of Afghanistan decades ago, and yet they had not discarded the outmoded methods of fighting, which were used when the CIA and the Pakistani Army were grooming them. Khalid preferred to think of their relationship as mutually beneficial: they were helping him to smuggle, and he was redirecting their energies to more commercial enterprises.

Khalid turned his attention again to the articles in the three papers. Perhaps the forces opposing the present government were responsible for shooting the schoolgirl—who had been flown to England for treatment. He found it hard to accept that the stunning valley of Swat still harboured the Taliban, despite the army's presence. He fought off the wave of depression that threatened to consume him by redirecting his thoughts to the problem at hand. Khalid had decided to raise money for his Iranian debt by selling three priceless works of art—works with which he'd never intended to part. He had already made the call. When the response came earlier than expected, it did not surprise him. The buyer wanted to purchase the pieces for a state minister's personal collection. The transaction would be made, illegally, through the national exchequer, and would be disguised to appear as an entirely different purchase.

Khalid handled the news with detachment. He was an art dealer; all that mattered was the sale and payment. The instructions for receiving the payment were very precise. An electronic transfer would be made to the bank account of his gallery in Bangkok. As soon as Khalid received confirmation, the vehicle that would collect the three works of art would be allowed inside his main gate.

"This is a big transfer, Abu. What have you sold?" asked his son Hamza, from the gallery in Bangkok.

"I have sold pieces of my heart, my son. Now listen to me

carefully: when the funds arrive, transfer them immediately to this account in London."

"Stay by the phone. I will call you back with the second confirmation," Hamza said, knowing his father would divulge nothing on the phone.

Like all corrupt government officials in Pakistan, Reza Mohsinzadegh had offshore accounts. Khalid maintained only one offshore account, and his son's residency in Bangkok legitimized it. Dubai was another hub for laundering money, but a business presence had to be established there, and Khalid instinctively disliked the Arabs, even though he had done business with them. As he waited to complete the sale and transactions, his anger at Adeel resurfaced. He had intended to live with these three paintings for the rest of his life.

Khalid rose and walked toward his Allah museum, seeking the solace of prayer. Faisal followed with his telephone, but maintained a discreet distance. Khalid walked past the rows of workmen toiling on the family burial tomb. Even if he lost everything, he thought, his burial place would never be removed or desecrated. His financial predicament had made him sombre. While walking past the gigantic Korans he kept in glass showcases, something caught his eye and he stopped. On a page of gold-painted Arabic script, a black dot had appeared. He moved closer to the case and widened his eyes. He withdrew his reading glasses from his pocket, pressed them into place, and stared at the dot again. The dot moved and his heart sank. It was a minuscule insect that had somehow found an opening in the case. He tapped the glass; to his horror, two additional black dots appeared from the corner.

"Faisal!" he shouted.

Faisal appeared by his side.

"The case is not airtight. Have it opened. There could be an infestation. This Koran is priceless and the insects will destroy it. Check the air conditioning, as well. I don't think it's working properly."

Upstairs, Khalid stood in front of his miniature *Ka'ba*, sank heavily to his knees, and began to sob. His recited prayers emerged as cries. Eventually, exhausted by the outpouring of emotion, he lowered himself on the prayer rug and fell asleep. An hour later, he felt hands on his shoulder waking him.

"Two calls have come. One from Bangkok—the money is deposited—and the other from Sher Khan. He wants you to call him. I'm sorry I did not wake you up," Faisal said apologetically.

Khalid rose immediately. He felt energized, as though he had slept for an entire night, and rapidly walked down the stairs.

"Have the gate opened. The transport for the paintings is waiting outside. Do it quickly. I don't want them to linger any longer than it takes to load the art."

He placed the call to Sher Khan, hung up, and waited for the return call.

"We have checked right up to Mansera and down to Bannu. No one has seen the brown truck."

"Please continue looking. He cannot hide forever," replied Khalid.

"Unless he changed the vehicle," suggested Sher Khan.

"Peshawar is the largest city. If he changed the truck, he would have had to do it there. He would have had to sell it."

"I am already checking. The hunt is well on its way; he will not escape me." Sher Khan laughed.

"Do we need more help? I can ask the ISI man to join in," Khalid offered.

"They are sons of jackals! No, do not involve them! I will deliver the man to you."

The line went dead. Khalid knew he had made a mistake. The Taliban loathed the army and the Intelligence Agency. The military penetration into the tribal areas and the resulting skirmishes had added a terrifying ferocity to the attacks on army checkpoints, personnel, and others who acted on their orders. It seemed as if the bands of unemployed and discontented men who joined the Taliban knew that a decent job and life was not their destiny. For them, pleasure only appeared at the sight of an enemy's corpse. The Durand Line might separate Pakistan from Afghanistan, but it meant nothing to the region's Pashtun culture. On both sides of the boundary, revenge was a time-honoured tradition. If a man did not take revenge, he was considered to be weak and without honour himself. Sher Khan — like the dons of Sicily — would hunt Adeel down because he had his own reputation to protect.

From a second-floor window, Khalid watched as a large, shiny van entered the front gates. It stopped near Faisal, who stood with two men, leaning against the flat cartons that contained the paintings. A sigh rose inside Khalid, but did not emerge from his lips. He seldom parted with paintings. He felt that the artist embedded a particle of his soul in every stroke of paint. With a fervour bordering on the mystical, Khalid felt he was the custodian of many spirits. Although he was familiar with his collection, the large air-conditioned vault housed works he had not seen for years.

KHALID RETURNED TO the house, hoping to put the day's unpleasant events behind him. As he made his way to the kitchen, he heard his wife's voice, and the familiar tone she used when speaking to her eldest son. Quietly, he picked up a nearby phone extension just in time to hear Safia confide in Hamza; Khalid, she said, was feeling some financial tension, but she had no idea about its cause.

Hamza reassured his mother, telling her that an enormous sale of art had just been made. Khalid heard him distracting his mother by asking when she would come to visit her grandchildren. After he heard Safia's response of "Soon," he quietly hung up the phone. He knew the rest of the conversation would be about the children.

After her call, Safia returned to her cooking, dicing turnips into julienne strips. Khalid leaned on the wall outside of the kitchen, enjoying the sight of his wife in her element. He knew she was preparing his favourite vegetables for dinner, and he loved the fact that she still looked out for him, even after years of marriage. When she reached up to the shelf that held her special frying pan, he moved forward, ready to help, but before he could, another hand shot up and brought it down for her. Once again he leaned against the wall, as Safia turned to see her son Hassan's mischievous face.

"I didn't hear you." She smiled indulgently at her youngest.

"Why are you doing this work yourself when we are so rich?"

"Hassan!" Safia pressed her finger against his lips.

"He will not let me do business. I need some money too. Hamza was given money."

"Oh, Hassan, please don't talk about your father that way."

"I don't care! I hate him! I hate all this! I want to go to America and never come back," Hassan shouted.

"I am going to make almond *halwa* just for you," said Safia, ignoring the outburst.

"Where does he keep the money? He made a big sale today," Hassan said quietly.

"Go away, Hassan. You are disturbing me." Safia leaned heavily against the kitchen counter, bracing herself with her hands.

Hassan left the room, unaware that his father had overheard the conversation. Khalid walked away from the kitchen and back to his office, too angry with Hassan to risk a conversation with Safia—she would realize he had eavesdropped—and smart enough to know that she, too, likely needed some time alone. Why did Hassan always have to torture his mother with his endless questions? Safia's anguish over her son pierced his heart, but he knew that it fell on deaf ears when he told her that the son with the face of an angel had the heart of a demon. She would always defend him. He was simply testing boundaries, she said; he never did any real harm. She insisted that Khalid get him a student visa even after he had dropped out of school. There were places in Pakistan where, for the right amount of money, papers were forged, including school and university degrees. And most colleges abroad allowed married students to bring their spouses along. But Khalid had refused to allow Hassan to study overseas last year, despite Safia's belief that he would return after a few years with some weighty professional degree. Khalid had no intention of looking after two toddlers for a few years, absolving Hassan and his wife from parental duties. Besides, Hassan still needed to deal with his secret second marriage. Unlike Safia, Khalid had a lot of experience in facing losses and accepting unfavourable outcomes.

Khalid spent an hour telephoning Reza both at his office in Tehran and at his country home in Shiraz. Neither one of the phones had voice mail, but Khalid knew that Reza would see the long-distance number and eventually call back. As he waited, Khalid's thoughts returned to Peshawar. Sher Khan's comment about a changed vehicle made sense. Adeel had sufficient money for expenses like fuel, food, and the allocated payments for the Afghans who had assisted, but not enough to buy a new vehicle. It would also have to be registered somewhere. Like Sher Khan, Adeel had been selected by Khalid for his success rate. The brigadier had vouched for him. This was not a man who would make stupid mistakes. Khalid wondered if he had lost control of the situation. Was it time for him to take a more active part in the search for the statue? He decided it was.

Having made up his mind, Khalid moved quickly. He told Safia that he was going to Peshawar for a few days and warned his son not to leave the estate — not tonight, or any other night until he returned. Then he retired to his room. He needed to pack and sleep. He would leave tomorrow.

WHEN THE SHABBY white sedan drove out of the front gates the following morning, Faisal was driving with Khalid by his side. Despite his enormous wealth, Khalid did not drive expensive cars. He believed they attracted undue attention. His manner of dress was also simple. He wore the Pakistani outfit of trousers and knee-length shirt but he clamped a Jinnah cap on his head. It gave him the air of a cleric and an offbeat dignity. His destination in Peshawar was not Sher Khan's hideout in Namak Mandi, but an antiquities dealer. There was a possibility that the marble sculpture, which he had yet to lay eyes upon, had been sold by Adeel. The dealer in Peshawar had his own network of people, and a discussion with him could be of value.

The three-hour drive was relatively uneventful, but on the last leg of the journey the phone rang. It was Ghalib.

"Mian sahib, you are the like the moon of Eid al-Fitr, hard to see," Khalid said boisterously.

"Politics, my dear Khalid. I am running for the National Assembly from my constituency. I am at the village. I have to be seen by my people," replied Ghalib in a lordly fashion.

"Yes, yes, we are all your supporters," Khalid laughed.

"If the party wins, I may be appointed as a minister," said Ghalib.

"Then you will have to behave yourself, Mian sahib." Khalid aimed his little dart by using the honorific of "Mian" and attaching "sahib" to it.

Ghalib did not respond. Khalid waited. Finally, Ghalib sighed.

"Small private pleasures, Khalid. Just games. You know that. Now, where is the new addition to my collection?"

"I am on my way to Peshawar to collect it," replied Khalid lightly.

"We will have to discuss the payment, Khalid. A lot of money is being spent for this political campaign. The construction of the local office has to be completed."

"Well, if you think you cannot afford it right now, I do have another offer."

"I am not in the mood for your games, Khalid. The sculpture is mine and you shall be paid on delivery," said Ghalib sharply. "Stay in touch."

Nothing would ever change Ghalib's greed, thought

Khalid. The political arena was full of men just like him—aging men with insatiable appetites who refused to clear the way for new blood. And now, a path to even greater riches was nearly open to Ghalib. If Ghalib were to be elected, Khalid knew that his rapacity would know no bounds. But it didn't matter. Not now. Khalid could not let his personal distaste for Ghalib's new political ambitions intrude on their business deal. Selling art was his business. He unwound the carved carnelian prayer beads from his wrist and slid them one after another through his fingers. There was only one prayer in his mind: that he would find the sculpture.

AN UNSEASONAL HIGH-PRESSURE storm gathered over the city of Peshawar. The workers at Sher Khan's restaurant in Namak Mandi spread a canvas awning over the cooking braziers. Rain or storm, people would still come to eat. Sher Khan stood on the rooftop terrace and gazed at the dark clouds. He had sent two of his men to the area of the city where trucks in need of minor repairs often ended up. Adjoining this area was another, where craftsmen stripped old American trucks and decorated them with murals and wooden trim. Sher Khan was following a hunch. Hours had gone by and there was still no word from Nadir; perhaps this assignment was going to be difficult.

Sher Khan took great precautions to remain anonymous. His name did not appear anywhere, and in his neighbourhood he was nothing more than the benign old man who watched over his sizzling kebabs and steaming naans. He was never seen at the local mosque for Friday prayers. Now, as the sky opened up, he retreated to his room where he found his phone ringing. He glanced at the number but did not answer it. His nephew appeared at his door.

"What is it?' asked Sher Khan.

"You have a visitor downstairs."

"How do you know the visitor is for me?" he asked.

"He gave me your name," the boy stammered.

A few minutes later, Sher Khan looked at the teacup in front of him. Gazing into its centre, he searched for an answer among the green tea leaves floating there. The visitor was one of his agents, who had come to tell him that he'd checked the truck stop and had found out that a local tea vendor had seen a brown truck enter the area around 10 a.m. that morning. However, the vendor never saw the truck come out. The agent told Sher Khan that Nadir had spent hours chatting up the mechanics; one man, who ran a truck-decoration business, was unusually aggressive when questioned.

"Bring out the motorcycle and take me to him," said Sher Khan, rising abruptly.

The two men blended into the snarl of traffic that had worsened because of the rain. Sher Khan was draped in an army-issue rain jacket. The man driving the motorcycle was soaked, yet he skilfully wove through the traffic. Finally, in a laneway where the road had disintegrated into puddles of water, the driver stopped the motorcycle.

"We need to walk from here," he said apologetically, gesturing to the overflowing gutters. "Otherwise, we will get stuck in the water."

"Let's go," said Sher Khan, striding through ankle-deep water.

They reached the large shed-like structure in ten minutes. It was padlocked from the front, but a light flickered from somewhere above. Sher Khan walked along the edge of the shed and saw a small wooden staircase. He climbed it quickly, tucking his holster further under his jacket toward his armpit. Sher Khan approached the wooden door and pushed it open. A man stood on a landing, facing him.

"Are you police or army?"

"Neither," said Sher Khan, pushing back the hood of his jacket.

"What do you want?" asked the man. "This is my property."

"I think you helped my friend this morning," replied Sher Khan.

"What friend?"

"It was the man who drove the brown truck."

"Many trucks come here. This is a small business. I would have noticed. There was no brown truck," the man replied.

"It is all right. He is in trouble and you helped him. He could not reach me or I would have given him one of my own cars," Sher Khan said, stepping closer.

"Who are you?" the man said fearfully, stepping back.

"We are all brothers," said Sher Khan as he pulled his revolver out.

AN HOUR LATER, Nadir received a call from Sher Khan.

"You will be looking for a needle in a haystack, Nadir," said Sher Khan, recounting all of the information he'd gathered from the man at the truck-decorating company.

"I will not fail to find him," Nadir replied. "There is only one road heading north."

SIX

Deep in the heart of Punjab Province, a tall man promenaded along the dusty lanes of a small village adjoining Ghalib's estate. His mission was to be seen so that he might create a combination of fear and awe in the hearts of the simple people. Nur Hyat, recently hired by Ghalib, fulfilled a time-honoured role in Pakistani politics: he ensured the vote bank. This meant that he guaranteed that the constituency, or *halka*, would deliver its votes on Election Day. Nur Hyat was six feet five. He sported glistening waves of short hair and a neat, clipped moustache. His pale-pistachio-coloured *shalwar kameez* suit was as theatrical because his cuffed, swirling trousers were made of nine yards of fine cotton instead of the usual three.

Nur Hyat was a jack of all trades. He sold carpets, supplied prostitutes, and even represented people when they sold their lands. Recently, however, he had fallen on hard times. Ghalib had summoned him, sniffed out his desperation, and promptly given him his current assignment. A modest expense account cemented the alliance between the two men. Nur Hyat was also given permission to enter both of Ghalib's residences, where meals would be served to him. On the odd occasion, he would also have the rare privilege of sharing a meal with Ghalib himself.

Nur Hyat's skills lay in his loquacious manner, twinned with his ability to argue a point to exhaustion. In order to escape the unchecked flow of his rhetoric, listeners acquiesced quickly. This was how Nur Hyat convinced the villagers to vote for his man. He often hinted at the great rewards that would come when Ghalib won. These false promises lit the flame of hope in the breasts of the downtrodden people who had been suffering silently since the creation of Pakistan. With his theatrical panache, Nur Hyat worked to build their confidence as well.

"Your needs are known," he would croon, "and they do not escape the eye of your patron. He is the only one who will take care of you." When some daring soul piped up and commented that this had never happened, Nur Hyat would promise that Ghalib would be the one to change all of that. He would get government money for them, but he would have to first win the election.

Nur Hyat's other task was to completely discredit Ghalib's opponents. Here, the storyteller in him rose to the occasion.

"The other party will seize all your farmland and build factories run by machines. You will not be able to feed your families!" he would roar.

Sometimes, he would pull out a wad of 100-rupee notes and put these in the hands of the women. This amounted to an extra three kilograms of vegetables. The money was always taken, confirming to Nur Hyat that votes were beginning to be secured.

At one of these speeches, a hard-eyed man with the body of a wrestler stepped forward.

"Other people have also come here to ask for our votes. Why should we give them to Mian sahib?"

"Because Ghalib is the best man for the job. He is like a father to all of you and his family has been here for generations. You see that great house?" said Nur Hyat, sensing trouble.

"Yes, we know all about that great house," said the man, and then spat viciously at Nur Hyat's feet.

"Hey! Watch your mouth," Nur Hyat said, slowly unbuttoning the cuffs of his shirt and pushing up his sleeves.

The two men faced each other while the small crowd stirred uneasily. Nur Hyat had been raised on the streets, and he was confident that a couple of blows would make the man retract his insulting gesture. Of course, he had no intention of getting into a physical altercation, but by rolling up his sleeves, he was indicating his ability to do so.

"*Dalal* pimp," hissed the man, spinning on his heel and swiftly walking away.

Nur Hyat smiled thinly, rolled down his sleeves—taking care to button them at the cuffs—and then raised his hand.

"That man is a fool. He will die poor. You," he said, pointing his index finger toward the crowd, "will give your vote to Mian sahib and reap great rewards."

GHALIB SAT ON his bed propped up by pillows, telling his cook which dishes he wanted him to prepare for a special lunch he was having. A disgruntled cabinet minister, Soody, who had resigned in a fit of pique, had joined a new political party. He was an acquaintance of Ghalib's, and the one who had convinced him to run in his constituency. The new party was garnering a lot of media attention, declaring its mandate to end corruption and give birth to accountability in a nation that had survived for almost sixty-four years without either. The leader of the new party was a Pakistani man named Ashiq Khota, who had existed on the fringes of the political arena before revealing his new ambition to lead the nation. Word swept through the country, and opportunists of every stripe joined his party. He had a youthful appearance and a tall, muscular body. This was a pleasing contrast to the country's heavily jowled, overweight, and greying politicians. AK, as he was called by everyone, had never held public office, and his record was clean. He blustered when at the podium, hurling colourful invective at the government and his various rivals. For close to a year, he had comically addressed his assembly of followers by mixing metaphors that his largely unlettered audience could not understand. He promised that a magic wand would clean up the nation, delivering a brand new Pakistan. His audience was made up of hordes of young, uneducated men who viewed political rallies as the prime venues for a new form of sanctioned hooliganism. They tore down barriers, jumped on the speaker's stage, and vandalized public property, all while terrorizing the more genteel attendees. They also waved party flags, danced to sentimental political songs, and created horrendous traffic jams. AK's canny social media team uploaded video footage and set the online world in Pakistan spinning. Facebook and Twitter support blossomed until, eventually, the artificially created popularity ratings became fact rather than fiction.

Ghalib, for whom opportunism was an act of both genius and survival, felt his new political aspirations would add lustre to his life. If he were to be gifted with a cultural portfolio, perhaps the seasonal depression that had plagued him for years would be lifted. He had to admit that the thought of riding around in a poster-emblazed car, lifting his hand to wave to the people, carried a certain seductive grandeur. The new party also had a modern buzz about it. The people coming for lunch would give Ghalib advice about campaigning for the new party and advise him on how to run his headquarters, or *dera*, as it was called locally. In return, Ghalib would dazzle them with his sumptuous country home and the copious amounts of food served at his table. The long dining table seated about sixteen, which in itself was an impressive display of china and flatware.

AN HOUR LATER, Ghalib greeted his guests with a lavish welcome. A smile flitted across his face when he heard the three party officials admiring the central salon. The abundance of ancient sculptures, vessels, and tapestries—lit perfectly by colourful, handmade wooden chandeliers—earned approving gazes. Ghalid could almost hear their thoughts: they knew they were in the home of a man who would serve the nation well. A local lawyer who had put in many hours to promote the party in the nearby town of Pakpattan was also present.

The lunch was a roaring success. A plan was immediately devised for organizing cricket matches for the local teenagers. These matches would be hosted by Ghalib, who would hand out cash rewards to the winning teams along with gilt-covered plastic trophies. Ghalib's visibility, including the brief speeches he would make, would be his training ground for the upcoming elections. When the lunch was over, Ghalib retired to his room.

As he sat in his bath, Ghalib fantasized about the

magnificent Buddhist sculpture Khalid would soon deliver. He had been perusing the new Sotheby's catalogue and planned to write a letter to an art dealer in London in order to ascertain the current value of the piece. He also thought about a slender fifteen-year-old girl in the village who had caught his eye. Ghalib knew that she would not be delivered to him. For her, he would have to indulge in a little courtship. The mother had made no secret of her loathing for Ghalib. As he soaked in the warm, soapy water, he decided to pay a casual visit to the girl's house later that evening, armed with a stack of presents to dent the mother's resistance.

DUSK WAS A mysterious time of the day. Pale light settled on the mud and stucco homes of the village. The whine of farm tractors ceased, along with the sound of small children playing in the lanes. Wearing a fresh outfit, Ghalib was on his way to the young girl's house. He sat in the back seat of his car, accompanied by squares of colourful fabric that rose in a tidy pile next to him. Each square contained enough material for a suit of clothes, along with a diaphanous length for the matching *dupatta*. The fabrics, carefully chosen by Ghalib, reflected his exquisite taste. The artist in him had selected vibrant magenta, turquoise, and emerald green. Next to the fabrics rested two one-kilo boxes of local sweets, wrapped in tissue paper fastened in place with gold ribbon. The pièce de résistance was a clear plastic box containing a cheap pink-quartz watch, along with two tubes of lip gloss. He knew these items would pierce the heart of a fifteen-year-old village girl like an arrow.

The car stopped at the end of the narrow lane. A tall, lanky man walked up to the car and greeted Ghalib.

"Ah Nilu, it has been a long time and I have come to visit your family," Ghalib said.

Nilu grinned as his eyes flickered over the gifts that the chauffeur was holding in his arms. This game was as old as the hills. Nilu knew his teenaged daughter would bring unlimited bounties to the family. All he had to do was wait and see how the negotiations would be carried out. He had been apprised of the landlord's interest weeks ago, but his wife had mounted a stubborn resistance. Over the years, an endless line of teenaged girls and boys had been selected and sent to the Ghalib's house, where they functioned as sex slaves and performed domestic duties. Once the novelty wore off, Ghalib would pay for a marriage to a more suitable local. Despite the unpleasant nature of these arrangements, most parents allowed Ghalib to have his way; they knew his displeasure could render them homeless and jobless in an instant. The girls who were selected would be fed a more nutritious diet than they would have at home, and be provided with clothes and gifts they could share with their families. It was the fathers who made these decisions about their daughters. In Nilu's case, however, his wife simply refused to entertain the idea. Unlike the submissive women in the village, she raged at the thought of this arrangement. The lack of social justice for women was a flame that consumed her. She loathed Ghalib, and she would not allow this to happen to her child.

Ghalib followed Nilu, who pushed open the wooden door embedded in the mud wall that encircled his tiny home. Two rope beds and a wooden armchair furnished the small central courtyard, along with a large tree to which a goat was tethered. Hidden under the lush, cascading foliage was a wooden wheelbarrow that Nilu filled with the local fruits and vegetables he sold on the main road.

"Please sit, Mian sahib. I will ask my family to greet you," said Nilu, gesturing to the wooden chair.

Ghalib asked the chauffeur to place the gifts on one of the rope-strung beds. A gaunt woman with dark skin emerged from inside the house. She threw a furious look at her husband and sat down on the bed that was farthest away from Ghalib and his gifts. She stared straight ahead, refusing to make eye contact with Ghalib. Then, a slender girl with her head wrapped in a black cotton shawl emerged. She sat on the bed where the gifts had been placed, but turned her back to Ghalib.

Ghalib murmured soft greetings to both the mother and daughter. He studied the girl's back and examined her dirty feet, dangling near the floor. When she'd entered the courtyard, her astonishing beauty had been clearly visible. She had an oval face with a small stud glinting on one side of her nose. Ghalib thought she could use a long soak in his bathtub. The thought of her rising, sylphlike, with drops of perfumed water dripping off her body made him dizzy.

"Look, Shehla. I have bought you some gifts. Why don't you show them to your mother," he cajoled in a soft voice.

The girl sat with her back to him, but the fingers of one slim hand pinched the lowest pile of fabric and then quickly withdrew. Her mother rose silently and walked to the open mud hearth. She squatted to light the fire for tea.

"I have already had tea. Nilu, please tell her not to trouble herself," Ghalib said. He noticed that the girl had turned sideways just a little, and her profile was now visible.

"Shehla. It is Shehla, isn't it?" Ghalib said.

She looked over one shoulder quickly and glanced at him. In the split second before he turned away, Ghalib saw laughter in her eyes. He smiled broadly at Nilu. The mother returned to her spot.

"Is Shehla going to school?' asked Ghalib, knowing full well that the girl was illiterate.

"She works with me in the fields at harvest," said the mother sternly.

Ghalib rose. He was not going to push his luck. His departure would determine if his opening gambit had made an impact. He knew the gifts would not be examined in his presence. But if he was permitted to leave them, the girl would fight for the watch and lip gloss and the mother would hang on to the fabric.

"Goodbye, Shehla," said Ghalib to her turned back.

She made a sound. He thought perhaps she stifled a laugh. Then, in a muffled voice she said. "You better take your things with you."

"They are gifts for you . . . and for the family. I will not take them back."

Ghalib walked toward the wooden door without glancing back. It was only a matter of time before another flower bud would be pinned on his lapel. Hunger, deprivation, and the complete absence of social justice had given rise to a reckless greed in this country. For the poor, any shortcut to the privileged life of the rich was acceptable — especially for girls, who were always a financial burden. The only obstacle to Shehla was her mother, but Ghalid knew this could be overcome. If the woman could no longer find work at Ghalib's estate, or at any neighbouring farm, she would likely change her mind.

Ghalib's chauffeur had witnessed many of these selection rituals, and had often played messenger while he ferried the girls back and forth in one of his employer's many vehicles. Tonight, though, as he eased the car over the dusty potholes of the village lanes, he had a sense of foreboding. The girl was so young, and the image of his corpulent employer plucking her virginity made him shudder. He had five children of his own. Ghalib's current object of favour was sometimes taken to the city home in Lahore, although her presence was concealed once there. The chauffeur knew that she stayed in a tiny room on the second floor, close to Ghalib's own suites. He also knew that male servants would often furtively proposition her, but he had no taste for this behaviour; he always kept his distance.

"What do you think?" Ghalib inquired from the back seat. "Is the mother really a problem?"

"Yes, she is. Let her go, Mian sahib, there are lots of other girls in the village," said the chauffeur.

"I cannot resist her. She is beautiful and I want her." Ghalib's tone was dismissive, matter-of-fact. "Tell Nilu there is a reward for him in this."

"Mian sahib, please ask your estate manager to talk to Nilu. I don't want to, I have children of my own..."

Silence filled the car. There was no need for Ghalib to respond. All it would take was a phone call to his household clerk, and a simple instruction: delay the chauffeur's salary this month.

RETURNING HOME EMPTY-HANDED irritated Ghalib. The night stretching ahead demanded some form of revelry. There was a female entertainer in the town of Sahiwal, thirty kilometres away. She was a singer who was not averse to being summoned on short notice. Ghalib fancied her easy charm, her husky singing voice, and her sexual compliance. The chauffeur—who would bear the brunt of Ghalib's displeasure for the remainder of his stay in the country — was dispatched to bring her immediately as Ghalib busied himself by ordering carpets and cushions to be brought to the rooftop pavilion.

Ghalib stood supervising the arrangements with a large beer stein in his hand. He was diabetic, and currently under the care of a somewhat untrustworthy naturopath in Lahore who had told him to drink as much beer as he wanted. This was Ghalib's third stein, and he felt a pleasant euphoria wash over him as he imagined that he was a Mughal prince waiting for a courtesan to entertain him for the night. Nur Hyat would handle the tedious detail of the singer's fee. His groom, who regularly beat him at snooker, would also be invited to the party, as well as two of the teenaged boys who were his current favourites. Ghalib's spirits rose even further when he heard the sound of the car entering the estate's gates. He clapped his hands in pleasure.

At midnight, Ghalib held a *mujra*, which had its origins in the Mughal culture of undivided India. Accompanied by musicians, courtesans sang innuendo-filled songs designed to arouse sexual desire. Whether it was a poem being performed, or movements from the classical Kathak dance, a strict etiquette was followed. The courtesan was treated with great respect, and the audience was given licence to make extravagant gestures of admiration.

The dark-haired singer settled on the carpet and tugged at her scooped neckline as she snapped her fingers at her accompaniment for the right rhythm. Then she cupped one hand, brought it to her forehead, and whispered *"adaab"* to Ghalib, who was seated right in front of her. Ghalib leaned forward, dropping strands of jasmine around her neck. The two teenaged boys giggled, while Nur Hyat let out a throaty sigh. The woman was more spectacle than songstress. From her wrists—encircled with tinkling glass bangles—to her henna-festooned feet, she heaved and writhed as she sang. Ghalib clapped and swayed in time with the music, occasionally indicating which songs he wished to hear. At 3 a.m., he told himself the night was still young. He knew he could last until dawn, when the singer's heaving bosom would become his pillow.

IT WAS 6:30 a.m. when the hysterical farm manager burst through the main gates of the estate, waking the sleeping guard and insisting that he lead him to Ghalib immediately. He raced up the stairs to the rooftop terrace where the carpets were littered with sleeping bodies. Ghalib's was not among them. The manager kicked Nur Hyat, who opened his eyes and scowled.

"Where is Mian sahib?"

"Be quiet." Nur Hyat whispered, pressing a finger against his lips. "He cannot be disturbed." He closed his eyes again.

The manager ran down the steps, where he spied Ghalib's valet sleeping outdoors.

"Wake up," he said, shaking the man. "There's been a catastrophe! Our master has been robbed! I have to speak to him at once."

"His door is locked. No one can enter," replied the valet.

"Bang on the door. Do it now," demanded the manager.

Ghalib heard the knocking. At first, he thought it was the workmen banging on wood. Gradually, however, he realized the sound was coming from his own door. He propped himself up on one elbow. The scent of cheap perfume surrounded him as the room spun and tilted. He was still drunk, and it was going to take him a few minutes to extricate himself from the mayhem in his bed—including the singer and one of the boys. He could hear the urgency in his valet's voice beyond the locked door. Thoroughly outraged at being disturbed, Ghalib bellowed at the door, then rose, knotted a sarong around his waist, and pulled on last night's shirt. The jasmine garlands that he had draped over the singer were now around his neck. He chuckled, pulled them off, and tossed them on the bed as he made his way to the door.

An hour later, the front courtyard had been transformed into a crisis centre. While Ghalib and his entourage had been enjoying their night of decadant pleasure, a sizeable portion of his fortune had slipped away. An entire potato crop—worth millions of rupees—had disappeared from his storage facility. Now, Ghalib sat with three phones spread on the table before him, along with a mug of scalding tea. He was still trying to digest the news. The sale of the valuable potato crop had been intended to make a dent in his enormous bank loan, but now it was not to be. Ghalid shook his head. One had to give credit where credit was due. The theft had been masterfully planned. The farm manager, aware of Ghalib's terrace bacchanal, had retired to bed early. When he awoke at 6 a.m., a villager reported that two long transport trucks had been seen at the storage area in the middle of the night. A visit to the facility had confirmed the news. The potatoes were, indeed, gone. Despite knowing that he'd probably be fired over the theft, the manager had run straight to Ghalib's house to confront his fate.

Ghalib spoke to the police in Sahiwal. Then he lined up all of his employees in the courtyard. He asked them to reveal any conversation or local gossip they might have heard about the theft. Calmly, he told his farm manager to keep an eye on the nearby markets: the thieves would undoubtedly try to sell the stolen potatoes, and that would lead to their arrest.

Ghalib dismissed the workers and the manager, and leaned back in his chair, cup of tea in hand. He had done all he could do for the moment, but the actions taken had not quelled his concerns. Would his present financial crisis hamper his purchase of the statue? How could it not, when such a sizeable amount of cash was required? Ghalib thought for a moment, formulating a new plan. He placed his mug on the table and rose from the chair, resolved that his day would not be entirely ruined by the theft. He would go visit his bank manager in town.

THE TWO MEN had an affable meeting. Ghalib did not reveal the true purpose of his visit. Instead, he hinted that his village could well do with a local branch of the bank. He had a choice corner plot of land that he could make available at a reasonable price, he told the manager. They decided that lunch should be had to discuss the proposition in more detail.

In a nation of gastronomical delights, Sahiwal had not been left behind. Chinese cuisine adapted for the Pakistani palate was a spicy favourite with many people in the region, and the town boasted a particularly good Chinese restaurant. When the sumptuous dishes of seafood, beef filet, and chicken arrived, accompanied by fried rice and soups, Ghalib tasted each one. The men ate for close to an hour in absolute silence, despite the crisis that had brought them together. Unbeknownst to Ghalib, the news of the potato theft had spread like wildfire. The bank manager had received the news by text as he drove to the restaurant, and he used the information to his advantage. He picked up the bill while Ghalib graciously inclined his head. As he settled with the restaurant's owner, he did so safe in the knowledge that his most fashionable and aristocratic client would be selling his land to the bank at an even cheaper rate than he thought. And, of course, it would now be the bank's duty to tighten the terms of Ghalib's outstanding loan.

SEVEN

ADEEL OPENED HIS EYES. The cold air had woken him up.
The small heater was not running, so he knew the electricity had been turned off at some point in the night. It was
almost dawn when he sat up and saw her folded like a child
in a fetal position against the wall. She had slept with her
shoes on. He entered the small toilet, peeled off his clothes,
and washed himself as best as he could in the cracked hand
basin. When he was done, he opened the faucet that was
stuck in the wall over the trough and clenched his teeth
as the cold water poured over his body. After drying himself, he dressed quickly. When he re-entered the room, the
woman was awake and seated against the wall; her face
was pale.

"We have to leave at once. Do you need to use the toilet?"

She got up gingerly and stepped across the room in her
new shoes. When she emerged a few minutes later, she
picked up the wool blanket and draped it over her head,
holding the edges of the blanket like a shawl. Her high

cheekbones stood out sharply—a physical confirmation of her Tibetan ancestry.

Not for the first time since meeting her, Adeel considered her body language; it seemed overly defensive, which made him wonder if she had experienced physical abuse at some point or another. Was it the husband she had run away from, or her father? A desire to console and reassure her overcame him, but there was no time.

"Let's go," he said, and led the way out.

They rolled out of the sleeping hamlet at 6 a.m. and headed to Chilas in the Gilgit Valley. It would be a 250-kilometre trek through the Babusar Pass and, factoring in road conditions, Adeel estimated a four-and-a-half-hour journey.

Adeel pulled out the round of cheese and the package of dried apricots he had picked up in Peshawar and put them on the seat next to her.

"Here," he said, pushing the cheese and his folded pen-knife toward her.

She unfolded the knife and examined it carefully. He wondered if she might decide to plunge its four-inch blade into his chest; instead, she sliced a perfect wedge of cheese and held it out to him.

"No. No. You eat first." He brushed her hand away.

"Food is given to the men first," she said quietly.

"Why?" he said angrily.

She scowled at him.

"I will not eat before you," he said more gently.

She turned her face away and gazed out the window. Adeel wondered how long she would hold out. He knew he could outwait her, but why was it so important to him that she eat first? He knew he had to control these feelings that she evoked in him. Again he considered dropping her off somewhere, but he knew it was too late for that. Every trace of last night's dinner had long since been digested; he knew they were both hungry, but her stubbornness won the day.

"Fine!" he said, exhaling heavily and reaching for the slice of cheese she had placed on the dashboard.

She immediately cut another slice and held it out to him. He grabbed it and jammed it against her mouth, the steering wheel spinning dangerously in the wrong direction.

She removed the pieces of cheese rolling off her chin, threw back her head, and laughed. Then she cut another slice and held it out to him. This time, though, she leaned away. In that moment, Adeel could no longer hold back his laughter. He had never engaged in such play with a woman before — only with his cadet friends at the military academy years ago. Every time his mother had suggested that he get married, he ducked the conversation. He did not want to make the same mistake as his brother and marry the wrong woman.

"What is in your truck?" she asked through a mouth full of dried apricots.

"What do you mean? Nothing," he said, shocked to be on the receiving end of such a direct question.

"I know there is something there. I can feel it. Here," she said, tapping her heart.

Adeel was dumbstruck. He knew she had not had a chance to look inside the back of the truck. She was just fishing for information.

"It is precious to you? Is this why you are taking it far away?"

He remained silent for a while, then cleared his throat. He knew he was about to take a great risk; what he didn't know was why.

"Do you want to see it?" he asked.

"Yes," she replied, carefully folding the bag of apricots.

Adeel drove in silence, staring at the mountains rising sharply ahead and the river splicing through the valley below. His reckless offer had aroused her curiosity, and allowed grave risks to enter his plans. Still, he knew that he wanted to show her the sculpture.

"Are you religious?" he said after a while.

"No. I cannot understand anything. The boys went to the mosque, but the girls stayed at home."

"You say the prayers?"

"No. I pretend if I have to."

He was surprised by her honesty and continued questioning her.

"Come on, your mother must have taught you something."

"My mother bled to death giving birth to me. I was raised by my father. He taught me how to light a fire and cook. That is all."

"Is your husband going to look for you? Did you give him a child?"

"No. He married another woman and his family threw me out of the house. I will live in these mountains and take care of myself," she replied, turning away.

"You will freeze to death. Nothing grows in the mountains," he said, slowing down the truck.

Adeel stopped where the road widened a little. A moment later, he and the woman stood behind the truck. He moved quickly, opening the back door and climbing in before he could change his mind. She followed right after him, and he reached to help, pulling her up by both arms. The shawl slipped from her head and she wound it around her neck like a long scarf. He turned, then, and slowly lifted the pile of woollen blankets. Behind him, her sharp intake of breath startled him. Her hands reached forward as she stared at the statue in wonder.

"I know what this is," she said as she stroked the neck of the sculpture, tracing the length of its marble drapery. Then she pressed her fingertips delicately around the face.

"What do you know about it?" Adeel asked.

"In Swat they destroy them. You must keep it hidden," she said.

"I will take care of it. It will not leave my side," Adeel replied.

"So you are like me. *Kafir!* Unbeliever?" She bent over the sculpture again.

"I have stolen it," he confessed.

"It's all right. I will help you. We will make a shrine for it with a big light," she said. "Then you will see how truly beautiful it is."

"We will both be hunted, and killed if we are found with it. Come on, we must go." He re-arranged the blankets over the quilt and made his way back to the cab of the truck.

Adeel knew that the hunt for him must have begun. He was placing his faith in the region he had chosen to travel, but he knew he would have to find shelter in the hamlet of Chilas. But what to do with the woman? She could not pass for a relative; she looked nothing like him. The people of Gilgit, where she was from, had distinct Indo-Aryan faces, in which Tibetan, Chinese, and Tartar bloodlines mingled. She would have to masquerade as his wife.

Adeel drove ahead, considering his new plan from every possible angle. For a while, the road was clear and they made good progress, but a little way outside Chilas, a

Jeep, heading toward them, did not pass. Instead, it stopped, blocking the path. The driver got out and ran up to their truck.

"Do not go to Chilas! Turn around," he shouted at them.

"Is there a problem on the road?" Adeel asked.

"Passengers were pulled from a bus and killed."

"Why?" asked Adeel, dreading the answer.

"They were Shia!"

Adeel did not press the man further, just pointed his finger forward and took his foot off the brakes. The driver, realizing that his warning was not about to deter Adeel, returned quickly to his Jeep and moved the vehicle aside. As Adeel drove on, he pulled an automatic rifle from under his seat and placed it between him and the woman. Sectarian violence was an aberration in the country. More and more often these days, blood was spilled in the name of Islam—and with each act, the pages of Pakistan's history book seemed to turn backwards. The Taliban, who were mired in medieval confusion and frustrated by a lack of political power, radicalized their brand of Islam by teaching men to sow the seeds of genocide. Murder was rationalized with phrases like "holy martyrdom" and "holy *jihad*." And now, in response to this latest act of violence, security forces would no doubt be rushing toward the area, looking for the perpetrators of the crime. Adeel and his passenger needed a place to hide, at least for a while.

OUTSIDE CHILAS, THE bus had shuddered to a stop. The passengers were unconcerned. Police checks were a way of life in this country. The two women who sat shrouded in their burkas, only half of their faces revealed, were the first to sense that the policeman who had jumped into the bus and pushed his way past the bewildered driver was not behaving like a real policeman. He went down the aisle barking a question: "Shia? Sunni?" Two turbaned men armed with revolvers followed him in. One by one, eight men were pulled from the bus and led to the road, where they stood in an uncertain clump. Within the bus, there was not a sound. The remaining passengers averted their eyes, looking out the windows at the mountains, the sweeping valley, and the stone-edged river below. The full-throated cry of *"Allah-o Akbar"* rang out as the three turbaned men, standing a mere foot away from their targets, lifted their revolvers. Eight bodies with blood-splattered heads fell forward, hitting the gravel-lined road. Not one twitched or moved. Somebody wept softly in the back of the bus. One young man had been saved by a woman who had claimed he was her son. The driver repeated a prayer for the dead under his breath.

Out on the road, another cry of *"Allah-o Akbar"* rang out. This time, it was the policemen's turn to topple. Their bodies fell on top of the men they had shot just moments before. Eight turbaned men darted over the incline at the side of the road, rifles bobbing on their shoulders. Within seconds, they had vanished.

When help finally arrived from the regional security force, some of the men vomited despite their training. White sheets were thrown over the corpses, but the blood seeped through the covering, making designs that looked like poppies and roses.

ADEEL DROVE RAPIDLY. He knew the woman had heard the news, but she had not reacted, except to nudge the rifle a little closer to him.

"They will be gone. They kill and hide quickly," he said, glancing at her.

She did not respond.

"We have to find a place and hide this truck. Do you know this area?"

"No. My father does not live in this region," she said quietly.

"I can leave you in the village if you are afraid, but I need your help for a little while longer," he said.

"Can you shoot the Taliban?"

"Yes. I am trained. Don't think about them," he said firmly.

"You have protection with you. The statue will protect us. Buddha," she said solemnly.

"Not Allah?" he asked, surprised.

"The Taliban, they are his people," she said scornfully.

"If anyone stops and asks questions, you have to pretend to be my wife."

"No," she protested. "You said they kill and run away!"

"I mean, if you are asked by the police, army, or people on the street. You have to be strong. Are you strong?"

"See that mountain," she pointed up. "I can climb that in my bare feet!"

"I mean in your head. That is what matters," he replied.

An army truck appeared behind them. Adeel knew it would be better to let it overtake him as soon as the road widened. He understood the confusion and frustration that must be rampant within a military continually sabotaged by the Taliban's surprise attacks. There would be solemn photographs in the newspapers with a figure from the High Command offering some lame excuse to the masses. The driver of the army truck leaned on his horn. Adeel moved his truck closer to the cliff side of the road. As the army vehicle shot past, Adeel turned his head sideways and lifted his arm to hide his face. The woman crouched lower in her seat. The man on the passenger side of the military vehicle glanced at them briefly. As soon as the truck had overtaken them, it slowed down. Eventually, it stopped completely, forcing Adeel to do the same.

"Don't say a word," Adeel hissed to the woman.

An officer got out and walked toward their truck, accompanied by two soldiers. Adeel rolled down the window.

"What's in the back of your truck?" the officer asked Adeel.

"Woollen blankets and shawls. I am taking them to a man who has a shop," Adeel responded smoothly.

"Who is the woman?"

"She is my wife. Her family is in Gilgit."

"There is trouble in Chilas. You have not passed a brown half-truck on the way? We are looking for a dangerous man," the officer said.

"Taliban?" asked Adeel.

"Yes," the officer replied slowly.

"I will keep my eyes open, sir," Adeel mumbled. "Can we go now? My wife has not eaten anything since the morning."

"Is this rifle yours?"

"It belongs to the man who owns the truck."

"Well, make sure she doesn't shoot you because she's become too hungry," he said, laughing and pointing his finger at the huddled woman whose face was turned away.

Adeel watched them walk away. So it was true; the hunt for him had begun. He needed to find a hiding place and stay off the road for a while. The only solution was Chilas: they would have to infiltrate the small community and try to assimilate, while somehow maintaining their anonymity.

"I have to stay in Chilas for a while. You must decide what you want to do. I cannot be responsible for you," he said, stumbling over his words.

"I have no home," she whispered.

"What about your father? He could be looking for you."

"You know that once you are given to a man in marriage there is no place back with your family," she said fiercely.

"If he knows you are in trouble he will take care of you."

"He will beat me."

Adeel felt a sudden rage at the truth of her simple statement. He took a deep breath, then looked at her.

"I will teach you a few things so that any hand that is lifted against you will break before it lands."

Adeel started the truck and they continued to Chilas together.

ADEEL WORKED OUT a plan in his head as they crossed the Babusar River Bridge in silence. But as they came around the last bend in the mountain road, a crowd of people milling about on the small main street outside Chilas blocked their path. Hundreds of men with angry faces shouted loudly and jostled each other. A handful of local police also raised their voices, trying in vain to disperse the crowd. The road leading into the main bazaar was jammed with parked vehicles. Their drivers had stepped out to investigate the situation.

Adeel leapt out of the truck and headed toward the crowd. These were Shia men, looking for revenge on behalf of the members of their community who had been killed. Adeel listened to the talk as he pushed his way through. There were dark rumours about the local police being complicit in the killings. The government had responded by immediately shutting down all of the mosques in the area— both Shia and Sunni. Most of the local shops had closed, the shop owners barricading the doors to protect themselves and their property from the angry crowds. Adeel moved farther along the main street. A small alley appeared on one side of the road, revealing a few box-like concrete homes. In front of one of them, an elderly man sat on a stool, puffing on a hookah. Adeel walked over to him.

"Baba, I am on a journey but my wife is not well. Do you have anyplace where she can rest for a while?"

"Don't stop. There is trouble here," the old man said, sucking on the hookah's stem.

"Everyone has blocked the road. Please help me. I can pay you," Adeel said, searching his pockets before realizing the money bag was still in the truck.

"There is space on the roof, but it gets cold at night," the man said reluctantly.

"We have blankets. Thank you. I shall bring her here." Adeel grasped both of the man's hands and clasped them within his own.

"What do you have? A car or a van?" asked the old man.

"I have a truck. It is not big. It is giving me trouble and I may have to leave it here and continue by bus."

"Do you want to sell it?"

"We can talk about it." Adeel smiled at the old man's opportunism.

"Behind the house there is a place where you can park it."

"I cannot move it. There are too many people in the road."

"We will see," the man said, rising up. "I will help you to bring it here."

Adeel watched him spit repeatedly in the hookah's small clay bowl. Once satisfied that the coals were no longer burning, the old man buttoned his long wool waistcoat with nimble fingers and rammed a wool cap on his head. He stepped off the small concrete stoop and gestured for Adeel to follow him down the lane.

They elbowed their way through the clumps of men toward the parked vehicles. In the time that Adeel had been gone, a new barrier had been erected on the path to the main road. Once again, a peaceful community had been shattered by sectarian violence. The real culprits would never be found, but an act of reprisal would be forthcoming. The bearded men with wool caps on their head all believed in this concept of revenge. Pakistan's security was threatened by shadowy figures who raised their faith like a cudgel and eradicated the notion of civil society. Adeel hoped that the man he followed could be trusted.

Before he left, Adeel had locked the truck and left the windows open a crack. As he approached now, the woman was not visible. For a moment, Adeel was worried, and he rushed to open the door. She was asleep on the seat, her face shrouded protectively with both arms. As the old man peered inside, a sense of tenderness flooded Adeel. He felt like a parent forced to wake a sleeping child. She stirred in her sleep, and Adeel quickly leaned forward and whispered in her ear.

"We have shelter, but do not look or talk to the man I am with."

The old man told Adeel that he would ride with him, and that a path would be cleared for the truck. Adeel sat behind the wheel and pulled the woman closer to him and away from the old man. As her rigid body pressed against his thigh, he shifted and tried to lean closer to the door.

Adeel tried to pull out of the lineup, but there were people and vehicles all around.

"Blow the horn and don't stop," the old man said. He stuck his head out the window and shouted at the people on the road, "Let us through! Let us through!"

It took them over an hour to finally escape the crowd of men and parked vehicles — a distance of only a couple of hundred feet. At last, though, their howling benefactor had cleared a path with the force of his unrelenting voice.

"Gilgit is changing," he said as they drove slowly toward the man's home. "Three generations of my family have lived here. But now we have to deal with the Taliban? We have all become afraid of them. The army needs to bring its big guns and hunt them down like dogs!"

Adeel made to turn into the narrow lane, but the man guided him instead to a dirt road that was full of potholes. The woman bounced up and down like a cork beside him, gripping his arm. The old man turned to her and spoke solicitously. "You will rest very soon."

After they parked the truck behind the house, the old man led them into a small room that had no furniture.

"The roof will be cold at night," he said. "I will bring you some quilts." He bustled from the room, leaving them behind.

The woman peered out of the small window. When she straightened up, she banged her head sharply on the cracked window frame. Adeel dashed over and pried away her fingers from her head. She swayed unsteadily and elbowed him away.

"Stop it," he said fiercely. "I want to see that you have not cut open the skin."

She took a step back and lifted her hand to reveal a large egg-shaped bump rising underneath. He started to laugh softly to himself. He couldn't help it; she looked like an angry bird. Almost immediately, her lips twitched and she began to giggle, oblivious to the rising pain.

The old man appeared in the doorway with a bundle of quilts in his arms. He placed them on the floor.

"I will kill a chicken for dinner. Is your wife a good cook?"

"The best," said Adeel, avoiding eye contact with her.

"Well, come with me."

They walked from the front of the house toward a small chicken coop. The old man knelt down and opened the mesh door a few inches.

"I think it should be the old one; she does not lay eggs anymore."

His hand shot in and grasped the squawking brown hen by the neck.

Adeel watched him the pin the chicken on a large rock, then expertly kill and feather it within minutes.

"What is your name?" The older man lifted the plucked chicken toward him.

"Adeel," he replied.

"Who is your father?"

"He is dead."

"Yes, but he gave you a name. What comes after Adeel?"

"Muhammad. Adeel Muhammad."

"The kitchen is on the roof. Take your wife there and let her cook our dinner."

THE KITCHEN SAT under a small cotton awning on the rooftop. There was a two-ring propane burner, some cheap aluminum pots, and a basket filled with mountain herbs. Adeel watched the woman stir the pot more frequently than he thought was necessary. She ignored all culinary rules, throwing long stems of uncut herbs over the chicken, after dousing it with two glasses of water. She placed the pot on one of the burners, but did not know how to control the gas flame. As Adeel bent over to help her, she looked up at him and smiled, rooting him to the spot. Eventually, he straightened up and turned away from her.

"I will go down to find some roti, if the bazaar is opened," he mumbled without looking at her.

As Adeel walked down the stone staircase, he heard the old man's voice, talking into the telephone.

"I think he is one of them. He has a woman with him, but he lies about her. Bring someone with you. I will keep them here."

EIGHT

KHALID REACHED PESHAWAR BY early afternoon, in a curiously optimistic mood. He felt that the key to the stolen sculpture lay in this city. Both Sher Khan and the brigadier were assisting with the search, but he needed a third option as well.

He watched Faisal weave through the chaotic traffic toward Hayatabad, the city's westernmost suburb. It was both a commercial and residential zone, and development in both areas was ongoing. Built along the road that headed to the Khyber Pass and Afghanistan, the area was a breath of fresh air compared to the snarl of the grime-laden city core. The residents were a mixed bag of prosperous Afghan refugees and local Pathans, and the homes reflected a degree of affluence. Khalid was on his way to visit a businessman named Karamat, who dealt in collectibles. The items he sold ranged from imported liquor to guns, antiquities, medication not available in Pakistan, and superb emeralds smuggled in from Afghanistan. Karamat was partial to Western clothing, old Egyptian films, and young wives.

His neighbours believed that he was a retired eccentric, but Khalid knew the scale of his business operations. His misleading public face had been created with great skill.

Karamat's nameless two-storey villa was the last house on a dead-end street. A guard swung open the gates immediately upon seeing Khalid's car; the man had been informed in advance of his arrival. Khalid got out of the car and began rotating his shoulder, which had started throbbing during the car ride. From within Faisal's pocket at telephone rang, but Khalid motioned for him to ignore it. Their host stood in front of the open front door, dressed in a cream-coloured three-piece suit and wearing a Turkish fez. Khalid smiled and embraced him.

Karamat welcomed Khalid warmly and led him into a book-lined room where an elaborate tea was laid out on a circular table flanked by armchairs. Pleasantries were exchanged over pastries and cumin biscuits. Khalid casually inquired about any new antiquities that might have come Karamat's way.

"Nothing after customs seized a truck at Karachi Harbour filled with fakes," Karamat said with a mischievous smile. The items in question were exquisite replicas, built by Khalid's craftsmen.

"Can you dig a little deeper?" asked Khalid.

"Certainly. I will call a few people. Why don't you take an afternoon nap. I have invited two diplomats for dinner tonight. They are both British," Karamat said, clearly excited with his plans.

Faisal—who had been sitting quietly, devouring sandwiches—finally pulled Khalid's vibrating phone from his pocket. He looked at the number, then spoke softly. "It is from the house. Madame Safia."

"I promised to call my wife when we reached Peshawar," Khalid explained to his host, reaching out for the phone.

Khalid stood up, stepping away from the table and turning his back as he dialed. He listened carefully, moving farther from Karamat and Faisal as his wife spoke. Suddenly, he jerked the phone away from his ear and spun around to face Faisal.

"Hassan... my son Hassan has been kidnapped," he yelled. "They want one *crore*—one hundred thousand dollars!"

"Is it confirmed? Are you sure?" Karamat rushed to Khalid's side, took his arm, and led him back to the table.

Khalid collapsed into an armchair. He dialed Hassan's phone, as he had been instructed to do, and waited. It was answered on the second ring.

"Do you have the money?" The voice was crude, rough. Before Khalid could answer, the line went dead.

Khalid called again. This time he was prepared. "Yes, but I am not in Barako. I need time and I want to hear my son's voice." The line went dead again.

Khalid held his head in his hands, struggling to contain his emotions. Safia had repeated what the guard at the gate told her—that a man on a motorcycle had delivered an envelope and then sped away. The envelope contained one bullet and a figure scrawled on a scrap of paper. Hassan, of course, had ignored Khalid's instructions the previous evening and headed out for a late-night jaunt to Islamabad. And Khalid, distracted with the preparations for his trip, had not noticed. He had not returned home. The cities of Karachi and Peshawar were notorious for a recent rise in kidnappings. Yet disaster, in Khalid's opinion, chose its victims irrespective of location. Of course, he did not dismiss the thought that Hassan may have orchestrated the stunt himself just to get his hands on some money.

Khalid could not raise the outlandish sum the kidnappers wanted without crippling losses. There would have to be negotiations, but first he needed proof that Hassan was alive.

"Inform the police immediately," said Karamat. "Nothing is going to happen to your son."

"I shall report the theft of the car," Khalid replied.

"Who is your enemy?" Karamat asked.

It was a practical question, but Khalid was in no mood to speculate — or to reveal that the whole incident could, in fact, simply be Hassan trying to extort money from him.

Hassan, his kidnappers, and Safia's maternal angst would all have to wait. Karamat had already dispatched a man to visit all the shops to which a priceless sculpture might have been sold, and the dull pain in Khalid's shoulder was becoming more severe.

"I am not feeling well, Karamat," he said. "I need to rest."

Karamat directed Khalid to a guest bedroom. He returned a moment later with a glass of water and a small white pill that he said was a muscle relaxant. Khalid swallowed the pill immediately, lay on his back, closed his eyes, and began a silent conversation with God. From outside his room, he could hear Faisal manning the telephones, repeatedly assuring Safia that it was probably all a prank orchestrated by the delinquent Hassan himself, and that he would eventually return home.

KHALID OPENED HIS eyes, surprised that the pain in his shoulder had disappeared, and that he had actually slept for two hours. He called for Faisal, who appeared instantly by his side, and asked him to telephone Safia.

"Now listen to me carefully," Khalid said to his wife. "Nothing is going to happen to Hassan. He is fine. This is all just a stupid game to try and get money."

"I want to see my son's face," she wailed.

"You will. But not just now, and you have to trust me," he said firmly.

"Promise?" She sounded calmer, but only slightly.

"Yes. I will be home tomorrow. Sleep well. Your son is safe," he reassured her.

After an hour, Khalid decided to rejoin his host. Arriving in the living room, he noticed the woman first. She was a slender blonde who was introduced as a diplomat from Britain. She flashed a practised smile and greeted him with a cooing, child-like voice. Her companion was tall and had the rugged looks of an athlete bundled up in a formal suit. He worked, Khalid was told, for a foreign aid agency. Karamat mixed drinks for his guests and handed Khalid a glass of freshly squeezed orange juice. Khalid had given up alcohol when he had decided that God was his only confidant. The current topic of discussion was Karamat's lavish display of ivory, spread over a glass table in the centre of the room. Khalid smiled as he took in the collection; he had sold most of the pieces to Karamat. When Karamat introduced Khalid as a fellow art collector, the female diplomat turned to him enthusiastically.

"My father was a curator at the Victoria and Albert Museum; I have grown up surrounded by art."

"In that case, you must visit me at my home in Barako," replied Khalid.

The woman bounced on the sofa as she talked, while her companion looked at Khalid with skepticism. Khalid noticed the man's expression and wondered briefly what was behind it. The man was here tonight with his friend, who, like most diplomats, seemed to enjoy meeting wealthy Pakistanis such as Karamat. They entertained lavishly, offering the privileges of their opulent estates in an unmistakeably fawning manner. What could possibly be wrong?

"Is there any further news from Barako?" Karamat asked him softly, pulling Khalid's thoughts away from the man on the sofa.

"I am going to call their bluff," replied Khalid.

"What bluff? Oh, do tell! This sounds interesting," chirped the blonde.

"It appears that my son has been kidnapped," said Khalid.

"Oh! Good heavens! How terrible!" Her little-girl voice was filled with concern.

"You don't seem overly concerned," said the woman's companion. The earlier look of skepticism had been replaced with outright curiosity.

"No," replied Khalid, refusing to elaborate.

"People are working on it," added Karamat. "The boy will be found."

Khalid simply lifted the palms of his hands upward in a gesture of prayer. With each minute that flew by, he was more and more certain that Hassan was behind the delivery of the envelope to the house. What infuriated him was that the boy had given no thought to his mother's response to the situation. This was especially upsetting to Khalid, since his own resolve so often faltered in the face of concern for his wife. He should have locked the gates of his home to Hassan a year ago, but he had no defence against Safia's reproaches. Wounding his wife was beyond his imagining.

During dinner, a server whispered something in Karamat's ear. He smiled broadly at Khalid, then leaned toward him and whispered in his ear.

"I think your missing sculpture has been found. I have asked for it to be delivered here."

After dinner, as the green tea was being served, news came that the sculpture had arrived and had been placed on the front terrace for viewing. Khalid allowed the others to walk ahead of him. He had known Karamat to pull many tricks out of his fez, but this, thought Khalid, would be the most magnificent. As Khalid approached the terrace, he saw the blonde kneeling in front of a marble statue, her head turned in his direction. Karamat, Faisal, and the man stood beside her. When Khalid reached the sculpture, his heart sank. He examined the fake sculpture with a still face. The marble-aging technique was the work of a craftsman whom Khalid employed. His work had deceived many serious gallery owners in Japan. He looked at Karamat and shook his head. Karamat shrugged in return just as the telephone in Faisal's breast pocket began to vibrate.

Faisal examined the phone with a puzzled expression, then silently handed it over to Khalid. He stared down at the message indicating a blocked number.

"Hello," said Khalid.

Sher Khan's voice came through the speaker. "I have news,'" he said. "Keep your phone with you. I will call back.

"Wait!" Khalid spoke quickly, before Sher Khan could disconnect. "I am in Peshawar. Give it to me in person."

A rendezvous was arranged and Khalid bid farewell to Karamat, explaining that he intended to return to Islamabad that night. The female diplomat said goodbye wistfully, as though he was carrying all the excitement of the evening away with him. Khalid took her card and promised to invite her to Barako.

SHER KHAN HAD agreed to meet Khalid in an outdoor location. This was out of character, as was the direct call Khalid had received. Khalid hoped this uncharacteristic behaviour was a sign of good news. He tried his son's telephone number again, but no one answered. He chuckled, realizing that the kidnappers did not seem to be in a hurry for the ransom. He planned to string them along for a while longer.

SHER KHAN WAITED alone at a closed gas station, his fingers tight around the butt of his revolver. He watched Khalid's grey sedan move toward his Jeep and relaxed his grip when Khalid stepped out of the car.

"There is word from Chilas that a man has arrived." Sher Khan spoke only when Khalid reached the Jeep's open window.

"Driving a brown truck?" Khalid asked.

"No. It is a local painted truck. But he fits the description of your man," replied Sher Khan.

"Where has the news come from?"

"A local source involved with the Taliban. He will keep him there."

"So he went north," Khalid said, amazed.

"There is something else. He has a woman with him."

"Then you have the wrong man!" Khalid shouted in frustration.

"Don't worry, I have sent my best person. He is a sword and will cut through any lie," Sher Khan reassured him.

"I should tell the man at ISI then," said Khalid.

"Don't even think of it. You will lead him to my people," Sher Khan replied.

"Yes, of course. You're right," Khalid said quickly, realizing his mistake. "Perhaps I should go there myself. I am curious about this man who stole my sculpture. He is either a common thief or very clever."

"You can't go there. The army is there. Shias and Sunnis are killing each other again."

"Then bring him back alive, please. I want to talk to him. I am returning to Islamabad tonight." As Khalid pulled a wad of currency from his pocket, Sher Khan quickly grabbed his wrist.

"What is this? You hurt my pride!"

"There are always expenses, Sher Khan. Men have to eat. Petrol is needed for cars. Bribes are needed for the police. Let us not forget that sometimes good hashish is needed before the trigger on the gun is pulled," Khalid said, smiling.

Khan released his grip and the money fell on the seat beside him.

Khalid walked quickly to his car without looking back. It was a negligible sum of money, ten *lakhs* for incidentals. Sher Khan's pride would hardly be dented. In a society where people who dispensed favours out of respect for each other were never deterred from biding time until they could pull in their markers, Khalid was an exception. He was a staunch believer in paying up front for services performed. He would often even pay in advance, simply to guarantee his faith.

The night journey back to Islamabad on the deserted motorway was uneventful. Khalid thought about his son. Where had he failed as a father? Was Hassan's visible hostility real, or just the protracted tantrum of a spoiled young man? Even as a toddler, Hassan had wriggled fretfully from Khalid's embrace. There was a trend in Pakistan of people discreetly seeking psychiatric help. Khalid wondered if this was what he required, but he knew he would never go through with it. He tried Hassan's number again, hoping that someone would answer. No one did.

WHEN THEY REACHED the Islamabad bypass, Khalid asked Faisal to drive to an address in the city. He wanted to visit the home of his son's second wife. Khalid was following a hunch. They parked outside the two-storey home and waited. A staircase led to a separate entrance on the second floor, where the young woman lived. Her mother lived downstairs. Khalid climbed the stairs alone. A light was coming from the flat. The door leading inside was not bolted. He pushed it open slowly and entered. In front of him was another door, this one to the bedroom. Khalid stood in front of the door for a moment, listening to the music coming from inside. He entered the room silently and stared at his son.

The young woman lying next to Hassan quickly pulled the bedsheet over her head. Hassan stood up slowly. He was naked. Khalid studied his son's physique as though he was examining a piece of sculpture. Then he moved his gaze upward, glaring at his son's stonelike countenance, which revealed neither fear nor embarrassment.

"Where is your car?" Khalid asked.

"I lent it to a friend." Hassan turned his back as he stepped into his jeans.

"Let's go and pick it up."

Hassan swung around, anger contorting his face. "Why are you following me?" he shouted. "You have frightened her! I will pick my car up when I want to!"

"I will be waiting downstairs," Khalid said, trying to remain composed.

Khalid waited outside by the car. He was smoking, and

trying to suppress his rage. His shoulder pain had started again. He had resisted the impulse to smash the palm of his hand into his son's handsome face. Now, he realized he felt completely detached from Hassan. How could this twisted young man be his flesh and blood? A profound sadness descended upon him. Was God punishing him? The faces of Hassan's toddlers flashed before his eyes. Would one carry the seed of Hassan's spirit? He longed at that moment to head toward Ghalib's Sufi shrine to search for answers. He wanted relief, as well as a permanent escape from Hassan's antics. As Hassan's shadow appeared near the gate, he wondered if his entire life was a house of cards.

For a time, they drove in silence, each contemplating his own thoughts. It was Khalid who spoke first. "What did you need the money for this time?"

"I wanted to buy her furniture." Khalid was gratified to hear the nervous tone in his son's voice.

"And who will pay for your mother's tears," Khalid replied.

"She doesn't know anything," Hassan said quickly.

"You are wrong! I was in Peshawar! She opened the envelope!"

Hassan's friend was not at home, and there was no trace of the car, so Khalid asked Faisal to take them home. Not a word was exchanged for the rest of the trip. The gates of the estate swung open to let them in, and Khalid told the guard they should not be opened again for anyone. He got out of the car and headed toward the house. Mounting the stairs, he paused halfway up and checked his watch. It was precisely 4:41 a.m. He had travelled for seven hours by car to two cities, and had accomplished only half of what he had set out to do. He'd had worse days, he thought.

Safia was curled up in her day clothes, fast asleep. The bedside lamps were still on. Khalid drew close, noticing that her eyes were smudged with kohl after weeping for her unworthy son. He leaned down and whispered her name. She awoke instantly.

"Your precious son is home safe and sound," he said.

She sat up and embraced him, sobbing on his shoulder with relief. He dried her face with the edge of his sleeve and said he needed some tea.

A short while later, Khalid sat alone on his terrace cradling a mug of tea. He had ordered Faisal to catch up on his sleep and had taken his telephone away from him. The night had flown by, and dawn was breaking in the east. Khalid loved to watch the sun rise over the hills. He sat quietly, taking in the sight and waiting for the call from Sher Khan. It was just after 8 a.m. when his telephone rang. He answered it, but it wasn't the voice he was expecting that greeted him.

"Khalid, my dear, we are working overtime to find Adeel and the truck," said the brigadier.

"Any luck?"

"Well, we have brought his mother to the office. She will be interrogated."

"Adeel's mother? Why?" This was an unusual tactic, even for the ISI.

"We have traced a call made to her telephone. The conversation was brief but the call was made by Adeel just after he entered Peshawar."

"Do you really think she will reveal his whereabouts? She is his mother, for God's sake." Khalid knew he could share his own information with the brigadier.

"His sister-in-law found a large sum of money in the

mother's room. We think Adeel gave it to her sometime in the past forty-eight hours," the man replied.

"He is not with his mother," said Khalid.

"How do you know?"

"I just have a feeling," Khalid replied. "Make sure you are not harsh with the woman."

"We don't mistreat mothers. But she will assist us in finding him. I can guarantee that. I will be in touch again."

Khalid sighed as he placed the phone on the table in front of him. A Taliban team had made more progress than the country's shadowy intelligence organization, with its deep coffers and complete autonomy. He trusted Sher Khan's innate sense of honour more than the brigadier's empty assurances. After all, it was the brigadier who had sent the wrong man; now he would have to save face. Sher Khan's people must have reached Chilas by now, Khalid thought. He was certain he would be called within the next few hours.

Faisal walked up to the terrace with the two morning papers he had picked up in the village. News of the massacre at Chilas covered the entire front page. Khalid wondered if anyone could accurately pinpoint the moment when sectarian violence had crept into the country. Regardless of when it started, it had become all too apparent that the people who indulged in this heinous crime were affiliated with the Taliban and other local warlords. Hordes of unemployed men from the provinces found their way into these shadowy terror clubs. Murder was synonymous with power, and the government looked the other way.

Sher Khan called earlier than expected, just as the heads of Khalid's two grandchildren appeared over the top of the staircase. He smiled at the sight of them — followed by

Safia, racing to catch up with them across the length—as he answered. He tried to savour this image of familial love, but Sher Khan's emphatic voice, hammering in his eardrum, made it impossible to concentrate on anything else.

"He has disappeared," Sher Khan said.

"Disappeared?" echoed Khalid, swallowing the bile that had instantly risen at the back of his throat.

"He can't be far away, Khalid. My man, Nadir, will find him. I give you my word. A few days more and we will bring him to you in chains!"

NINE

THE CLUB IN LAHORE hailed from the colonial period and had a tainted history. The days of the British Raj had ended sixty-six years ago, but the club had insisted on preserving some of the more outdated touches of its bygone era, including one polished-teak door with a sign that specifically barred women from entry. These days, membership included businessmen, retired civil servants, and the offspring of feudal families. The lush-hipped matrons of Lahore — the wives of the club's members — had never mounted any objections to the sign, aware that alcohol was stored beyond the door and the men enjoyed the privilege of drinking themselves into oblivion.

Ghalib, wearing well-pressed khaki trousers and a crisp, long-sleeved shirt, entered the club. He nodded at some of the familiar faces as he marched toward a pair of armchairs, one of which was occupied by a strikingly good-looking man. His leonine grey hair and sparkling dark eyes seemed to create a magnetic field around him, drawing people in.

Soody — or Sulieman, if one was being particularly formal — shared both spiritual links and distant blood ties with
Ghalib. He sprang up to embrace his friend warmly.

The gentlemen of the club who consumed alcohol had
their bottles stored at the bar, and the bartender made it
his business to know who drank what. Soon after Ghalib
arrived, a double whisky and a lime juice diluted with mineral water appeared instantly on a small tray, carried by
a formally clad waiter sporting a ceremonial pleated, fan-
like turban. The club afforded its members great privacy.
The injunctions of the Islamic Republic of Pakistan may
have been observed everywhere else in the country, but
they tended to stop outside these gates. A few years ago,
the club's alcohol-laden New Year Eve's fete had drawn the
ire of the mullahs, who gathered outside and threatened
to storm the building. After that, the fetes became tamer
affairs. Soody, who had held several cabinet portfolios, never
consumed alcohol in public, even at the club. He sipped his
lime juice diluted in mineral water chastely, and allowed
Ghalib to take a few sips from his drink.

"AK, the chairman of the party is holding a rally in Sahiwal tomorrow," Soody said. "I expect you to attend. The
time has come to harness all the voters of Punjab."

"I shall be there. I have ordered posters to be made,"
replied Ghalib. "Your great leader was still a teenager when
he used to trail behind us on our shoots."

"Well, now he has formed a political party that could
easily win this election," Soody replied.

Ghalib knew that Soody had recently been replaced as
a cabinet minister by a beautiful young woman who was
partial to expensive handbags. The portfolio he had been
offered instead was lacklustre, and Soody, outraged, had

promptly tendered his resignation. Being a man of burning ambition, he then switched his allegiance, and AK had welcomed him with great respect. Ghalib had joined the party at Soody's behest, after he had promised to deliver the votes from his constituency.

"Yes, but is he an intelligent man?" Ghalib asked.

"He does not have to be. He draws people, and that is what counts."

"He's very popular with the ladies, I am told," Ghalib added.

"Women are voting as well, Ghalib. He is quite a visual relief from the average politician in this country. He'll be very popular at tomorrow's women's rally in Sahiwal."

"Well, this is revolutionary. So our presence is to back the ladies?"

"You will be part of the reception committee and then attend a lunch afterwards. He draws a great deal of media attention," replied Soody sharply.

Ghalib concealed his ire. There were no ladies in Sahiwal, only a handful of women who were the wives of civic administrators. Rural women would be brought in by the busload, along with female party volunteers. Men would not be allowed to witness the rally or the speeches. He wondered why Soody was even requesting his participation. Yet Ghalib knew that a prosperous landlord with a car emblazoned with posters would be an asset to any public display of strength. How would Soody, who had commanded centre stage for most of his professional life, feel about playing second fiddle to the party leader?

"I am happy to host a lunch for the party leader," Ghalib offered.

"A lunch has already been arranged. He will not have

much time," Soody said, patting Ghalib's forearm in appreciation.

Soody did not linger, so Ghalib fortified himself with two more drinks and looked around the room. His geriatric companions, trussed in Western clothes, sat in the ruined splendour of their faded lives. Many would even stay to dine in solitude. Ghalib found them depressing. He knew that his decision to enter politics would save him from a similar fate. He quickly summoned a waiter and ordered dinner, informing the man that his chauffeur would collect it in half an hour.

WHEN HE ARRIVED home, he gave quick instructions to his staff for the departure. They would have to leave tonight in order to arrive in the country and prepare for the next day's rally. A little over an hour later, two cars rolled out of the gates carrying supplies and many members of his staff.

During the drive, Ghalib thought of Khalid. He wondered why he had not heard from the man and decided to call for an update.

Faisal answered the phone.

"He is asleep, Mian sahib. We travelled to Peshawar and back in one day."

"Wonderful! Wonderful! Tell Khalid I am heading to the country and when I return I will come to Barako to collect the sculpture myself," said Ghalib.

"Of course," replied Faisal.

"Also tell him that I expect a huge donation to my political party. He may need a favour one day."

THE NEXT MORNING, Ghalib dressed quickly in a pristine white suit and stepped outside to behold a colourful sight.

Nur Hyat stood beside two cars plastered with political posters. The photos of Ghalib's face had been touched up with a generous spill of hair. A red, green, and black party flag sailed out from the side mirror near the driver's door. The entire domestic staff was milling around in the front courtyard, looking at the cars, while a clutch of villagers stood outside the front gate. The estate manager's black Jeep, also festooned with posters, was parked nearby. Ghalib adjusted his dark sunglasses and climbed into the back seat of the car. As he raised his left hand, waving in a stately fashion at the villagers, he began to feel the excitement of the carefully constructed pageantry. The villagers waved back, believing that greater glory would appear for their region through Ghalib's political success.

As they approached the city of Sahiwal, a snarl of more poster-emblazoned vehicles reduced the speed of Ghalib's mini-cortège to a snail's pace. Ghalib preened in the mirror, imagining the sensation of success he would feel once the elections were over. Politics, he thought, was a lot of fun. When they reached the property where AK would be received, Ghalib's cars were stopped. He got out, waved to the gathered crowd, and walked with his chauffeur toward the main gate, where the party officials greeted him respectfully. Cameras clicked and television stations filmed his arrival. AK appeared at the entrance soon after, with a head of windblown hair, a gaunt face, and an air of unease. An aide beside him pointed to Ghalib, and AK stopped and clasped Ghalid's outstretched hand in both of us own. Ghalib simply smiled, realizing that he had nothing to say.

The women's rally was conducted in a large space behind the house under a tented marquee, complete with a stage and microphones. The day was hot, and Ghalib was still tired from his preparations and drive the night before. He pulled a carefully pressed handkerchief from his pocket and patted the sweat from his face. Was it really worth it, he wondered, to wait for the rally to end and then partake in a crowded lunch—where the invited few would fight with the gatecrashers to get close to the leader? He lingered for half an hour and then immediately walked out and headed to his car.

Twenty minutes later, Ghalib's car was driving toward Harappa, a small village located twenty-four kilometres west of Sahiwal. Harappa dated back to 2500 BCE; it had been the most vital part of the Indus Valley civilization. It was a place Ghalib visited secretly. He had managed to purchase an entire hillock just before the government sealed off the area to any speculative land sales. Archaeological excavations in Pakistan were now state-sanctioned, and relied heavily on resources from developed countries. Ghalib, however, had acquired a vast collection of antiquities by teaching the local people how to dig and what to look for. His long-term plan was to secure his political power, and some international interest, so he could unearth an entire treasure trove through a more professional excavation of the area.

Reaching Harappa and walking along the side of the hill was almost a spiritual experience for Ghalib. He was more comfortable here than at any political rally. As his footsteps left imprints on the baked earth, he imagined he could feel vibrations from the vast collection of artifacts buried beneath. The museums in his country were a scandal, he thought. There was little respect for antiquities. The three main museums of Pakistan, still housed in colonial buildings, had never beened modernized — and the collections suffered. Graduate degrees in museum sciences were not sought in this country. Museum directors drank copious amounts of tea in their shabby offices while semi-literate men acted as custodial staff. Many senior museum bureaucrats regularly dined in the homes of people who had pilfered entire collections, yet no action was ever taken.

Ghalib almost wished for a shovel so that he could dig for himself. His ownership of this mound of earth — which, he believed, held an unimaginable fortune — could solve some of his more tedious financial problems. Keeping his dreams close, Ghalib paced the perimeter of the knoll for an hour, drawing curious looks from his chauffeur, who was no doubt wondering why they were here. Eventually, Ghalib reluctantly climbed down from the hillock and returned to his car.

Ghalib was exhausted on the drive home. He had consulted his naturopath in Lahore about his fatigue and had been prescribed a special diet. He found the regimen distasteful, however, and so did not follow it. In addition to diabetes, there was also the possibility that he had kidney stones. For years now, Ghalib had concealed most of these infirmities from others. He refused to air out any of his health concerns in public. As a result, a kind of denial had set in, and he had not been entirely truthful with the psychiatrist he saw in Lahore. In weak moments, he often worried that the full canvas of his life might suddenly fold up without any warning. This was one of those moments. Instead of heading directly home, Ghalib asked his driver to take him to a local Sufi shrine.

Ghalib climbed the long flight of marble steps leading up to the shrine with some difficulty. He felt his heart flutter and he sank breathlessly onto a bench in a pillared arcade where a group of musicians sang Sufi songs. Clusters of visitors strolled in the shrine's the top pavilion, often dropping money down at the musicians. The small chamber that housed the burial site of a saint drew the biggest crowd. Ghalib was usually led to this chamber by staff. Today, however, he was content to just sit quietly and listen to the devotional songs. His chauffeur had positioned himself in the long line of people queuing for the shrine. While waiting for his elevated heartbeat to slow, Ghalib watched a man dressed in black with a drum and ropes of beads strung around his neck. Rows of bracelets encircled his wrists, and his fingers were encrusted with silver rings. He moved toward Ghalib and joined him, sitting cross-legged on the ground.

"Something has been stolen from you," he said softly.

This statement startled Ghalib. For a moment, he looked ahead silently, sorting out his thoughts. Then he turned to the drummer and spoke. "What do you think it is?"

The man slumped forward and pressed both hands to the side of his head. Ghalib watched him curiously, wondering if it was a game to earn some money.

"*Buth* . . . statue . . ." The man breathed heavily, his head still bent.

"Did you say '*buth*'?" Ghalib asked.

"Yes." The man raised his head and fixed his eyes on Ghalib. "It comes from far."

"Who has stolen it?" asked Ghalib.

"I have seen it in the back of a truck. I see a man and a woman." The man's pupils were dilated.

Sufi mystics often claimed to follow the path of divinity. But Ghalib knew that they also indulged in the use of opiates. Ecstatic fervour, they believed, was the path to God.

"Perhaps you know something about me?" Ghalib ventured. He wanted to keep the man talking without revealing too much.

"I am the messenger. I have been sent to you," the man said, pointing a finger at Ghalib.

"Do you sing?"

"Only my drums sing. I will make you dance." The man looked up and smiled at him.

"Come to my house. You can play your drums for me there," Ghalib said.

Ghalib headed toward the burial chamber and stood at the marble latticework window embedded in one wall. He cupped his palms and recited the *Fateha*, the prayer for the dead, and savoured the peace this exercise induced. The drummer had not followed him, but was waiting for him outside. Local folklore insisted that miracles did occur at Sufi shrines, and Ghalib felt that the saint had singled him out for his encounter with the Sufi mystic. When his chauffeur appeared by his side, Ghalib told him that the drummer would be coming with them. He then instructed the chauffeur to give alms to some of the people sitting against the walls of the shrines.

THE DRUMMER SAT in the front seat next to the chauffeur. When the huge wooden gates of the estate swung open, he turned around to Ghalib and gave him a large smile. In that moment, Ghalib realized that the man had not chosen him in the shrine because he had any prior knowledge of who he was. When Ghalib got out of the car, he ordered refreshments for the drummer, then excused himself so he could call Khalid again.

"Khalid, I want the truth. Do you have the sculpture?"

"Yes. It is coming. It will be here soon," replied Khalid briskly.

"Was the person whom you sent to collect it travelling in a brown truck?"

For a moment there was silence.

"I will check and let you know. Relax, Ghalib. Sometimes delivery takes longer than we anticipate. All is well. Do you have the payment?"

"Yes, I do. I have sold land for it, my friend!"

Khalid laughed, then said goodbye quickly, leaving Ghalib to wonder if his friend was lying to him. Ghalib was now convinced that something was wrong. All of his recent conversations with Khalid were briefer than they had ever been in the past. Ghalib decided to rest for a while, in order to gear himself up for the long evening ahead that he would share with the drummer from the shrine.

THAT EVENING, FADED carpets were spread over the bricks in the front courtyard. The household domestics sat on the ground in front of the drummer, while an armchair was brought outside for Ghalib. Next to him on a table rested a bottle of inferior whisky, Pakistani vodka, and numerous cans of beer. Ghalib nodded to his valet, who dipped his hands into a large straw basket and drew out garlands of miniature roses threaded with jasmine. As he distributed them, the drummer held up his hands, wanting the garlands to be wrapped around his wrists. Then he rose and fixed his eyes on Ghalib. He began to play a familiar Sufi elegy, swaying from side to side with the rhythm. Ghalib was hypnotized by the flowers that encircled the drummer's wrists, and by the gentle voices of his staff, who had joined in by singing the words. Within fifteen minutes, they were on their feet, pulled by the drum's steady beat. Ghalib's staff circled, dancing around the drummer as he twirled.

Ghalib sipped his beer and watched the faces of the dancing servants. Each of them wore a smile, as the party was a release from their assigned chores. Two of the teenaged boys broke away and danced together. The drummer encouraged them by quickening the music's pace. Mesmerized, Ghalib joined in, circling each boy's head with a 100-rupee note before tucking it safely into a shirt pocket. A generous amount of whisky was mixed with cola in a glass and offered to the drummer. He emptied the glass in one long swallow before flinging it away, not once breaking the frenzied rhythm. Ghalib sank back into his chair and enjoyed the concert for the next two hours.

When the performance ended, a chair was brought out for the drummer. He set his drums aside and proceeded to down another glass of watered-down whisky.

"You are blessed. You have a great gift," Ghalib said, before dropping a five-thousand-rupee note on his lap. The drummer ignored the money and fixed his bloodshot eyes on Ghalib.

"There are those who would harm you," he whispered.

"Me? Why?"

"There is a curse. I see it in this great house of yours."

Ghalib laughed, trying to lighten the mood. He had to determine if the man's earlier prophecy was valid.

"I have a friend—"

"Your only friend is up there," the drummer interrupted, pointing to the sky.

"Yes, but we also have to live here," Ghalib replied, indicating the ground.

"This world is nothing. People come and go. This also goes." He picked up the money and tore the note in half.

Ghalib ignored the uncivil gesture. "I want to thank you for playing the drum for all of us."

"Give me more whisky and I will tell you how you can thank me."

"Let us talk," Ghalib said, then caught his valet's eye. "Bring another drink for our guest."

The valet threw an angry look at the drummer. He mixed a weak drink and placed it down with hostility before collecting the two halves of the note that had been thrown on the ground. Ghalib took a sip of his beer and wondered for a moment if he had not been generous enough.

"Tell me what you saw in your mind. It is important to me."

"You are a sick man."

"No, I am fine," Ghalib said coolly. "Tell me about the truck and the man who is in it."

The drummer emptied half of the glass and then set it down on the ground in front of him. Again, he slumped forward and pressed his hands to the sides of his head. He took longer this time, and after a while his shoulders began to twitch, as if he was trying to get rid of something that disturbed him. Finally, his movements stopped and he straightened up, facing Ghalib.

"This 'buth' will save them. He is looking for escape. He is a warrior. He will reach the other side, but the woman will put him into trouble. There is so much light around them. So much light," the drummer murmured.

"But where are they?" asked Ghalib.

"I see them on the other side of the world. I am tired, Mian sahib. I must sleep," the drummer said as he rose from the chair.

"You can sleep in my house. You will be comfortable," Ghalib said, getting up as well.

"Do not harm them, or an even bigger curse will fall on your house."

Ghalib instructed his valet to find a place for the drummer to sleep. He knew the session was over and that it was not wise to push his luck further. The valet whispered that it was not a good idea to let the man stay indoors. Ghalib refused to accept his suggestion and walked back into the house, where he telephoned Khalid again.

"How was your political rally?' asked Khalid.

"A waste of time, but I had to show my face. When are you expecting delivery?"

"I would say in two days. I have never known you to be so impatient before," Khalid said irritably.

"I hope there was no act of violence with respect to the statue's acquisition or delivery," Ghalib added.

"Violence?"

"Yes. I mean that no one was killed."

"Well, I had to get some help from our special friends, but they always respect my instructions," replied Khalid.

"There will be an election soon. I am running for office and cannot have any links to the Taliban," Ghalib said curtly.

"There have been some unforeseen expenses. I think you should send half of the payment to me now, Ghalib," said Khalid.

"Don't discuss payment with me, Khalid. I will make the entire payment on delivery," Ghalib said furiously.

"Then you'll have to wait."

Ghalib walked to his dressing room and searched amongst his jumble of medications. When he found the correct vial, he shook a Valium into the palm of his hand

and swallowed it. He returned to his bedroom to find his valet standing at the side of his bed.

"The drummer has left," announced the valet.

"Why? Were you rude to him?"

"Saqib has left with him," the valet said nervously.

"This is impossible. Search for them at once," Ghalib commanded.

Many hours later, it was confirmed that the drummer and Ghalib's favourite teenaged companion had indeed disappeared together in the night. To Ghalib, both losses were insufferable. He fought off the consoling effects of the Valium, organized a search party, and posted a large reward. No one could fathom why the reward was so high. Everyone knew that there were many drummers hanging around at shrines, and that a sixteen-year-old pampered village boy could be replaced by at least a dozen others.

TEN

THE PAPER BUNDLE PRESSED under Adeel's arm was comforting. The freshly cooked chapattis wrapped in newspaper allowed him to blend in with the other men lined up at the shop. He walked away quickly after his purchase, then jogged back to the house. When the threat had presented itself, there'd been no time to plan an exit without arousing suspicion. He wondered now if the woman would follow his cues without instruction.

Two motorcycles were parked in front of the house. He entered the small back room and headed toward the stone staircase leading up to the roof, curious as to whether his companion had managed to cook the chicken or ruin the meal. Two men stood at the foot of the staircase; in his peripheral vision, he caught sight of another two men standing with the old man. He calculated the risk. Five men pitted against the round of bullets in his revolver and his speed in letting the chapattis slip to the floor so he could raise the gun.

"My wife has cooked chicken. Let us go up and eat it."
He nodded to the men and transferred the bundle to the
front of his body.

There was a small sound behind him, then the pressure
of something against his back. He did not have to turn; he
knew it was the muzzle of a rifle. He looked up and saw the
woman standing at the top of the staircase, looking startled.

"What is the problem, Baba," he said lightly, standing
very still.

"Who are you?" said a voice behind him.

Adeel swivelled on his heel, letting the chapattis slide to
the ground. Their host stood between the two men, pointing the rifle at Adeel.

"I am taking some provisions, blankets to my wife's
family," Adeel said, casually brushing the rifle away.

"There are many people looking for you," said a tall man
standing behind their elderly host.

"We do not talk in front of women," Adeel responded,
glancing up at the top of the staircase.

She had disappeared. Adeel bent down and picked up
the chapatti bundle.

"Let me go up and give her these. We have had a long
journey and she needs to eat."

One of the men blocking the staircase moved aside.
Adeel darted up the stairs. She was crouched just behind
the door.

"There is no time to explain. You eat first. I have to go
down and settle something."

"What do these men want?" she asked, ignoring the
bundle he pressed toward her.

"Do not come downstairs. Stay here. Nothing will happen." He turned away.

Six men crowded into the small room. The old man sat on his bed. The four motorcyclists lounged against the walls. Adeel stood with his back to the door. He knew exactly who the men were, and he had no option but to do what they wanted until he could escape.

"There is news from Peshawar that a man just like you is being looked for," said the old man.

"It is a mistake. I am not from Peshawar," replied Adeel.

The men were silent. Then one moved closer to Adeel.

"Is the truck yours?"

"No, it belongs to my family. My brother lent it to me," Adeel replied.

"We need it," came the startling reply.

"What do you need it for? How can I help you?" Adeel asked.

"We will put something in it and you just need to deliver it."

"How far do I have to go?" Adeel asked, to keep the conversation going.

"There is only one army checkpoint in the area," the tall man said, smiling at him.

Adeel faced the man steadily. He knew he was in the presence of the Taliban, and that these men wanted him to detonate explosives at the checkpoint.

"You should be a comrade. If you help us, no one will know that we have found you," the leader of the group offered.

Adeel moved closer to the bed and sat on the edge.

"I am your comrade. I have been trained in this work. Tell me the plan."

They studied him carefully while he wondered where in the house the explosives were stored. He already knew that a mobile phone with a timer would activate the device. These men were typical of their type: all in their late thirties, and all steeped in the traditions of sectarian warfare, completely deluded by the men who controlled them. Adeel was not surprised that his host was involved with them. He also knew that the sculpture had to be removed from the truck and hidden.

"You may have something to hide from us," said the leader, "but we have nothing to hide from you. Just follow our instructions and leave."

"I understand. I believe in your cause. But I must take my wife away from here first. Then I will be free to help you."

"She is safe here. When you complete the task for us, you can come back for her," replied the host quickly.

"No, I will take her with me," Adeel said firmly.

"She is a woman," replied the tall man.

"She is a *jihadi* like me," replied Adeel.

"If you take her, the bomb will sit at her feet," the tall man said.

"She is very brave. She has been trained," Adeel said, staring down the man.

The next half hour was spent going over the details of the plan. The target was the army checkpoint around the area where the two mosques had been cordoned off. The explosive device would be in a bag that would have to be taken beyond the wooden barrier. It would be detonated by the two men on motorcycles, who would follow Adeel. The mission was to kill as many soldiers as they could, so they would wait until the morning when the checkpoint was fully manned.

Adeel took over the planning. He asked questions, voiced concerns, and quickly came up with solutions. He also noticed that two of the men had left the room.

"You should go to Waziristan; they need people like you," the tall man said, admiring Adeel's input.

"Yes, but do they pay you good money?" Adeel asked. He knew it wouldn't hurt for them to think he was a mercenary.

"More than you can imagine!" The host threw back his head and laughed.

"You can work for both sides: the Americans pay for information and the Saudis send gold in bags." The tall man smiled at him.

"This country is covered in filth. It must be cleansed. You understand, brother, the Holy Prophet guides us," the host proclaimed.

"We have four hours to sleep. I will come down then," Adeel said and got up.

"It will be cold on the roof. Bring your wife and come sleep in the room."

Adeel climbed the short staircase and found her sitting on the floor against the wall. He pressed a finger against his lips and crouched down next to her.

"There is trouble. But I will handle it. You have to do exactly as I say," he whispered to her.

She looked up at him fearfully.

"Let us leave now while they sleep."

"No. We cannot. It is a short wait. Have you eaten?"

"I was waiting for you," she said and turned to the pot.

They shared the pan of stringy chicken with the cold chapattis. He found her cooking almost inedible and was surprised that she did not know how to cook. She glanced at him, sensing his lack of enthusiasm for the meal.

"The chicken was tough. It was old and hard to cook," she said defensively.

"This is fuel. Not food. It's all right," he said gruffly.

They finished quickly and rinsed the cooking pot. Adeel then casually unbuttoned his woollen waistcoat, drawing the automatic pistol out of its holster. She muffled a scream and pressed herself against the wall. Stifling his laughter, he quickly placed the weapon on the ground between them.

"I am going to show you how to use this," he said softly.

She watched him silently as he loaded the chamber with bullets and explained the parts of the gun. Then he extended it toward her.

"Hold it. Then you can point it and shoot at anything you want."

"It is this easy to kill?" she asked, pressing her hand directly over the muzzle.

"No!" He jerked the pistol away. "Like this." He wrapped her fingers around the stock and held her hand in place with his own.

"Why do I need to know how to use this?" she asked, looking at him reproachfully.

"We are in the company of killers and we may need to defend ourselves."

She shrugged his hand away, lifted the revolver, and slowly aimed it at his head. He did not move; he only turned his face away.

"Is this the way?"

"Yes, but you will never get that close. You will have to calculate where the head or the heart is and then fire."

He held his hand out and said, "Give it back to me. We have to go down."

ADEEL DID NOT sleep. He watched the woman, curled up in her shawl and fast asleep. The small room was cold despite the number of bodies inside. Adeel listened to the even breathing of sleeping people and went over his plan. He had decided that they would bury the sculpture. He calculated how much force it would take to drag it to a safe site. He had ropes in the truck and a harness, but he would need her help as well. Then he calculated the time it would take to dig a large enough hole. He had seen a shovel by the side of the house when the chicken was being slaughtered. He got up quietly and walked to the door, where two of the Taliban were lightly snoring in their sleep. He swung his leg over the first man. For a minute, he straddled him without contact. Then he swung his other leg over. Thankfully, there was enough space between the two men for him to clear both. He walked to the back entrance and stepped out quietly. He grabbed the shovel from the side of the house and quickly made his way to the truck. As he pulled the keys from his pocket, they slipped through his fingers. He knelt down to pick them up and noticed a wire dangling under the truck.

He set the keys on the dirt and crawled under the truck for a closer look, but it was too dark to see where the wire led. He pulled out his mobile phone and turned the flashlight function on. The wire led to a package that was securely taped to the underside of the truck. The thin film of plastic covering it could not hide the fact that it was an explosive. Adeel knew that the lethal package had the ability to reduce the truck and everything around it to nothing more than mangled iron and torn flesh. He also knew he could easily disconnect the wire leading to the timer, but he didn't touch anything. He crawled out, opened the padlock, and carefully hid the shovel under a pile of blankets next to the sculpture.

He spent another half hour sliding the leather harness over the wrapped sculpture and attaching the ropes. He tested the device by pulling the weight — which he estimated to be close to seventy kilograms — toward the edge of the truck. The progress was slow, but it worked. He climbed into the truck, reversed the straps of the harness, and pulled the sculpture back to its original resting place. He shut the padlock and returned inside, once again stepping over the sleeping men.

Just before dawn, Adeel woke the woman up, and their movements woke the sleeping men. When they walked outside together they saw only one motorcycle and two men standing by the truck. On the ground next to them rested a small straw basket. A paper cover concealed the contents. The men watched Adeel and the woman get into the truck, and then they placed the basket at her feet.

"Follow us. We will stop one kilometre before the checkpoint. You drive right up to it and tell the soldier this is fruit for the officer inside. Then call on this phone and tell us you have made the delivery." He held out a small mobile phone to Adeel.

Adeel faced his would-be executioners squarely and took the phone. "God will protect us," he said over his shoulder and started the truck.

Adeel followed the motorcycle. It headed toward the main road, keeping a safe a distance from them. The woman sat by his side, calm and wide awake. Adeel wondered when she would leave.

Soon, the moment he had been waiting for presented itself. A small road veered off to the left, heading to the mountains. He slowed down, watching the motorcycle disappear around a bend ahead. He swung the wheel and shifted gears, accelerating up an unpaved road. He knew it would take a couple of minutes for the men on the motorcycle to realize that the truck was no longer following them.

Within seconds, a copse of trees appeared at the side of the road. He continued driving until he reached a heavily forested area and slammed on the brakes.

"Come, I need your help." He jumped out of the driver's seat and raced to the back of the truck.

Quickly, he grabbed hold of the two ropes attached to the harness and pulled the sculpture to the edge. When the woman appeared behind him, he told her to hold one of the ropes. Together, they eased the sculpture over the edge of the truck and allowed it to slide onto the ground. They dragged the sculpture toward the coniferous undergrowth at the side of the road. The ground was soft and covered with vegetation he did not recognize. He raced back to the truck for the shovel. They took turns digging, and within a very short time, the sculpture was buried and covered with earth and layers of branches. Adeel was astounded by how quickly the task had been accomplished, and how effectively she had helped. Not a single word was exchanged between them, even after they raced back to the truck and Adeel reversed down the path to the main road. The truck and the motorcycle reached the turnoff from the main road at the same time. The driver waved furiously. Adeel drove up to him.

"You were supposed to follow us," he shouted.

"My wife had to go to the toilet so I needed a less public place," Adeel replied.

"You bloody fool! This is a mission! If you do this again we will shoot you."

Their journey resumed and Adeel focused on the next part of his plan.

"We must let this truck go," he explained to the woman. "It has become very dangerous. A time will come when I will slow it down so you can jump out. I will tell you when to jump. Can you do this?" he asked, looking at her.

"Jump where?" she asked, confused.

"If you don't jump, you will die."

"And you? Where will you go?"

"I will also leave the truck. Don't worry, I will find you," he said softly.

"I will jump," she said gravely.

Twenty minutes later, the motorcycle ahead slowed down and then stopped. Adeel brought the truck up beside it.

"The checkpoint is the next thing you will see on the road. You must make the call on the phone. That is the most important thing," said the driver, whose face was now completely concealed by a black scarf.

Adeel lifted his hand to indicate that he understood. When he cleared the motorcycle he noticed that the man riding pillion had also concealed his face. He kept his speed low until he saw the wooden barrier and small adobe structure ahead. He could see three military men standing around the barrier. He geared down, slowing the truck.

"Now! Jump!" he shouted to the woman.

She gave him a terrified look, opened the door, and jumped. He had no time to see where she had landed. He kept his eyes on the road ahead as the truck moved closer to the checkpoint.

He stopped at the barrier and handed over his driver's licence and registration. The soldier nodded, lifted the barrier, and allowed him to proceed. Adeel drove through, accelerating until he was almost five hundred feet away from the checkpoint. He moved toward the side of the road and stopped the truck. There was no one on the road behind him. On one side of the road was a sharp drop into the valley, and on the other the ridge of a low hill. Adeel stepped out of the truck, crossed the road, and ran up the hill as fast as he could. Finally, he dropped down flat on the ground. He had a safe, bird's-eye view of both the parked truck and the army checkpoint. He punched out the number he'd been given on the cellphone.

"I have done the job," he said.

Five seconds later, a deafening explosion rent the air. It was quickly followed by another. For a few moments, billowing dirt, flames, and ricocheting metal eclipsed his vision. Then he heard the welcome sound of voices; he knew he had saved lives. The motorcycle riders would be halfway back to the village of Chilas by now, where they would report his death. It was a perfect solution to Adeel's predicament.

When the air finally settled he could see people standing around the shell of the truck. A military Jeep raced up to the site, then turned around and sped off in the opposite direction. As he followed the truck's progress, he noticed a slight, bundled-up figure in the distance. He saw her stumble as a soldier pushed her away from the scene. The blood pounded in his head as he slid down the hill and raced toward her. Chunks of tire rubber and strips of metal littered the road. He ran through them, removing his wool cap and dark glasses and pushing them into his waistcoat pocket. He did not want to be recognized by the soldiers who had checked his licence only a few moments ago. All he wanted to do was reach her so she could see that he was alive.

"Halt!" A barrier guard stepped in front of him. It was not the one who had checked his licence.

"My wife and I were waiting by the road for the bus.

Then this explosion! I had just walked ahead of her," he said, pointing to the woman.

"Leave this area at once! Go back! The road will not be open for a while."

"Yes, sir," Adeel said, stepping aside and heading toward her.

She moved slowly. Her arms were folded across her chest; he knew she had been hurt from her fall. He closed the few feet that separated them, resisting his desire to scoop her into his arms. When she saw him, she collapsed on his chest and burst into tears. He placed both his hands on her shoulders to steady her.

"I don't know your name." These were the first words that came out of his mouth.

"Norbu," she sobbed.

"Norbu? What kind of name is that?"

Her demeanour changed instantly. She drew herself up stiffly.

"It is an old name from my grandmother's family," she replied.

"A Tibetan name?" he said, amazed.

"My family is from the time before. When people were Buddhist and not Muslim."

"Are you all right? We have to walk now." For the first time since they'd left the house, he was nervous.

"When I jumped I thought I had died. When the bomb exploded I thought you had died. I came to look for your body." She wiped her tears with the back of her hand.

They began to walk back to the spot where the dirt road led up the hill. She moved so slowly, slower than Adeel had expected. He knew she had been badly bruised; now he just prayed that she had not sustained a fracture. When he asked her to let him check for broken bones, she refused, drawing her two woollen shawls tighter around herself.

Adeel struggled to hold off a creeping exhaustion. It had been three days since he'd left Barako to execute his assignment, and he had not had much sleep. He needed a new plan, but he also needed to rest. When they finally reached the path and saw the trees, her pace quickened, and he followed her to the spot where the statue was buried.

It took them ten minutes to erect a small tent. Three branches pressed into the soft earth became the support for a canopy made of her two woollen shawls. He lay down, removed the pistol from its holster, and placed it to one side. There was enough space for Norbu to rest as well, but the last thing Adeel saw as he turned on his side and fell into an exhausted sleep was her hunched form, standing next to the spot where the sculpture was buried.

WHEN HE WOKE up three hours later, the afternoon sun had begun to recede. He looked at the dun-coloured woollen shawl overhead and savoured the relaxed state of his rested body. Then he glanced beside him; she was not there. He sat up and immediately reached for the pistol that lay undisturbed by his side. Crouching low, he crawled out of the makeshift tent.

She was in the same spot she'd been in before he fell asleep, though she was now sitting cross-legged on the ground. He wondered why she had left the enclosure. For some reason, her independence irked him. As he walked toward her, his footsteps made a sound. She turned around and gave him a nervous smile. Adeel looked past her and saw what she had done. The mound of earth covering the statue had been removed, and a border of leaves now circled the hole. She had used her bare hands. He sank on the ground beside her and together they looked at the sculpture. The feeling that he'd had in the cave in Bamiyan resurfaced. Somehow, the ancient marble transformed itself into a living entity, one that pulled him into a new consciousness. For Adeel, the face of the statue represented a perfect universe.

Norbu cast him sideways glances as he continued to stare.

"I am resting with him," he explained, pointing to the face. "I could do this all day long. It is the only thing that makes me feel normal."

"My grandmother told me stories of a different life," Norbu replied. "Perhaps you are looking for that life as well." She opened her palm and let a few wildflowers drop onto the sculpture.

Adeel watched the little pink flowers settle on the forehead of the Buddha. A caterpillar poked his head up from the petals and crawled to the head. Adeel moved to swat it away, but Norbu was faster than him. She cupped her palm protectively around the insect.

"You must not kill it," she said solemnly.

"I was just going to flick it away," Adeel protested.

She did not move her hand, and he knew that she did not trust him. He was overwhelmed by her gesture and desperately wanted to change her impression of him. This slight, resolute woman had somehow entered places in his heart that he did not even know existed. He thought of his mother and what her response would be to a woman whose name was Tibetan and not Muslim. When he rolled her name over in his mind, he envisioned caves and cascading mountain waterfalls.

Adeel told her then that he would have to remain in this area for a few days, but that he would put her on a bus bound for Skardu so she could go home to her father. He spoke in clipped sentences, stifling all that he felt.

"I do not wish to return to him." She released the caterpillar onto the grass beside him.

"I cannot take care of a woman. I have to take you down to the place where the bus stops. I will give you money for food," he said, avoiding her gaze.

"I do not know your name," was all she said.

ELEVEN

KHALID STUDIED THE PIECE of paper Faisal had extended to him. The instructions were precise. His attendance was not requested but demanded, and couched in a very clear threat. Faisal had tried calling Reza in his Tehran office as well as at the country villa in Shiraz, but had been unable to make contact. The rendezvous had been organized not by Reza himself but by a diplomat from the Iranian Embassy in Islamabad. It appeared that the partial payment had not satisfied Reza; in his greed and impatience, he had pointed a gun at Khalid's head all the way from Tehran.

Khalid headed to the large pavilion that housed his Kashmir collection. Although he generally preferred not to mix his antiquities, he had made a notable exception years ago. Two enamel brooches from the early sixteenth-century Safavid period sat on a piece of black velvet flanked by two silver-embossed Kashmiri waterglasses. The brooches represented the earliest display of enamel craftsmanship in Iran and were fashioned as large, shimmering, turquoise and indigo butterflies. Khalid carefully lifted the brooches, placed them in a black velvet box, and handed it to Faisal to wrap in a square of silk organza. An hour later, after changing into a formal suit, he walked outside to the car with the box tucked under his arm, remembering his father's advice: never get attached to a work of art.

The rendezvous destination was the playground of the Rawal Lake park. The lake, situated a few miles from town, offered boating and picnic spots for families. Faisal took the Murree Road exit and stopped the car near a fleet of taxis waiting on one side of the road. Visiting diplomats were constantly under observation, and Khalid did not want his licence plate number in anyone's file. He grabbed a cab and gave the driver the directions, barking out rapid instructions to the park. Khalid's supressed fury at Reza's muscle-flexing was heightened by the odour of the unwashed body of the driver. He attempted to ignore it, and focused instead of the task at hand. The rendezvous had to be as covert as possible. When the taxi reached the park, Khalid got out and immediately bought two balloons mounted on sticks and a paper cone of fried chickpeas. He could have passed for a father indulging his children. The cloth-wrapped package tucked under one arm might have been a box of sweets.

Khalid handed the balloons to the first child he saw, then skirted the children's recreation area and headed to the edge of the water. He stood on the concrete embankment staring at the lake, which had been created by a nearby dam. A few hardy souls had ventured out onto the water, rowing little boats that were not equipped with life jackets. He glanced at his wristwatch and, suddenly, a hand brushed his shoulder.

"You are Reza's wizard?" said the small, impeccably dressed man who stepped in front of him.

"Is that what he calls me?" Khalid raised his eyebrows.

"We shall go for a boat ride, Mr. Khalid. I hope you are not afraid of the water?"

Khalid studied the ambassador for a moment before turning his attention to the man who had accompanied him—obviously part of the ambassador's security detail. He wore well-pressed trousers with a light windbreaker; there was a slight bulge in one pocket.

"Hameed will be our oarsman," the ambassador said before heading down toward the water.

Khalid followed, amused by his host's playfulness. The security man walked down the line of boats, chose one, and handed a generous sum of money to the owner. He helped the ambassador in first and then assisted Khalid's rather precarious entry. Once the two men were settled on the plank seat, the bodyguard sat himself in the middle and began expertly rowing away from the shore.

The ambassador drew a cigar from his suit pocket and fussed for a few minutes before clipping and lighting it.

"El Presidente! Mr. Castro's cigars are wonderful, don't you think?" The man's eyes glinted behind his spectacles.

"I've never been to Cuba," Khalid replied.

"So, Khalid, can you tell me why my good friend Reza Mohsinzadegh is disturbing my peace?" he finally asked.

"All agreements with him have been honoured by me. He is an impatient man," replied Khalid.

"What business are you in, Mr. Khalid?"

"A little bit of import and export," he replied.

"Yes, but it appears in this case that you have imported and not exported," the ambassador said pointedly.

"Come now, Ambassador. You know how government presents obstacles one does not expect."

"Yes, yes. But this artifact is worth a lot of money. Reza is most upset. How can we change his mood?"

Khalid knew the joust was about to begin. Many foreign diplomats did not shy away from privileges; they considered them to be the perks of their "hardship postings." If this tidy man enjoyed the delights of a Cuban cigar, then his response to the contents of Khalid's black box was assured.

"Ambassador, you are the expert at changing moods. It is what you are trained to do. Let me change your mood first, sir, then perhaps you will convince Reza to change his."

Khalid held out the box. The ambassador shifted his cigar to his left hand and reached forward with his right.

"Let me hold your cigar for you, Your Excellency. I think you will need both hands." Khalid reached forward and plucked the cigar from his fingers.

The ambassador offered an approving smile as he peeled off the organza covering the box, the tip of his tongue caught between his teeth in anticipation. When he lifted the lid he drew in his breath sharply. He lifted one brooch, then replaced it immediately. He pulled off his glasses, rubbed them with a handkerchief, put them back on, and lifted the brooch again.

"Qajar dynasty." He hunched over the brooch. "Magnificent! Beauty of the sort numbs the brain. Two! My God, you have two of them!"

"They are from Safavid dynasty," corrected Khalid.

"Safavid!" the ambassador repeated.

"Yes, they have been authenticated," Khalid said, smiling at him.

There was silence. The only sound was of the oars dipping in and out of the water. The boat glided across the lake's surface in a lazy arc. Khalid waited, observing the excitement of the ambassador, who turned the brooches over one at a time, examining them up close as well as at a distance. Khalid hoped his costly gamble, and the ambassador's greed, would halt Reza's assault.

"Khalid, you did not present me with a gift, you've given me a fragment of Persian history. These brooches belong in a museum, but my wife will show them off to better advantage." He grinned.

"But, of course, Ambassador. Our women should always be adorned in the finest jewellery."

"I must return. I have a reception to attend. Our dear friend Reza will not be difficult. I give you my word," he said as he patted Khalid's shoulder.

"There is an election coming up. I know the entire cabinet will change. Perhaps there will be a new admiral," Khalid said, hoping the ambassador would pick on his meaning.

"I see."

"The outgoing government will not leave a scandal behind." Khalid drove the point home.

"We are private citizens at this moment, Khalid. You have nothing to worry about."

"You know better than that, Ambassador. Your vehicle will have been followed."

"What about yours?"

"I travel by taxi," Khalid replied.

Upon returning to shore, Khalid waited a few minutes for the ambassador and his security man to leave the park before he headed for the taxi stand. Walking slowly, he purchased tea from an outdoor stall. He took his time drinking it before finally hailing a taxi to take him back to his own car. He was certain that he would be invited to some gratuitous function at the Iranian Embassy in the days to come. Personal telephone numbers had been exchanged. Khalid reassured himself that the loss of the brooches would be made up for at some later date.

Faisal was waiting in the car.

"There is some bad news," Faisal announced as Khalid slid into the passenger seat.

"Then don't give it to me," Khalid said, looking straight ahead.

Faisal remained silent.

"I want to do some shopping. Drive to United Bakery. I want to buy some lemon tarts for my grandchildren and the almond cake that Safia loves," said Khalid.

The bakery was an airy emporium of glass display cases. Well-heeled Pakistanis shopped there because the baked goods resembled the kind they'd eaten on their trips abroad. Khalid pictured the faces of his grandchildren as he examined the cream-filled concoctions and made his selections. He bought almond cake for Safia and blocks of imported cheese for Hassan. He collected all the items and reflected on the simple pleasure this small exercise provided.

"We will go home and have a wonderful tea with Safia. You may as well give me the bad news now, Faisal. I don't want to carry it home."

"There was a call from Sher Khan. The brown truck exploded at the side of the road," Faisal blurted.

Khalid plucked his phone from Faisal's breast pocket and dialed Sher Khan's number three times in rapid succession, hanging up after only a few rings. It took Sher Khan five minutes to return the call.

"Khalid! My people have reported that the truck exploded," said Sher Khan.

"Was a body found?"

"I cannot tell you that. The area has been sealed off by the army."

"I told you I wanted him alive. You were asked just to find him," Khalid said furiously.

"My people fight many battles, Khalid. Your agent Adeel offered to help them."

"I want details. I want you to find out what happened to the sculpture," he shouted before hanging up.

"What is the ISI man's number?" he asked Faisal.

"It is under *B*," Faisal replied.

Khalid scrolled down the phone list and punched the number he wished to call.

"Khalid, we have a problem," said the brigadier. "Did you get my message?"

"Yes."

"Did you ask anyone in Peshawar to help you?"

"No," Khalid lied.

"This is a classic Taliban strike. Fortunately, no one was killed. The truck was far away from the army checkpoint, which was the target."

"How do you know it was my truck?"

"We already knew that it had been painted over in Peshawar. There were no body parts or any trace of a human being in the truck. No sculpture either. I can assure you."

"I will lose a great deal of money on this, Brigadier. Adeel must be found. "

"Please don't use names on the phone, Khalid," the brigadier said sharply. "I have army connections in the region. When I have news I will call you."

As the car approached the house, Khalid jumped out and banged on the gate in anger. He stumbled through the opening, ignoring the startled expression on the guard's face, and walked rapidly along the path that led to his outdoor sculpture gallery. There, he paced up and down, trying to analyze the situation. Adeel had betrayed him. Sher Khan had sent his Taliban squad to look for him and they had blown up the truck. The brigadier was conducting his own private search. And although he had managed to stall Reza's payment, having a greedy ambassador on board might be a problem for him down the road. And of course there was Hassan to deal with. Khalid headed to the sanctuary of his Allah museum.

Khalid sat on the prayer rug in front of his miniature *Ka'ba*. This time, he came as a penitent and not a hope-filled supplicant. Day by day the country was savaged by lawlessness. Foreign investors and tourists gave Pakistan a wide berth. In the pristine white buildings of the nation's capital, the government was desensitized to the prevailing chaos, so much so that it had become totally disconnected from the 197 million people it ruled. Khalid realized that he was guilty of an error in judgement. Sher Khan was no longer only a carpet dealer and restaurant owner; he was a Taliban operative. He commanded men and loyalties and was singularly aware that Khalid was an extremely wealthy man. Khalid should not have trusted him. He should have gone to Bamiyan himself to retrieve the sculpture. Five years ago he would have considered such a trip an adventure, but he had grown soft with age. Now Khalid feared that his dream of creating the world's finest collection of Islamic art — right at his estate — would never materialize.

Khalid sensed a shadow behind him. He cupped his hands and uttered a simple prayer for strength.

"Father," came the tentative whisper.

Khalid turned around and saw Hassan, standing barefoot.

"What is it now?"

"Faisal says you are having some trouble. I want to help," Hassan replied.

Khalid rose, cupped his palms again, and murmured a prayer for clarity. For the briefest moment imaginable, he felt as though he had detected something different in his son. Although his experiences with Hassan were laced with heartache, he never stopped longing to repair their relationship.

"How brave are you, Hassan?" Khalid asked.

"As brave as you want me to be."

"There is a man hiding somewhere in Gilgit who has to be found."

"Let me help you, Father."

They walked from the museum in silence. Their destination was not to the elaborate tea Safia had prepared but to the room that Khalid used as an office. He sat behind a large antique table flanked by filing cabinets and narrated the entire situation to Hassan, whose face remained still. Khalid watched his son absorb the information without flinching or asking questions.

"Why is it, Father, that with all your wealth you cannot trust anyone?" Hassan finally said.

"When one decides to break rules, Hassan, one has to walk alone. This is a dream that will support another six generations of this family."

"I am going to help you. I don't want you to suffer," said Hassan.

"And are you going to get kidnapped along the way?" Khalid muttered.

"I want to restore your trust in me," Hassan said.

"Where is the expensive camera I brought you last year?"

"Somewhere in my room," Hassan replied.

"This is what I want you to do. Go to Gilgit. If anyone asks, you are a college student interested in photographing the region for a project."

"All right," agreed Hassan.

"That way, you can go anywhere and talk to anyone. Travel until you find the person I am looking for," said Khalid. "I am going to give you a new phone and you will call me on it daily."

As he spoke, Khalid noticed that Hassan's habitual indifference to his business had suddenly disappeared. He sat on the edge of his chair, alert and focused. His eyes glowed with excitement.

"What happened to all the gym equipment I imported for you from Dubai?" asked Khalid.

"I use it every morning," Hassan replied.

"So I am sending a strong man?"

"I think so."

Khalid was amazed at how his own sprits had lifted after talking with Hassan. He rose and clapped an arm around his son's shoulder, and they walked out together.

"Go pack a few clothes. Faisal will have a car ready with instructions and money."

As Hassan headed to his room, Khalid quickly grabbed his arm and pulled him back.

"You are not to discuss this with anyone — especially your mother."

Hassan agreed.

KHALID TURNED TOWARD the large pavilion that housed the family's gigantic swimming pool. His family sat on cane armchairs, watching Hassan's two children play with their toys. Tea had been arranged by Safia, and she looked expectantly at Khalid as he approached.

"You pamper everyone with these treats, but you stay away yourself," she said.

"I had some business with your favourite son," Khalid said as he sat down next to her.

"Good. He should be part of your entire life," Safia said, pouring tea for him.

"He will be all right," Khalid replied, wanting to reassure her.

Safia looked at him silently. Khalid felt as though he was looking at Hassan's face, the resemblance between his wife and son was so striking. Yet Hassan had a height and an angularity that reminded Khalid of his own father.

A few minutes later, Hassan joined them. A bulging black gym bag swung on one shoulder and a camera bag on the other.

"I have come to say goodbye." He spoke to both his mother and his wife.

His children shrieked with joy at the sight of him, and abandoned their toys to run to his side. Hassan dropped the bags and took them, one at a time, and tossed them into the air before ruffling their hair and releasing them. Then he scooped up his bags and smiled at Khalid, who was sipping his tea.

"Where are you going?" Safia asked as she stood up.

"I have to take some photographs for father's art brochure," he said.

"I am sending him to Gilgit," Khalid added.

"Well, it is a beautiful place. Take your wife with you,

Hassan. Have a little holiday with her," Safia pleaded.

"I will take her next time. I am going to be in rough places. This is not a family trip."

Safia walked to her seated daughter-in-law and hugged her from behind."He will take you next time," she whispered in her ear. "I will see to it."

Khalid glanced at his silent daughter-in-law. He knew that she no longer loved his son. Yet the young ages of her children and the genuine love she displayed for both him and Safia prevented her from leaving. Like Safia, she was fascinated by Kahlid's dream of completing all of the museums on his property. Khalid knew that she resented being supported by them; he also knew that she had no say in the matter as Hassan flitted from one hare-brained scheme to another. The baroque splendour of the estate had seduced her when she arrived as a bride, yet Khalid knew that one day she would want to be free of her gilded cage.

Khalid spent the rest of the afternoon with his frolicking grandchildren, and savouring the peace of Safia's companionship. He knew he had gambled on his son Hassan. If Hassan was successful in finding Adeel, Khalid would leave for Gilgit immediately to reclaim his sculpture. He now viewed Adeel's actions not as theft but as just another deal he had to make. Adeel knew the sculpture was valuable, and he would never make the mistake of selling it in Pakistan, thought Khalid. The man had to know that Khalid's own network would immediately report any such sale, regardless of where the deal was made.

Khalid's thoughts were interrupted when Faisal appeared by the pool. There was a car outside with two men—obviously from the ISI—who insisted on seeing him.

Hoping it was news about Adeel, Khalid left the family tea and hurried out to meet them.

THE TWO MEN shifted uneasily in the ornate chairs placed before Khalid's desk. One had a pockmarked face with a drooping moustache. The other had oily, slicked-back hair and a bulging stomach that strained against the confines of his cheap leather jacket. Faisal hovered in the background, holding a tray of green tea. The teapot was Turkish. It had an ornate dragon's-head spout that was intended to disarm visitors. As Faisal poured the tea into fine china cups, the men stared in amazement.

"Mr. Khalid, you met with the Iranian ambassador today?" said the man with the moustache. He balanced his teacup on his knee, unable to take his eyes off the pot.

"I had promised to take him boating. Show him a place right in Islamabad where one can relax," replied Khalid.

"Yes, but ISI wants to know what you gave to him." This time, it was the man with the bulging stomach who spoke.

"Nothing but the pleasure of my company," replied Khalid sharply.

"Um . . . the box. . . ." The man's voice trailed off.

Khalid was stunned. The ambassador had been followed. These men had probably watched the boat with binoculars. He could feel the bile rising in his stomach.

"Why am I being watched?" Khalid said angrily.

"All diplomats are watched, Mr. Khalid. We cannot be too careful, you know. Pakistan has many enemies." The man with the moustache shrugged.

"Why don't you ask him what was given to him?" Khalid said, resisting the urge to throw both men out.

"The government of Pakistan wants you to co-operate."

The moustached man spoke sternly.

"Let's settle this. Faisal, call the brigadier," Khalid ordered and then got up from his chair.

Both men shot up from their seats. They stood silently watching as Faisal dialed the phone and handed it to Khalid.

"I am serving tea in a seven-hundred-year-old teapot to two of your baboons," shouted Khalid into the phone as soon as the brigadier answered.

"Khalid, control your temper. They are just doing their job. Give the phone to one of them."

Khalid handed the phone ceremoniously to the man with the moustache. The exchange was brief.

"Mr. Khalid, I am just doing my job. There is no need for insults," the man said as he placed the phone on the table.

"Well, I have more important things to do. My private life is no concern of yours. Faisal, show the gentlemen out." Khalid skirted past both men and left the room without looking back.

AT DUSK, KHALID sat on the parapet of the half-constructed burial tomb and looked up at the violet sky. Piles of bricks and tools were littered about, but if he raised his eyes, he could see the distant hills that surrounded his property. For a moment, he felt that his universe was under control. When the stars came out, he thought, Safia would release her hair from her long braid, and the paintings in their bedroom would light up like fireflies. He wanted to climb the stairs to their bedroom, but he could not budge. The day had sucked every ounce of energy out of him.

He heard the soft patter of Safia's slippered feet behind him.

"I don't like this burial tomb. It is very depressing. What is the hurry, Khalid? We will live long lives. *In sha'Allah*," she said.

"I want you by my side forever. Come sit with me."

"I don't like this talk of death. I have come to give you a message."

Khalid turned and smiled at her. As her hair shifted around in the evening breeze, he sighed. Did she know, he wondered, that she was the most treasured thing in his life?

"Hassan just called from a strange phone and asked me to give you a message," she said.

"Yes."

"He has reached Peshawar and is spending the night in a small modest hotel and will drive to Gilgit in the morning."

"Good!" said Khalid.

"Why is he staying in a small hotel? They never have clean sheets. Is he trying to impress you by not spending too much money?" she asked.

"Did he tell you the name of the hotel?"

"No."

"It's all right. I have a surprise for you. We are going to throw a party. I will give you your surprise there," Khalid said, and slid down from the parapet.

"A party! " Safia clapped her hands like a child.

"Yes, with dancers and musicians. We will invite Ghalib from Lahore."

"I don't need anything, Khalid. I have everything I need," Safia said as she wound her arm through his.

As Khalid looked at her hand, resting on his arm, he saw it spin away. He tried to move — to reach out and clasp it — but the world continued to spin, as if in slow motion. He struggled to stand, to gain some sort of purchase, but to no avail. He was falling, away from Safia, away from everything.

TWELVE

GHALIB HAD DIFFICULTY WALKING up the winding staircase of the Alhamra Art Gallery, but his desire to see the
second-floor exhibition spurred him on. At the entrance,
the Middle Eastern diplomat who had opened the exhibition
was surrounded by a flurry of press and television cameras.
A large crowd had also gathered. Rather than lingering to
see who was in attendance, Ghalib hurried past; offering
early would give him an advantage when it came to buying
what he wanted.

Ghalib stood before the large canvasses, utterly mesmerized. The artist in him was completely humbled by the
masterful control displayed in the brush strokes. *This man
is a genius*, Ghalib thought to himself. He felt sure that the
work would be avidly collected. There were close to fifty
canvasses mounted, and it took Ghalib five minutes to purchase four of the best works. The artist came up to him,
conveying his gratitude, and invited him for a private tea
downstairs. Ghalib offered his congratulations but declined

the invitation for tea; he had a snooker match at his club in half an hour.

As his driver pulled away from the gallery, Ghalib thought of Khalid and wondered if he should call him to suggest investing in the new artist's work. Although he was peeved with Khalid, who still hadn't delivered his sculpture, he decided to call.

"There are delays at the border, Ghalib. Don't worry, it will be here soon," said Khalid.

"How are you, my friend?" asked Ghalib after the issue of the sculpture had been addressed.

"A little like a woman. I have these dizzy spells."

"Have you seen a doctor?"

"Yes. He called it labrynthitis. It happens once every few years. It will go away by itself." Khalid chuckled.

"Well, be careful. You don't want to fall and break something,"

"Not to worry. Safia kept me in bed for a day. It's the best way to deal with it. Ghalib, I am throwing a party for Safia. You must attend."

"What is the occasion?"

"A *Guth Jamai*."

"Good heavens, Khalid!" Ghalib was intrigued.

"I have acquired the ornament from one of my Indian dealers. It is twenty-two inches long. Safia has not seen it yet."

"I have to see it. Who have you invited?"

"I have invited the family and a few close friends. You have two days to get here. Your rooms will be ready for you."

"Well, let's hope the sculpture gets there in two days as well."

The *Guth Jamai* dated back to the Mughal period. During the ritual, a solid gold, jewelled ornament was used to cover the braid of a queen or royal princess. Ghalib shook his head; Khalid's acquisitions never failed to amaze him. With the current price of gold, the piece must have cost a fortune. Besides, Mughal gems were not readily found anymore. Some had wound up in museum collections; others had simply vanished. Ghalib admired Khalid's romantic heart as well as his loyal adoration of his wife. An event of this nature would require some pageantry. It would be a chance to dress extravagantly. Ghalib knew exactly the outfit he would take along. The pristine air of Islamabad and the surrounding hills would be a good change, he thought. Khalid, a fellow nocturnal soul, was delightful company for Ghalib, and even his staff members loved visiting the estate in Barako; Khalid was a generous host.

The invitation to Khalid's extravaganza, combined with the acquisition of four new works of art, lifted Ghalib's spirits considerably. He played a superb game of snooker at the club. Not even the memory of his missing teenager disrupted his concentration. He had taught Saqib to play, but the boy's act of disloyalty had changed everything. Rather than dwell on it, Ghalib reduced his thoughts of the teenager to specks of dust and mentally brushed them away. The Sufi drummer had obviously offered something to Saqib that Ghalib had not, and thinking about it was a waste of time.

THE NEXT AFTERNOON, Ghalib was absorbed in the morning papers that accompanied his late breakfast. The new political party to which he belonged seemed to have cornered the press. The media was in love with the party's leader. AK had done a bit of a U-turn, switching seemingly overnight from a lightweight womanizer to a born-again Pakistani. From every paper a half-page photograph of his craggy, lined face and ruffled hair peered out at Ghalib. He hoped that Nur Hyat was succeeding at gathering votes. Ghalib felt that change was in the air. His habitual boredom was beginning to vanish. Politics heralded excitement and promised a new lease on life.

That evening, Ghalib was on his way to a dinner party at the home of a powerful woman named Qudsia. She was the special adviser to the top bureaucrat of his province and belonged to a competing political party that hoped to win in the upcoming elections. Ghalib knew the stocky, white-haired woman would serve not only dinner but also a heady amount of political gossip. It would be marvellous for Ghalib just to sit and listen.

"How are you, my dear Ghalib." Qudsia greeted him warmly upon his arrival and led him to the living room.

"I feel splendid! You know I have decided to run in my constituency for the new party," he replied.

"Yes, I have heard. Is this wise?" she said, looking at him sternly.

"Wisdom is not my strong suit, Qudsia. I think it is guile," Ghalib replied, laughing.

"Well, then you would be a fool not to run with the winning party. It will be a clean sweep," she whispered.

"Is that so? But our chap is gobbling up all the press," Ghalib replied.

"Whoever takes Punjab takes Pakistan." She raised her head and faced him squarely.

"Has Punjab been taken?"

"Yes. You can say it has been delivered!"

"Well, there's nothing like a good fight," Ghalib replied

with a smile, though he now wanted nothing more than to escape from her smugness.

"With our party, your entire village will get electricity. Perhaps even a new school and a medical clinic," she added.

"I believe I am part of a *new* winning team," Ghalib said, knowing he was being courted.

"Rubbish! If an election was held tomorrow, the Punjab would deliver the country into our hands for the next five years."

"So, money has already been spread around?"

"Running for elections always has expenses. You know that, Ghalib."

"Well, I am ready to serve my country. A cultural portfolio was what I had in mind. Perhaps it may come my way."

"Yes, I know all about Soody's reckless promises. Think about joining us. Come, we must meet the others," she said, holding her hand out toward the dining room.

"Who is that beautiful creature standing in the corner?"

"She is somebody's niece who is wasting her life writing poetry," Qudsia snorted.

Ghalib immediately changed direction and walked toward the lanky girl who leaned against a door in the corner of the room. As he approached, she looked at him with large brown eyes. Her face was framed by a chin-length cap of shining dark hair that caressed the edges of her jawline.

"'She walks in beauty, like the night,'" recited Ghalib.

"'Of cloudless climes and starry skies,'" she carried through.

"'And all that's best of dark and bright meet in her aspect and her eyes,'" Ghalib finished.

She gave him a faint smile.

"I hear you write poetry."

"The real poet is coming. His name is Ghalib something or other," she replied.

"Are you waiting for him?"

"Not really, but Aunt Qudsia mentioned him." She was looking over his shoulder toward the other people in the room.

"I am Ghalib something or other."

"Oh, I am sorry." She flushed.

"Can you recite one of your poems to me?"

"No, I am not very good." She flicked at a strand of hair that fell across her eyes.

"You should be painted," Ghalib said, pointedly ignoring her discomfiture.

"Do you paint?" she asked.

"Yes."

"I hate these people. I am supposed to become a doctor or study law," she said suddenly.

"Here is my card. My email address is on it. Send me a poem and then we can see where you are going. Don't worry about other people."

She took the card and carefully tucked it in the bag slung over her shoulder.

Ghalib observed her angular beauty and felt a current of desire whip through him. Then she lifted her head and met his gaze. "I may," she whispered, before darting away.

Although he felt like dashing after her, Ghalib saw Qudsia advancing toward him accompanied by a powerful bureaucrat.

The pair approached him and the man struck a playful punch on his shoulder. "So, Ghalib, I hear you have entered the political fray, but with the wrong group."

"This nation is ready for a change and I intend to serve

the nation," Ghalib replied with a flourish.

"Don't tell me you have been duped by all the media hype."

"Well, today's papers indicate that my party is picking up steam," replied Ghalib.

"We have a bored press. Attending a political rally is entertainment for the hordes of unemployed, illiterate young men. The circus does not come to town so this is the next best thing. Never make the mistake of thinking the public will know how, or for whom, to vote." The bureaucrat spoke with an air of contempt.

"The 'whom' has already been decided, Ghalib. Proper guidance has been arranged," chimed in Qudsia.

"Who knows? With the right allegiance, your last book of poetry could wind up being part of the curriculum in the English departments of all our universities," said the bureaucrat, a faraway look in his eyes.

Ghalib was not at all surprised by their comments; it was all part of the parry and thrust of politics. He looked over their shoulders, trying to see if the girl was still in the room. His chauffeur had informed him earlier that Qudsia's party had been delivering envelopes of money to the homes of rural Punjabis. With soaring food prices and inadequate salaries, mothers with an average of five children would leap to spend the money on groceries and clothing. Then they would turn up to put a thumbprint on the ballot paper for the party that had sent them the money.

Ghalib's university days at Oxford, which the cynical bureaucrat had also attended, flashed through his mind. They had returned to Pakistan armed with progressive liberal ideals; over the years, however, these ideals had all but eroded. Personal ambition, greed, and ego had nudged aside the heady dreams of nation building. For the briefest moment Ghalib felt a twinge of revulsion for both himself and the posturing buffoon who stood before him. Murmuring excuses, he excused himself from the conversation to go look for the young poet, but she had disappeared. He lingered for another half an hour and made a mental note to remind his secretary to check his emails regularly.

GHALIB LEFT FOR Islamabad and Khalid's estate at Barako the next day. His valet sat in the front seat with the driver. A fourteen-year-old named Billa—the replacement for the runaway Saqib—sat next to Ghalib in the back seat. Spirits were high as they headed for the motorway. His staff of three had been told to wear fresh, neat clothing. Billa's wardrobe had been personally selected by Ghalib. The boy wore snug brown trousers and a fitted white cotton shirt. On his head sat a jaunty American baseball cap. When the car stopped at a petrol pump, Ghalib took him into the gift shop and lavished him with potato chips and chocolate bars. Spying a pile of embroidered cloth caps hailing from the province of Sindh, he bought six and made his staff, and Billa, wear them. For Ghalib, the pageant had already begun.

WHEN THEY ENTERED Barako four hours later, the gates were wide open. Khalid, wearing a wan expression, was seated in the little garden near his office, waiting for them.

"Are you still having the dizzy episodes, Khalid?" asked Ghalib.

"I am getting better. Let's have some lunch."

It was a leisurely lunch. Khalid announced to Ghalib, and the other guests, that the party would begin at nine that evening. The musicians and dancers would arrive at eight, and his Mughal pavilion would be illuminated at sunset.

Two of Ghalib's close friends from Islamabad had arrived for the party, as had the brigadier.

After lunch, Khalid escorted Ghalib to his suite in a poolside pavilion that housed three bedrooms. When Khalid swung open the heavy wooden doors to the bedroom, he noticed Ghalib's avaricious glance at the collection of Kashmiri enamel and silver vessels displayed on a shelf. For years Ghalib had wanted to purchase items from Khalid's Kashmiri collection, but Khalid had always refused.

As his valet unpacked, Ghalib amused himself by taking in Billa's awe as the boy looked around the gigantic forty-foot bedroom. It was a remarkable backdrop for the boy's nubile beauty, he thought.

"What do you think of all this, Billa?"

"Is this how all the rich people live?" he asked.

"Yes. But what is here is not just money, it is history." Ghalib laughed.

"What is history?"

"You have to go to school for that," said Ghalib, sitting on the edge of the bed.

"You promised that I would not go back. I will never go to school." Billa's voice rose in panic.

"It's all right. Come here. I give you my word I will arrange some other kind of education for you."

The boy stood in the centre of the room. His eyelids fluttered before closing for a moment, but not before Ghalib saw the memory of pain in his eyes. Billa had been sent to a *madrassah* outside the village, a place where he had been regularly exposed to corporal punishment and sexual abuse by the sole teacher. One evening, he escaped and walked the fifteen kilometres back to his home. His devastated mother ended up at Ghalib's country home, begging the estate manager for justice. The manager had brought the boy to Ghalib, who had ordered that Billa be taken care of in his personal household. The deeply traumatized boy had started to heal only when he was confident that all he would receive from Ghalib and the house staff was gentle affection. Within days of his arrival, the sparkle in his mischievous eyes was restored. The boy was illiterate and Ghalib's plans to have him home-schooled had yet to materialize.

"There will be music and dancers who will entertain us tonight, Billa," said Ghalib, trying to cheer him.

"I will dance with them," announced Billa, walking toward the bed.

"Would you like to play cards?"

"Yes."

Reclining on the bed, Ghalib dealt out cards and watched his young pupil master gin rummy. It was an exercise laden with affection and some tutorship. When the card games were over, Ghalib dozed off as the boy silently massaged his feet. Eventually, Billa crept away to explore the mysteries of Khalid's house of many pavilions.

THAT EVENING AS the festivities began, Ghalib walked toward Khalid, who was sporting brocaded clothing complete with a turban decorated by a gem. Safia stood by his side dressed in a pale green chiffon dress with gems blazing at her throat, wrists, and forehead. Ghalib circled her to examine her braid, which hit at her waist and was encased in links of solid gold encrusted with minute gemstones. Ghalib looked at Khalid, who stood proudly beside his wife.

"It is exquisite. I dare not even ask its value."

"Oh." Khalid rolled his eyes theatrically.

"Where is your son Hassan?" asked Ghalib.

"Can you believe it, Mian Sahib. Khalid has sent him to do some work in Gilgit," said Safia with sadness.

"Gilgit?" Ghalib looked at Khalid, who avoided his eye contact.

"I think the dancers have arrived," Khalid said quickly, ushering them toward the path that led to the white marble pavilion.

The footpath led them to a square space that featured walkways and bridges arranged over a square marble pool. In the centre of the pool, a fountain shot up a spray of water. Coloured lights strung along each column illuminated the main pavilion. Circular tables, sprinkled around the area, were set for dinner with white linen. A gilded settee, where Khalid and Safia would sit, was placed in the centre of the square. Ghalib was led to a front table next to Faisal. Another guest was already seated—a man sporting a dinner jacket and puffing on a pipe. They shook hands, but before they could be introduced, something colourful caught Ghalib's eye. He squinted and then smiled. Four stunning transvestites with manes of shining hair and voluptuous bodies stuffed into shimmering outfits clapped and swayed like courtesans as they arrived and began to entertain the guests.

As the sumptuous buffet was served and a troupe of musicians played, the dancers took turns giving solo performances. Ghalib spied Billa hiding behind a column, intensely studying the dancers' movements so he could duplicate them later. Ghalib rose to his feet as Billa materialized by his side, mimicking the feminine movements of the dancers perfectly and filling Ghalib with uncontrollable mirth. Khalid, Safia, and their family members began to dance as well. The only person who was not dancing was the pipe-smoking man. He sat sipping whisky and watching the frivolity with half-closed eyes.

"Come on, man. You need to dance," Ghalib said to him when he returned to the table.

"I'm not much of a dancer, I'm afraid."

"Are you from the government?" asked Ghalib.

"I am with the service," he replied.

"Are we talking about the army?"

"I do special work for the government," replied the man evasively.

"Are you Khalid's brigadier?" asked Ghalib, certain he had hit the nail on the head.

"I don't know what you mean. His art collection is spectacular, isn't it?" said the man, deflecting the conversation.

"Do you collect?" asked Ghalib.

"No. Khalid acquired quite a fine piece recently, and I have been assisting him with it. It's been a difficult undertaking," the brigadier whispered.

"That is most unusual. Khalid is an old hand in the art business. Are we talking about a painting or sculpture?" Ghalib pressed.

"It is a sculpture. Quite old," the brigadier said. "Would you like a whisky? I am going in to refresh mine."

Ghalib watched him head toward the main pavilion with a mixture of anger and sadness. Khalid had not been truthful; he did not have the sculpture in hand. Meanwhile, the sale of Ghalib's land had gone through and the money had been deposited in his personal account. Ghalib had to get to the bottom of the situation right away. He rose to find Khalid and saw him disappearing into the white marble salon where a bar had been spread out. He walked in and found Khalid narrating an anecdote to an admiring audience, including the brigadier.

"Khalid, it has been quite a party. I think I may turn in early, but just need to tear you away from your friends for five minutes," Ghalib said.

"Come on, Ghalib. I have brought in entertainment just for you. We are going to be up all night," Khalid cajoled.

"Well, come by my room later then. That's where I will be," Ghalib said and walked out.

Ghalib did not have to wait long. He was sitting next to the pool near his rooms when Khalid approached.

"Well, I hope you enjoyed the night," Khalid said, sinking into the chair next to him.

"What are you hiding from me, Khalid?"

"The person who went to Afghanistan for the sculpture returned to Peshawar and has disappeared with the sculpture," Khalid replied.

"I thought this was properly organized, Khalid. My God! Has the wretched man stolen it?" Ghalib asked, outraged.

"That is the mystery. He has the best reputation in the country for this sort of work. I fear there has been a double-cross somewhere."

"Have you checked with the person who arranged this for you? Perhaps another buyer has surfaced?"

"I thought of that myself, and I have people looking for him, but the situation has become a little wild. I think the Taliban has gotten involved as well."

"What do you mean, the Taliban?" Ghalib almost choked.

"Ghalib, I am going to find the agent. He left Peshawar and headed north toward Gilgit."

Ghalib was speechless, but he was certain that Khalid

was now telling him the truth. He knew Khalid had the resources for the hunt. It was common knowledge that the Taliban were utilized periodically by the ISI as well.

"What does your bloody pipe-smoking brigadier have to say about all of this?"

"Not much, but I have also used my old friend Sher Khan in Peshawar," replied Khalid.

"Oh, Khalid! I know the leading Pathan family of that region. You should have told me," Ghalib said in despair.

"It is too late for that. Sher Khan blew up the truck, or his Taliban cohorts did. So the agent is hiding somewhere and has the sculpture with him. I will find him."

"How?"

"I have a new plan. I have sent someone there to locate him. I will go myself to negotiate."

"Well, your brigadier has failed and so has your Taliban friend. Who is helping you now?" asked Ghalib.

"I have sent Hassan."

"You are mad!" Ghalib exclaimed.

"Not really, Ghalib. Sometimes it takes a thief to catch a thief."

THIRTEEN

ADEEL HAD ALWAYS BEEN the master of his own destiny. Now, however, he found himself facing an unpredictable challenge: Norbu refused to leave. He had been determined to find a bus he could put her on, but when he told her of his plans, she darted away and disappeared into the thicket. He searched for half an hour without finding her. She was an expert at hiding, he realized, a woman who had learned to hide from men when she feared abuse. He was saddened to be mistrusted in this way, but he knew he would eventually find her. For the time being, he would let her hide. Their survival in the forest required a few essential items, so he decided to venture into town to pick them up.

The ride into Chilas was relatively quick, thanks to a van that picked him up and dropped him off near the outskirts of the town. He quickly bought what he'd come to buy and made his way back to the road, intending to return to the campsite the same way he'd come to town—by hitchhiking. Unfortunately, no ride was forthcoming, so he set off on his own, alternating between walking and jogging.

As he neared the cutoff, he thought about Norbu. He suspected that she was probably near the sculpture and so he headed straight for it, hoping to catch her unawares, before she could disappear again. As he approached the spot, however, he sensed movement behind him and turned around. Norbu was standing there with her arms full of tree branches.

"What is this for?"

"I'm making a shelter," she replied.

"You are a madwoman. You cannot stay here."

"They will not find us here," she said.

"You cannot stay here with me," he cried out in frustration.

"I have found a little stream. It is close by," she replied, ignoring his outburst.

He sat down wearily. She moved toward the temporary shelter he had created with the shawls and placed the branches on the ground. Before he could say anything, she walked away again, in search of more branches. He watched her movements silently for about ten minutes—back and forth, back and forth—and wondered if he should tell her that a fire could not be lit with the branches she had collected. Finally, he walked over to where she had settled, next to the shelter. She was sitting on the ground braiding a length of vines and branches. He was amazed at her skill. She raised her head, smiled at him, and patted the ground next to her. She knew that they would have to stay hidden for a while, she explained, so she was weaving walls for a forest dwelling. Adeel noticed for the first time how slender she was. Her fingers darted in and out as she wove, and when her palms turned outward, the sight of her chapped hands constricted his heart. He lowered himself and settled in beside her. He picked up the thin, leaf-laden branches and tried to duplicate her technique. The exercise was more difficult than he'd imagined. His clumsy labour could not match either her delicacy or her speed. When they were finally done, her shawls were replaced by the new "walls," and the shelter was much more welcoming than it had been. It wasn't much larger than a child's playhouse, but there was enough sleeping space for two.

She got up and surveyed her work proudly. Then she crawled in and placed one of her shawls on the ground inside.

"Are you hungry?" Adeel asked.

"It does not matter," she said.

"I will light a fire." Despite her evasive answer, he knew she must be as hungry as he was.

"What will we eat?" she asked.

"I bought a few things," he said, pointing to his black nylon bag.

Norbu clapped her hands with joy when she discovered the clay pot, two spoons, rice, lentils, and small cone of spices that Adeel had bought in Chilas. As Adeel constructed a hearth out of three large stones, and built a fire beneath, Norbu busied herself with preparing the rice and lentils. Before long, the pot was boiling merrily. Both ravenous, they sat by the pot, unable to tear their eyes off it. They shared one large bottle of water and drank it sparingly. She examined the bar of soap that Adeel had also bought with curiosity, casting a dark look his way.

"You can use this to wash in the stream," he said, handing it to her and trying not to laugh.

"I washed already," she said.

"Without soap?" he inquired mildly.

"That is none of your business." Her voice was defiant and angry.

"As long as you are with me, Norbu, everything is my business," he said sharply.

When he thought the food was cooked, Adeel lifted the pot with his scarf and placed it between them. He dug both spoons into the pot and slid it toward her.

She pushed it back. "You eat."

"You taste it first. Tell me how it is," he said.

She relented, raised the spoon to her mouth, blew on it, then tasted it and made a face.

"What is wrong?"

"No salt!"

"You don't need salt," he said.

She threw him a scornful look and slid the pot back toward him.

"You eat it! I don't want a woman around who is going to faint from hunger," he said, annoyed.

"After you have finished I will eat," she said, clinging to her traditional ways.

He spooned some of the gelatinous mass into his mouth and chewed slowly. When he finished half, he slid the pot back to her.

"Eat. I am tired. I have things to do before it gets dark."

For once, the fight seemed to have gone out of her. She swallowed a few mouthfuls, then flung the remains to one side. She stood, manoeuvred the pot into the crook of her waist, and grabbed the bar of soap.

"I will go wash the pot in the stream," she announced.

"I'll do it in the morning." He pointed his index finger at her. "You have to get on the bus and go to your father's village."

"You must be peaceful after you eat or you will not digest the food properly," she said primly from a safe distance.

He watched her disappear through the bushes, waiting until he knew for certain that she was gone. Then he retrieved his bag. His small portable phone was dead. He counted his money; he was down to twenty thousand rupees. His shaving kit was untouched, as were a small comb, a bottle of almond oil, and two pairs of socks and underwear he had wrapped into an extra pair of cotton khaki trousers. His mother had gifted him with the small plastic bottle of oil, and he used it sparingly on his hair, his sole concession to vanity.

Dusk was slowly darkening the sky and Norbu had still not returned. Once again, his anxiety about her made him uneasy. He threw his bag in the little tent of leaves and moved toward the forest with his small flashlight. It was only a minute before he heard her singing in s high, birdlike voice. The knowledge that she was close by caused him to exhale in relief, and he walked toward the sound. A moment later, she materialized in front of him with the damp clay pot resting against her waist. The song died in her throat when she saw Adeel approaching.

"It's getting dark. I came to look for you," he explained.

She held out the pot for him to inspect. "Is it clean?"

"It's fine," he said gruffly.

They walked in silence until they arrived at the spot where the sculpture lay lightly covered with earth. She sank down and began clearing the earth with her bare hands.

"Look into its face. See, there are no eyes."

As Adeel sat next to her, gazing at the face of the statue, the stress of the entire day receded. He heard only the sound of his breath and the rustling of the leaves through the trees.

Norbu sat across from him, her face outlined by her woollen shawl. Looking at her—almost statuelike herself in her stillness—Adeel realized that he was on the threshold of a new existence. The bestial faces of the Taliban men on the motorcycles, the violent assignments that he had completed in the past, as well as his act of thievery and betrayal weighed heavily on his mind.

The marble lips of the statue appeared to move, murmuring in a tongue that Adeel could not decipher but still seemed familiar. Memories of his past eight years in the army filled him with revulsion. Adeel knew that Norbu, his strange companion, had become inextricably entangled in the choices he would have to make. He was going to have to completely abandon his personal history. No longer was he just a gun for hire; he was a questing soul. All he wanted was to fully embrace this peace. He realized with a start that the mystical feeling of calm that the statue elicited was something he had been seeking for many years.

"Norbu, tell me about your grandmother's religion," he said.

"Buddha," she said simply, pursing her lips as she spoke the name.

"Not the prophet Mohammad?"

"No," she said emphatically.

"You believe in Buddha?"

"Yes."

"Why?"

"Because Buddha has salt."

He burst out laughing. She was brighter than he thought.

"Can you read and write?" he asked hesitantly.

"I reached middle school in Skardu and then they married me," she replied.

"Is that where your father lives?"

She looked away.

"Are you finished with your husband?"

"He has another wife. His mother brought me the divorce paper. He will never see my face again and neither will my father."

He considered her words and hesitated a moment before he spoke again. He knew she would not want to hear what he had to say, and he had no wish to hurt her. But he needed to be clear.

"Please do not make a fuss in the morning," he said. "I am a man who has to be alone. I have nothing to give you. It is better for you to go home; it will be safer for you."

Her face was expressionless. She looked away without saying a word. He wanted to reach out and shake her, to force her to acknowledge his words. There was no way to know what she was thinking—and he was no longer entirely sure of his own thoughts. Did he really want her to leave because she was a burden, or were there other reasons?

Norbu crawled into the tent of leaves and branches and wound one of the woollen shawls around herself like a blanket. Without a glance in his direction, she turned and faced the wall. He followed her into the shelter, removed his revolver from his holster, and placed it near his side, where her second shawl rested. He covered himself and lay in the dark, listening to the wind outside, unable to fall asleep. An enormous sense of responsibility for Norbu plagued him. There were elements of compassion tucked into those feelings, certainly, but he also knew he was attracted to her. Somehow, he needed to clarify their bizarre and undeniable bond. But all he knew for the moment was that their companionship and shared attachment to the sculpture was a solace. Adeel listened to her breathing in the dark. He ached to reach across the small space that separated them and unwind her shawl, but he put those thoughts aside and eventually fell asleep.

ADEEL WOKE UP at dawn. On the other side of the shelter, Norbu stirred as well. Slivers of light filtered in through the leaves and branches. Adeel did not look at her, but crawled out, dragging the woollen shawl with him. The morning air was cool and he walked toward the three stones on the ground and lit a new fire. Then he measured out water, tea leaves, and powdered milk into the clay pot and waited for it to boil. Apart from the two spoons he had bought on his trip into Chilas, there was nothing with which to drink the tea. There was, however, a small army-issue enamel mug in his nylon bag. He normally used it for shaving, but it would have to do. He crawled back into the shelter to retrieve it.

Norbu was sitting up, trying to smooth the knots in her hair with her fingers.

"I have something for you," he said.

He pulled out his comb and the bottle of almond oil. He placed them next to her, then retrieved his enamel mug and revolver. She glanced at the revolver for a moment. He did not see fear in her eyes, only curiosity.

"I am making tea," he said over his shoulder as he crawled out.

A few minutes later, when she stuck her head out of the enclosure, she looked different. Her hair was pulled back from her face and fashioned into a gleaming braid that trailed over one shoulder. The woollen shawl hung loosely around her neck, its ends cascading down the front of her body. She reminded Adeel of the Sherpa guides he used to see in the high mountains. He poured the steaming tea into the enamel mug and held it out to her. She sat on the ground next to him, but did not take the mug.

"There is only one mug. Drink it and then I will have some," he said.

To his surprise she did not make a fuss. She took the mug, had a sip, and then grimaced.

"What is it now?"

"No sugar," she said, and handed the mug back.

He took a sip then promptly extended it again.

"Drink it. There is some sugar," he said in a low voice.

She looked at the mug for a few seconds, and, to his surprise, drank it all.

"You are a very bad cook," she said.

"I have been trained to do other things," he replied, amused.

"Do you shoot with that?" she said, pointing to the revolver tucked in its holster under his arm.

"Yes. It could save our lives," he said.

"I can save my own life," she said, rising and grabbing the pot.

"Don't move from here. And don't hide again. I have to do something. I will be back in a little while."

Adeel collected his phone, charger, and some money from the shelter. He put the revolver back in the black nylon bag and then set off for Chilas and the small bazaar he had visited the day before. He jogged lightly, picking up his pace as the sun rose over the mountains and warmed him. There was no traffic on the main road, and nothing to distract him from his mission: find the bus schedule for Skardu and make one call to his mother.

He heard the car before he saw it. He looked around

quickly for a place to conceal himself, but this was a flat stretch of road and nothing presented itself. He stopped immediately, wound the heavy shawl around himself, pulled a woollen cap low on his head, and continued to walk slowly. When the large beige sedan with a flag fluttering on the hood came into view, Adeel knew it was the staff car of some very senior army official. The car pulled up by his side, a window rolled down, and a face under a peaked cap turned toward him. Adeel found himself staring into Major Zamir's topaz-coloured eyes. He froze. The major tapped the chauffeur's shoulder and the car stopped.

"Captain Adeel!"

Adeel walked over to the window, raised his eyes, and braced himself. The major was now a general, he noticed, taking in the man's uniform.

"Congratulations, sir!" he murmured.

"My God, it *is* you! I had heard you were discharged eight years ago. Why?"

"It was suggested, sir. I am performing some other duties."

"Those ISI hawks! You would have had a fine career with the regular service. I would have seen to it."

"I am fine, sir."

"What are you doing in this deserted spot? No transport?"

"I need to get going, General. I am expected," Adeel replied, wanting to get away as fast as possible.

"What is your destination?"

"Skardu, sir," Adeel said quickly.

"Well, you are in luck, Captain. I am headed there myself. Do you want a ride? I have room."

"Thank you, sir, but I have made arrangements with some people already."

"Pity," Zamir said, extending his hand.

Adeel reached forward and clasped it.

"Are you all right?"

"Yes," replied Adeel, trying to disengage his hand.

"I don't like your appearance," the man said, looking him up and down and taking in his worn clothing. "You could have been a major by now, Adeel. Do you know anything about the truck that exploded in Chilas?"

"No, I don't. But I need a favour, sir. I have to call my mother and my phone is dead."

"Of course." Zamir handed his phone to Adeel.

"I will be very quick. She worries, you know." Adeel nodded his thanks and moved away from the car.

He dialed his mother's number. After eight rings, she picked up.

"Adeel?"

"Are you all right? Did you receive the money? I have to be very fast. Don't worry about me." He spoke rapidly.

"Where are you, my son?"

"Far away, but I cannot talk just now. Are you alone?"

He heard a soft moan accompanied by a sharp intake of breath; there was someone with her. They had gotten to his mother. He hung up the phone immediately and walked back to the car.

"I have to go, sir. Good to see you," he said, shoving the phone back at the general through the window.

Zamir lifted his hand in a salute. Adeel saluted back.

"Is she all right? Adeel? Do you need my help? You can trust me. I know you know that."

Adeel looked at the general, willing his face to remain expressionless.

"Where are you posted these days, sir?"

"I'm seducing and battling with the Marri tribesmen in Baluchistan. We all do the best we can." He leaned forward and tapped the driver and, after a small wave, they drove away.

Adeel watched the car until it disappeared around a bend in the road, then raced toward the bazaar. It was no longer safe for him to communicate with his mother; this much he knew. Were they still at the house, or had his phone call prompted them to take her somewhere for interrogation? Either way, he was confident that she would endure whatever was coming. Borrowing Zamir's phone had been a stroke of genius, he decided. These men would track the phone call to try to reach him. When Zamir answered, someone would fill him in on the situation. And then, Adeel felt sure, the general would step in and protect her.

Adeel reached the small bazaar to find only one of its five shops open. A green sedan was parked in front. A young man with a camera around his neck was waiting for the tea to be brewed. Adeel ducked instinctively. He hid until he saw the man return to his car with his tray. It took the man about ten minutes to polish off his breakfast before handing the tray back, paying the server, and driving away.

As the car began to move, Adeel caught a better glimpse of the man's face. The chiselled profile and the jet-black hair seemed familiar. He had seen the man's face somewhere before. He squeezed his eyes shut and concentrated. After a moment, an image exploded in his mind with the force of a thunderbolt. The assignment to collect the sculpture from Afghanistan had been given to him at an estate in Barako. The brown truck, fake identity cards, cash, and instructions were handed to him there. The truck was parked close to an ornate marble gazebo. Before Adeel left, he watched a young man in the gazebo tossing and catching a small toddler. It was the same young man who had just driven away. So his employer was hard on his heels.

Adeel slowly walked up to the teashop, ordered some breakfast, and spoke casually to the server. "Journalist?" he asked, nodding at the trail of dust kicked up by the car that had just departed.

"No. He is a student of photography," the man replied. "But I think he is a rich man's son. His watch was very expensive."

"What's he photographing?"

"All of Gilgit, he said." The man shrugged.

"Is there a bus for Skardu today?" asked Adeel.

"It will leave here in three hours. It's a five-hour journey but can take up to nine hours, depending on what's happening on the Karakoram Highway."

Adeel nodded. "Can you make some omelettes and rotis for me?"

"You'll have to wait. I have to find more eggs."

ALTHOUGH HASSAN WAS frustrated by his lack of success in finding the man his father wanted him to locate, he was entirely enchanted by the region he was visiting. The area was a photographer's dream, he decided, and since he was posing as a photographer, he dedicated himself to taking many pictures while driving around and searching for the man with the statue. After his breakfast, he set out to find higher terrain where he could take some panoramic views of the valley. He drove along the road from the town until he saw a small, forested area up an incline. An unpaved path led from the main road toward the trees; he turned his car onto the gravel path. A line of trees with heavy foliage appeared in front of him, creating a canopy of branches over the path. It was beautiful sight. When the gravel road ended, he got out of the car and took some photographs as he moved toward a clearing. The smell of smoke was in the air, and it made Hassan curious. He kept walking until he reached a small encampment with an ebbing fire and a cooking pit. He peeked inside the small shelter that had been erected and saw a black nylon bag and a shawl. A foreigner's camping site, he figured.

Hassan walked past the camp and, a few minutes later, came upon a stream. A woman was bathing there. As she rose from the water Hassan dropped to the ground, lifted the camera, and focused the zoom on her body. The powerful lens picked up the sheen of her water-soaked braid as it swung against her fair skin and ended at the curve of her slender hips. He sought out and located her clothes, piled nearby on a flat rock. Hassan inched backwards until he was hidden from view. He did not photograph her; he only observed through the lens. He watched her dry herself with a length of cloth, then step into rustic cotton pants and a tunic. She leaned down and picked up a pair of shoes and held them in one hand. Hassan was mesmerized. He felt as though he had stumbled upon a wood nymph. This woman with her shining braid and damp skin looked as if she had stepped out of a painting. Eager to see more, to keep watching, he rose a little higher from the undergrowth. She turned her face then, and saw him.

Norbu had not known she was being observed. The man startled her, and she took in only his presence and the black object in his hand as she turned and ran toward the shelter. She could hear his footsteps close behind her and his voice in her ear, shouting words she couldn't make out over her own tortured breathing and the pounding of blood in her head.

When she reached the enclosure she stumbled over Adeel's black nylon bag. She ripped open the zipper and pulled out the revolver. She held it in both hands, turned, and pointed it straight toward the opening. A second later, Hassan's head poked in. Norbu closed her eyes and pulled the trigger.

FOURTEEN

KHALID STUDIED THE EMBOSSED card. The summons
from the Iranian Embassy had arrived two days earlier
under the guise of an invitation to a cultural reception. He
longed to ask Safia to join him, but she was uncomfortable
at events of this nature. Unfortunately, there was no denying
his need to attend; it might be a good opportunity to meet
a wealthy art collector or two. He would have to dress for
the occasion, and for that, he needed Safia's help. He found
her getting out of bed.

"I have to attend a reception. I need to wear a Western
suit. Can you help me choose a tie?" Khalid asked.

Safia nodded her agreement, then shook her head as if to
clear it. "I took a nap and had a terrible dream," she said, her
eyes widening in alarm. "I thought my heart had stopped,
but then I woke up."

"What sort of dream?"

"I was being buried alive. I shouted but no one could
hear me." Safia shuddered at the recollection.

"Does this have to do with the burial shrine I'm building?" Khalid asked.

"I don't know. Hassan has not called today. I'm worried about him."

"He is doing some work for me. He will let me know when he is finished. It will take another two or three days," Khalid said, and planted a kiss lightly on her forehead.

"Which suit are you wearing?" she asked.

"I think it should be the black suit with a white shirt. I don't want them to think I'm a savage. You choose the tie," repeated Khalid. Safia's words and worries had distracted him. He found himself wondering, not for the first time, if Hassan had made any progress.

THE IRANIAN EMBASSY'S sprawling villa was located in Islamabad's diplomatic enclave. Barriers and checkpoints cordoned off the entire area. High concrete walls with barbed wire surrounded all the buildings. After a bomb had been detonated in a nearby five-star hotel, the security protocol had changed. The American compound was a perfect example of the new order. It was vast, with a three-storey parking structure and a cluster of solid buildings. The Americans had imported both their contractors and their building material—not a single nail or security guard had been provided by the host country. Even the passports of those simply applying for visas were scrutinized at the main barrier. These days, though Khalid, the entire diplomatic enclave was a fortress city, set apart from Islamabad's benign hillside sprawl. Surprisingly, the atmosphere did nothing to discourage visitors. The United States, Canada, France, and Britain all had social clubs in the area, where nationals could drink alcohol in peace and eat the foods of their respective countries. Local Pakistanis avidly sought invitations to these exclusive spots, ignoring the subtle resentment their presence always seemed to engender.

Khalid showed his invitation and national identity card at the gate to the Iranian Embassy. The main foyer gleamed with polished marble floors, covered here and there by exquisite Persian carpets. Khalid slipped inside the large reception room, which was filled with foreign diplomats and clutches of the locals who had managed to wrangle an invitation. He spied the ambassador, who immediately waved him over. Khalid walked across the room, unable to take his eyes off the plump woman who stood by the ambassador's side. His two Safavid-period butterflies nestled against each other on the black silk of her unfashionable jacket.

"Ah, my dear, here is the wonderful Mr. Khalid," the ambassador declared.

Khalid shook the limp hand extended to him and pasted a smile on his face.

"Madame, your brooches are beautiful," he said deliberately.

"Yes, they are Persian antiques," she said with a hint of pride.

"Khalid, let us show you our little display." The ambassador ushered Khalid to the far side of the room, where a few people had gathered around a large mahogany table covered with white felt. The collection of handblown Persian glass — fashioned into perfume bottles, goblets, and lamps — was brilliantly lit. Most of the pieces were blue, and they practically glowed under the carefully arranged spotlights. Despite the care that had gone into the display, the collection was mediocre at best, thought Khalid. There was a glut of Persian glass in the collectors' market at the moment. The only item that caught his eye was a bird-shaped fragrance bottle. He spent another moment or two looking at the items, then moved away. Many of the other guests were doing the same, he noticed. They seemed more interested in accosting the servers carrying silver trays of Iranian hors d'oeuvres. The caviar bowls emptied faster than any other items. Khalid was planning his escape, and edging ever closer to the door, when he walked right into the ambassador, who was standing near the entrance.

"My dear Khalid sahib, I have some news for you." The ambassador directed him to the hall outside the reception room.

"I am being recalled to Tehran. I could be assigned a new posting, but there is also a rumour of some pressure being exerted on my department by another ministry."

Khalid stood silently. He knew exactly what was coming.

"Someone has pulled a very senior card here, Khalid," the ambassador said, looking apologetic. "I must have the remainder of your payment in hand when I leave next week."

"You shall have it. Thank you for your hospitality. Unfortunately, I cannot stay longer. My wife is waiting for me." Khalid said coolly before turning on his heel.

The ambassador's hand shot out and grasped his shoulder. Khalid stopped.

"Reza Mohsinzadegh has gone over my head. Unfortunately, he is very close to the ayatollah. I'm sorry," the man whispered.

"You shall not return empty-handed," Khalid said as he brushed the hand from his shoulder and headed toward the door.

ONCE HOME, KHALID set his contingency plan into motion. He called a shipping agent in Karachi and inquired about the earliest-possible delivery of a twenty-foot container to Bangkok, then instructed Faisal to summon his packers to the house immediately, even though it was 9 p.m. Next, he personally supervised the crating of twenty-two works of two-thousand-year-old Gandharan art, most of which were manifestations of Buddha, in either frieze or statue form. The packing work continued through the night until, finally, a container rolled up to the gates of the estate on the bed of a tractor-trailer. Khalid wired payments while Faisal arranged for a security detail to escort the truck the entire 713-mile route to Karachi. By 3 a.m., the container was filled and securely padlocked. From his terrace, Khalid watched the truck snake its way down the winding country road. It was only when the lights of the vehicle disappeared that he finally sat down and lit a cigarette.

Khalid's thoughts were as cold as ice. His mission was to raise a large sum of cash within four days. He had discussed the shipment with a businessman in Bangkok a few days earlier. An entire photo file had been sent to the buyer months ago. Khalid knew the buyer would accept the shipment and was capable of releasing the container into Thailand without it being examined. Khalid also knew he would pay promptly. Yet this daring transaction was not without risk. In the past three years, he had successfully sent many smaller consignments. Recently, however, his network of people at the Karachi ports had changed, as had the shipping rates. Khalid had, of course, taken precautions. A specially prepared bill of lading would be attached to the container the moment it reached the outskirts of the city, using a carefully selected business alias. The bill would specify that the famed Hala ceramic tiles from Sindh were being exported to Bangkok. Khalid's arrangements were meticulous, but the entire venture was a colossal gamble nonetheless. But Reza Mohsinzadegh had to be silenced. Khalid would conduct no further business with him.

When he finally entered his bedroom to go to sleep, Khalid noticed his wife's mobile phone lying next to her face, on her pillow. He switched it off and placed it in the night table drawer. If there had been word from Hassan she would have told him. And at the moment, the only call he wanted to receive was the one that told him his container had been safely loaded onto a ship.

THE TRUCK CARRYING the artifacts followed a black SUV at an even speed of sixty kilometres an hour. The security company Khalid had hired to guard the shipment was a slick operation owned by a retired army officer who trained discharged military men for this new line of work. It had branches in three of the nation's main cities. A tractor-trailer with a twenty-foot container was not an easy vehicle to secure, so Khalid had also paid a team of men for their time and skills. The four men travelling in the SUV were heavily armed.

The driver of the truck behind the SUV knew that something other than ceramic tiles was travelling in the container; there were more economical ways of transporting tiles, certainly, and the wooden crates were all different shapes and sizes. And the black vehicle in front of him — carrying four armed security guards — suggested that the cargo had value. But his job was to drive, not to ask questions. The manager of the security company had made it clear that the client was an extremely wealthy man and that the timely completion of this delivery, in exactly the way the client had specified, would result in more business.

The driver was a veteran in his profession. He had shuttled vehicles and merchandise from one end of the country to the other for thirty years. He was also a man blessed with luck. Twice his trailer had jackknifed and the containers he was delivering had slid off onto the road. He had walked away with only minor bruises and cuts. The tangle of spiritual amulets worn around his neck and the prayer beads wrapped around his rear-view mirror were his guardians. His eyes never strayed from the road as he considered this strange assignment. He had never been summoned on half an hour's notice before and had never seen a trailer loaded in the dead of night with such efficiency. Even though it was not his business, his curiosity about the cargo gnawed at him for hours.

After many hours of travelling a brief stop was made. The truck driver strolled over to the driver of the SUV with his mug of tea. The man was stretching his legs.

"We are both travelling much faster than we should," the truck driver said companionably.

"I know, but we have to reach Landhi on time. Someone is waiting for us," the man replied.

"We are going to the port in Karachi?"

"Yes."

"And all those lucky Sindhi tiles are going abroad?" the truck driver said, fishing for information.

The SUV driver flashed a sharp look at him and remained silent.

"Come on. What are we really carrying? I won't tell anyone."

"They are export items. It is not our business."

"As you say, brother." Masking his anger, the driver returned to his truck with his tea.

THE SMALL CONVOY cut through the heart of the Punjab, heading toward the southern end of Sindh province, where the seaport lay. The road—a modern motorway that often separated into narrow bypasses—was crowded even at this realitively late hour. Buses, trucks, and cars fought like gladiators both for space and the ability to drive at top speed. On the outskirts of Karachi, the signpost for the town of Landhi appeared. The mobile phone sitting on the dashboard rang and the truck driver answered.

"We are going to pull into the first filling station that will appear on your right," said the driver of the SUV. "Follow us and stop when we do, but do not get out."

The suburb of Landhi was a war zone for local administrators. It was filled with mud tenements and sewage-strewn lanes, and it boasted a shockingly high crime rate. The Taliban had infiltrated the area, and gang warfare erupted weekly. The gas station appeared on the main road outside the colony. The truck driver followed the SUV halfway into the filling station lot and stopped. It was 1 a.m.; nearly twenty-four hours had passed since the trucks pulled away from the estate in Islamabad. Despite the time the gas station was ablaze with neon lights, which illuminated both an open-air restaurant and a small area for prayers. As the driver watched and waited, a black Mercedes appeared beside the SUV. A slim man got out, walked over to the security vehicle, and had a quick exchange with the driver. Then he made his way to the tractor-trailer. He handed the driver a brown envelope encased in plastic.

"This is what you will give them when you reach the

port entrance. They will tell you which loading dock to use," he said, then raised his hand and walked away.

Next, it was the SUV driver's turn to approach the truck. "We will take you all the way to the port," he said, "but will not be able to go inside. Once the container has been loaded, we will meet you outside the gates. Do you understand everything you've been asked to do?"

"Yes. Let's go," replied the truck driver impatiently, putting his vehicle into reverse. He was tired from the long journey, tired of this job, and tired, most of all, of the security man's condescension. As they resumed their trek toward the port, he made a decision: if an opportunity presented itself, he would try to make some extra money on the side.

Karachi Port, when it at last came into view, looked almost like a city. Ships lined the wharves jutting out into the Arabian Ocean, piles of shipping containers loomed everywhere, and cranes swung back and forth, loading and unloading cargo. A warship idled in the distance. The truck driver thought about the long journey home and wished he were already there, nestled in bed with his wife. The sooner he completed this task, the sooner he would be on his way. He followed the signs to the entrance, extended the envelope to the officials when they approached, and watched them rifle through the paperwork.

"You are to stay on your right and head toward the west wharf," said one of the men, waving a large white sheet of paper at him. "You will show this paper and be given instructions about where to proceed with the container."

The driver took the paper and the envelope and placed them on the seat. He drove on a concrete path along the water, heading toward the cranes and ships farther ahead. At each checkpoint, he showed his papers and did what he was told. Finally, two customs officials stood with the truck driver, watching as a giant crane lifted the container and placed it on the wharf. The driver watched the younger official looking through the papers again and realized this was the moment he had been waiting for.

"What is the system here, sir? Do you check the cargo?" he asked.

"There's no need. The bill of lading gives a description of the contents, along with a value," the customs official said, his eyes glinting through his wire-rimmed glasses.

"What if the papers lie?"

"Are you trying to tell me something?"

When the driver didn't immediately respond, the customs agent walked away and spoke to his colleague, handing him the envelope that had, just a short time ago, been sitting on the tractor-trailer's passenger seat. The driver wondered if money was changing hands. If his hunch was accurate, he had just witnessed a bribe being offered and accepted. He hoped they would come back and offer him some of the money as well. He watched as both men walked up to the container and secured the padlock. Then the shipping agent walked quickly over to him.

"Your job is finished. You can leave now," he said curtly.

"I can't stay to watch the crane lift it and put it on the ship?" he asked, hoping for an offer of money to go away.

"No. That will take a while. The ship will not leave until noon. The containers have to be placed according to their destination. You are not allowed to stay here anymore."

The driver reluctantly walked back to the trailer, not realizing that his sole comment to the custom's official would be the source of a newspaper headline the next day.

From their vantage point on the dock, the two officials

watched the driver reverse the truck, execute a perfect turn, and head toward the exit.

"Sir, I think there is something we should check," said the younger of the two men, the one with the wire-rimmed glasses.

"There is nothing to check," the older man said, throwing his arm around his colleague and directing him away from the container. "Come, I need a cup of tea."

"In my opinion, sir, we need to open this container. We need to do a routine check," said the young man, shrugging off the arm draped around his shoulder.

The older man came to a stop, irritated by his colleague's defiance. "You have worked here for six months. Do you really think your judgement is better than mine?"

"Part of our training is also to pay heed to our instincts, sir! As a customs officer, I am exercising that privilege."

"I used to train people like you! Breaking a sealed locker is an official customs act."

"I am certain about this," said the young man, unable to dismiss the driver's comment.

"You want to orchestrate a customs seizure? A big drama so your career rises?"

"That is what we are trained for, sir."

The veteran looked at his partner, wondering if this fresh young recruit had the potential to jeopardize his long career. In that moment, he made a tactical error.

"Listen, there is a system here. A certain amount of petty smuggling goes on because the government can be unreasonable. It is more convenient to look the other way," he explained, attempting to take the young man into his confidence.

"But what if the items being smuggled aren't petty? What if the act breaks the laws of our country?"

"What is your salary? Are you married?"

"I do not have to answer these questions!" replied the younger man, confused.

"Sometimes we are given little gifts to facilitate things. If a container misses a ship, the wait can be a disaster for a businessman. I am in a generous mood today. Let me reward you for being so conscientious." The older man pulled out a roll of currency from his pocket.

"You keep it, sir. I am going to find my superior," shouted the junior officer, walking away rapidly.

"I *am* your superior!" the older man bellowed after him.

Within an hour, the junior officer had dented the armadillo-like hide of the customs bureaucracy. He did it with courage and unwavering resolve and the assistance of the department's near-retirement senior officer, who heard the young man's impassioned tale and felt that one redemptive act might save the morale of a government office that had been steeped in corruption for decades. The seal on the container was broken, and the contents of the first three cases opened sent the entire loading dock into a frenzy. The shipment, which clearly contravened the Antiquities Act, was immediately seized—and the press instantly summoned (the seizure would do wonders to boost the custom department's sullied image). In the end, however, the name of the shipper could not be discovered. The customs agent who had accepted the large bribe was protected by his colleagues, while the younger agent found himself transferred to another department. In their haste to open the crates, and due to their abysmal lack of expertise in handling antiquities, the customs officials managed to damage some of the statues.

KHALID SAT BEFORE his breakfast tray as Faisal placed a bundle of newspapers on the table beside it. Safia had been quieter than usual this morning, and he knew she was worrying about Hassan. But thoughts of his son and his wife evaporated as he smoothed out the rolled-up national paper and saw his seized shipment on the front page. He examined the other papers and found the same thing. While Faisal looked at him nervously, Khalid felt laughter bubbling up inside of him. Finally, he gave in to it.

"Faisal, Faisal," he wheezed, trying to catch his breath. "You know only two were real."

"Yes, but there was a lot of money and labour wasted. Those fakes were stunning," Faisal said sadly.

"You think our ship is sinking, Faisal?" Khalid asked, composing himself.

"You don't need enemies in the government."

Khalid wondered how long it would take for the antiquities department to decide where to place the seized shipment. There was less than a handful of people in the entire country who had the credentials needed to make such a decision. The craftsmen he had employed for years were serious artists, and their talents had been honed by years of practise. Khalid considered himself a patron of the arts in a country where, with the notable exception of Ghalib, few cared about Buddhist antiquities. However, the business at hand was to make sure that the diplomat flying back to Tehran had a large bank draft with him. Khalid would have to dig deeper into his pockets to make the payment.

Before he left for his office, he checked in on Hassan. The telephone rang, but his son did not answer. The voice mail had not been activated so Khalid sent a text message: "Progress? Call your mother." He was in such a rush that he didn't notice the delivery of the message had failed.

KHALID PAID A visit to the bank that afternoon. He opened his briefcase in front of the senior bank manager and theatrically fanned out the deeds to his properties. Two were located in the most expensive residential areas of Islamabad. The other two were in the city of Lahore: one was a three-storey shopping plaza in Gulberg; the other was an entire street of food shops in the old city. Khalid asked for a huge loan, offering the real estate as collateral. The bank manager studied the documents carefully, made a few calls, and then informed Khalid that it would take another day to get evaluations on the Lahore properties. Mentally, the bank manager sliced off a third of the sum requested. He knew that Khalid was a wealthy man, but defaulting on loans where real estate was concerned was a common occurrence. There were standard directives issued by his bank that could not be ignored. He was also aware of Khalid's huge estate in Barako. While construction was an ongoing affair at the estate, the bank loans that had been taken out to ensure its progress were always paid on time. Khalid had a superb credit rating.

"You know, sir, every one of these properties will go up in value day by day," Khalid advised, not pleased with the figure the manager had suggested.

"Banks have to be conservative, Khalid sahib. We are not averse to small risks, but this is quite a large one," he replied uneasily.

"Well, I could do some comparison shopping. This country seems to be cursed with an abundance of banks," Khalid stated, motioning to rise.

"Khalid sahib," the bank manager said, "there is no need

for that. We have a long relationship. Let me see how I can come closer to what you require."

"My dollar account certainly makes your bank happy. I am a man in a rush. I shall give you twenty-four hours. Don't disappoint me." Khalid got up from the plush armchair and walked to the door.

"The matter will be handled," the bank manager reassured him, reaching out for a handshake.

Khalid stared at his outstretched hand.

"I shake hands only when I first meet a person, never when I say goodbye. Please indulge my personal superstition. We shall embrace when you have the right draft for me."

It was only on the drive home that Khalid acknowledged the enormity of what he had done. The five real estate parcels and the structures on them were meant to be for his two sons, his two grandchildren, and Safia. All of the properties generated revenue, and the notion that he had provided for his family in case some misfortune befell him was a comfort. Yet he had casually fanned the five title deeds at the bank like he was handling a deck of cards. Khalid had spent a lifetime staying under the radar of his inept government. And now, Reza's vindictiveness had exposed him to serious hazard. For the first time in his life, Khalid felt completely alone.

On the ride home, Khalid continued to try Hassan's phone. Despite the new-found confidence Hassan had exhibited before his departure, Khalid was worried that his son was still prone to distractions and temptations. It was entirely possible that this exercise in trust would end in failure. When he arrived home, Khalid headed to his Allah museum. He studied his little altar, feeling no desire to kneel. He gazed at the bowl of water that was changed daily.

He stooped down, lifted the bowl, and drained it completely. Not a single prayer came to his mind. There was nothing to ask God for. The one thing Khalid knew for certain was that he was alone; the consequences of all of his actions rested only on his shoulders. God had other things to do.

That night, he received a call from Sher Khan in Peshawar.

"I am sending another two people. They will bring back your man and your property."

"What has changed, Sher Khan?" Khalid asked.

"I have a promise from a man in Waziristan, and he does not need your reward."

"You cannot say that on the phone," Khalid said, shuddering at the indiscretion.

"He never fails. It is a question of honour. Tell your army dog to go home," he said before hanging up.

Khalid had a sudden urge to see an old photograph of his parents, who had died years ago. He found the framed picture in his office and looked at their familiar faces. His tall, lanky father wore a crumpled suit, locally made. He was standing next to Khalid's mother, who was also simply dressed. Her hands, folded across her stomach, were broad, and the strands of hair escaping from her *dupatta* gave her a dishevelled appearance. The photograph had been taken outdoors in the little dirt yard of his childhood home. He mistook the uneasy expressions on their faces as personal censure. Then he reminded himself that his gargantuan acquisitiveness had stemmed from his rejection of his parents' willingness to live in relative poverty. He loved his parents, but he had long ago decided to rise above their circumstances. While his timid father operated his business on a very modest scale, Khalid's aspirations knew no limitations. He had travelled abroad and visited museums and galleries to learn how art was valued. The first two decades of his career were spent servicing clients outside his country. That had been the beginning, the root of what was now an immense fortune. Even so, Khalid had learned a few valuable lessons from his father. He kept his own collection to use as a bargaining chip, if the need arose. He hated financial losses, and always sought to balance his books as soon as he could in their aftermath.

When he received the call from the bank, advising him that the loan had been deposited to his account, he was relieved. He knew he would stay in the game forever.

FIFTEEN

GHALIB HAD A NEW pain at the side of his back. Worried that it might indicate the presence of kidney stones, he had visited his doctor. The man had recommended a surgical procedure, but that kind of treatment did not interest Ghalib at all. And so, he'd travelled to the office of his *hakim*. As he sat in an office at the busy clinic, his spirits lifted considerably.

"My dear sir, doctors know nothing," said the portly man who sat behind the desk, writing out directions for a homeopathic course of treatment. "In six weeks it will be all over."

Ghalib felt a burst of affection for his medical saviour. "Hakim sahib, you must come and dine with me tonight," he said as he made his way out of the office.

Ghalib arrived back at his home to find that Nur Hyat had called many times while he was out, and had sounded quite hysterical by the time of the last conversation. The valet handed the phone to Ghalib and asked him to call the man back immediately.

"What is it, Nur Hyat? I gather the food bills at the constituency office are quite substantial. Are you throwing parties at my expense?" asked Ghalib by way of greeting.

"Mian sahib, we have to speak. I am on the bus to Lahore. I shall be there by 9 p.m. and will come to the house."

"Hakim sahib is coming for dinner,' said Ghalib. "You can join us."

WHEN GHALIB WALKED into his seldom-used formal dining room at 9:30 p.m., the two men were already seated. Two dishes of vegetables, lentils, and a platter of fresh chapattis had been arranged on the table. The *hakim* eyed the dishes and gave an approving smile when he saw that his dietary instructions were being followed. But Nur Hyat, who was starving after his long journey, was shocked by the absence of meat.

"Come on, Nur Hyat. Eat the vegetables! They are good for you," encouraged Ghalib.

"You know, the holy prophet was partial to vegetables," said the *hakim*, ladling a large amount of slivered vegetables onto his plate.

"Really," murmured Ghalib, wondering why the dish appeared to be drenched in oil.

"Mian sahib, I need to speak frankly with you," Nur Hyat burst out.

"His digestion should not be disturbed," said the *hakim*, looking sternly at the other guest.

"It is a private matter, sir," replied Nur Hyat, scowling back.

"It seems he will not be able to swallow his food until he has told me about this private matter," Ghalib said to the *hakim*.

"I can wait until you have finished your meal," Nur Hyat said, and then rose from his chair.

"Hakim sahib is my guide now. We cannot hide anything from him."

"It is not a good idea to air one's dirty linen in public," Nur Hyat said, slumping back into his chair.

Ghalib chewed his food slowly, ignoring Nur Hyat and musing over his comment. When the meal was over, he requested that green tea be served in the living room and asked the *hakim* to excuse him for a little while.

"Well?" Ghalib said after the *hakim* had left the room.

"I don't think you can run in this election, sir," stated Nur Hyat.

"Is this your way of telling me that you have failed at the task you were hired for?" Ghalib asked sharply.

"There is a man who is making up stories about you. If your rival hears the rumours, he will shame you." Nur Hyat stroked his hair nervously.

"You are seated at my dining table and not a barbershop! What is this rubbish you are spouting?" Ghalib said furiously.

"It has been said that you have a bad reputation in the village. Or that the house has a bad reputation," Nur Hyat said delicately.

"Get out!" Ghalib shouted. "I will speak to you in the morning." He stood up abruptly, struggling with the heavy dining chair.

Ghalib felt a knot in his stomach. He curtly informed the server standing in the corridor to tell the *hakim* that he would not be joining him for tea because he was going to go to bed. On the way to the stairs, he told his valet to ensure that Nur Hyat stayed in the house and did not leave until the morning. Ghalib heard footsteps behind him and, as he reached the top of the stairs, Billa darted in front of him.

"Are we going to watch television in your room?" he asked.

"No, I have to think. I need silence. I need rest."

"Would you like me to press your legs?" asked the teenager.

Ghalib marched ahead to his bedroom and changed into his pajamas. Billa scooped up his discarded clothes, folded them neatly, and put them in the large hamper in his bathroom. When he returned, Ghalib was sitting on the edge of the bed with his head cradled in his palms. He looked up for a moment and stared at the boy. A long-buried fragment of his discarded morality burst from his subconscious and beat like a storm upon his brain. He felt tears prick the corners of his eyelids.

"Leave," he said, pointing a wavering finger at the boy. "Go sleep downstairs with the others."

IN THE MORNING, Ghalib interrogated Nur Hyat. He discovered that the veil of secrecy he had assumed he was operating under was simply an illusion. Despite the artful duplicity of the employees at his country home, despite the precautions he had taken, the villagers knew all about the teenagers he had exploited over the past twenty years, and readily discussed his exploits amongst themselves. In the time of elections, such information had a price tag, and loyalty was absent.

In the span of that brief conversation, all of Ghalib's fantasies about being appointed a weighty cultural portfolio in a new government came crashing down. Mercifully, he had ample time for damage control. He would simply withdraw his candidacy, citing ill health. If Soody was displeased, he would simply suggest another possible candidate from the area.

A few hours later, when his secretary came to attend to his correspondence and work on an art catalogue that was being compiled, an email was delivered. The young poetess whom he had found so enthralling at the party had sent him a poem. He read it over several times, and decided she had talent. He sent the young woman an invitation to tea.

For the remainder of the day, Ghalib stayed upstairs, behind the locked the door of his suite. He opened his liquor cabinet, pulled out a bottle of red wine and, between measured sips, took stock of his life. He uncorked a second bottle, and did not respond to calls on his bedside intercom for dinner. Several hours later, when he rose to go to the bathroom, he collapsed on the floor.

At midnight, Billa, who had found the behaviour of his benefactor incomprehensible, crept up to the room from the back entrance. When he entered the lit bathroom, he found Ghalib crumpled in the corner, and screamed for help until he was hoarse. An ambulance tore through the star- and dust-laden night to answer the call.

Hours later, when Ghalib opened his eyes, he found himself lying in a hospital bed hooked up to two intravenous drips. A nurse bent over him, murmuring something, but he could not understand what she was saying. There was a delicious languor to his entire body, as though he were swaddled in soft clouds, or resting in that perfect space between the lines of a poem. He noticed the solemn faces of his staff members standing at the door, and he chuckled.

"Go home. This is a holiday for all of you. Who was the fool who brought me back from the dead?"

"I did, Mian sahib. I found you," said Billa, wiggling past the older men.

A nurse put her arm out, preventing Billa from coming closer.

"It's all right. He is just a boy. Like a son," Ghalib said, shaking his head at her.

"The doctor has said you must rest. There are too many visitors. They have to leave now."

"The nurse is the boss here, Billa," he said gently to the terrified boy. Then he raised his head and spoke to his valet. "Go buy him some clothes for school. That is where he is going soon."

Billa let out a howl of anguish. The word *school* was like a bullet that had pierced his heart. Although he was restrained, the boy fought like a caged animal, straining backwards to look at Ghalib as he was pulled from the room.

Ghalib closed his eyes. He could not bear the look of terror on Billa's face.

Five days later, when Ghalib was discharged, the attending physician summoned him to his office. Ghalib sat in a chair and heard the list of health issues that the doctor declared had now become a permanent part of his life. New medications and dietary guidelines had to be followed if he wanted to live. At the age of seventy-three, Ghalib was now perched on the slipperiest of slopes. Only caution would allow him to enjoy a reasonable span of old age. Ghalib took the news like a gladiator.

"Well, Doctor, I'd better follow your suggestions. I have invited the prettiest girl in Lahore for tea. I need to be alive for that."

The doctor burst out laughing.

"You will be in good form," he replied, and then handed over a sheaf of prescriptions.

THE NEXT DAY, Ghalib visited his psychiatrist. They had an open-ended agreement, so that if Ghalib felt he needed to see him, he could just stop in. A few years back, he had had a prolonged bout of depression, and had initially gone abroad to seek treatment. In this country, there was still a stigma attached to mental health problems, and Ghalib kept this part of his life carefully concealed.

After recounting details of the hospital stay, and giving the psychiatrist time to complete his notes, Ghalib approached the issue that was truly uppermost in his mind.

"For years there have been catamites in my life," he said, using the word to broach the subject of his pederasty. But the psychiatrist was not impressed. He simply unfolded his crossed arms and looked passively at Ghalib, waiting for him to continue.

"Some are here in the house in Lahore, others are at my country home."

"How old are the boys?" asked the psychiatrist.

"They are between the ages of fourteen and sixteen, others perhaps a year or so older or younger."

"How do you procure them?"

Ghalib knew that the answer to this question lay at the heart of what was troubling him. The doctor waited silently.

"After my wife's death and my long depression, I felt happier in the country. You know, I live the life of a gentleman farmer in that glorious house."

"So the village became your feeding ground?" the psychiatrist asked.

"I suppose it did. I am seen as their benign father. A type of patriarch—"

"Is this continuing? Do you want treatment?" the psychiatrist interrupted.

"No! I have stopped," said Ghalib.

"Is that so? Are you being truthful?"

"Yes. This is a part of my life that I have decided to end."

"So, you intend to control your impulses?"

"Yes! That is why I am here. I needed to tell you this. I needed to admit it," Ghalib said in a low voice.

"Well, your impulses may be helped by some of the medications you are on. They should quiet your libido for a while," said the psychiatrist.

"I take care of them, you know," added Ghalib.

"Sex with minors makes you a pederast, Ghalib. Even in this blighted country you could end up in prison."

"I feed and clothe them. I have taught them how to play snooker and cards. We sing and dance together as well. They have never complained," Ghalib said, reciting his own familiar justifications.

"Have you not been able to find mature adults to have sex with?"

"Youth is like wine, Doctor."

"Are you still dabbling in politics?"

"No. I don't have the energy."

"Would you like to meet again?"

Ghalib nodded. The psychiatrist gave Ghalib an appointment card and ushered him to the door. Ghalib examined the card, nodded, and walked out. His confession had not provided the catharsis he'd expected it would. And the doctor's lack of advice troubled him. Did the man not know that desire was an unassailable force, especially for someone — like him — with an artistic disposition?

LATER THAT EVENING, as Ghalib watched television in
bed, he discovered that every news channel was carrying the same lead story — a political march that was being
organized by a fiery theologian to take place in the nation's
capital. Ghalib was spellbound by the man, who declared
that the current government in Pakistan was not fit to rule
and that the Election Commission, which was overseeing
the coming vote, should be dismantled due to corruption.
The man's name was Tahir-ul-Qadri, and he had a large following in other countries as well as in Pakistan. According
to the reports, Qadri had no desire to run for office, but his
crusade for change, in the middle of pre-election fervour,
was impressive. Ghalib immediately called Soody.

"Who is this new messiah?" Ghalib asked.

"You mean Dr. Qadri? He has been around for a while.
He's currently living in Canada and is expected back in Janu-
ary for this march," said Soody dismissively.

"Yes, but he is addressing the same issues as your party."

"And your party as well," Soody reminded him.

"Does he have a large following?" asked Ghalib, ignoring his comment.

"Marginal! He thinks he will steal our thunder. But it is
not going to happen. How are you, by the way?"

"Not well. I have to be careful. Doctor's orders," replied
Ghalib, not yet wanting to break the news that he was bowing out as a candidate.

"Well, take care, for God's sake. This is not the time for
any problems. People are waiting for me, I have to go," said
Soody briskly before hanging up.

Instinctively, Ghalib knew that Soody's judgement was

wrong. This fiery orator had a masterful knowledge of constitutional law, and he looked like a patrician. He wore a small, handsome cap and well-tailored robes. He bore no resemblance to the long-bearded mullahs so common in Pakistan. And his timing was superb. The elections were still three months away. Did Dr. Qadri have the ability to inspire the thousands who would travel from Lahore to Islamabad to see him? he wondered. The appearance of a potential new catalyst for change would dent the complacency of the political machine. The party Ghalid had joined, with its inexperienced leader and its host of recycled opportunists, should brace themselves, he thought. He continued to make calls, anxious to discuss this new development, but each person he spoke to dismissed the man as yet another religious charlatan.

As Ghalib simultaneously chatted on the telephone and flipped channels on the television, Billa crept into his bedroom. When Ghalid at last heard a sound and noticed the boy, he hung up the phone.

"Ah, Billa. We have to have a chat. Come and sit here," Ghalib said, pointing to the small couch next to his bed.

"Can we watch television instead?" Billa asked.

"No," said Ghalib, switching off the set. "This talk is very important."

Billa threw him a mutinous look and sat on the edge of the couch. He was neatly dressed in khaki trousers and a striped shirt, which clung to his slender waist. There were brand new sneakers on his feet but the laces were undone.

"It's time for you to return to school. I am sending you home to your mother. All of the arrangements will be made for you to attend a good school," said Ghalib.

"No!" Billa shouted.

"It will not be a terrible school like the last one. You will go in the daytime and return home to your mother in the evenings."

"This is my home," the boy cried.

"You need to play with boys your own age. Everyone in this house is old! You can still come for a visit during the holidays," Ghalib said.

"I will die." Billa wiped away tears.

"You run faster than anyone. You eat like a horse. Don't be silly." Ghalib laughed.

"What if the teacher beats me?"

"It is not that kind of school. I will give your mother money for the fees and for new clothes."

"Who will press you?" said Billa, his voice choking. "Someone else will take my place."

"Thank you for worrying, Billa, but I will be fine. You will always be my friend," said Ghalib gently.

"You don't like me anymore?"

Ghalib closed his eyes. Billa's accusation weighed heavily on him. Yet redemption was also close at hand. Time would heal both of them. When Ghalib opened his eyes, the couch was empty. He could hear the boy's footsteps racing down the hall. Ghalib pressed the intercom and instructed his valet to keep Billa with him and to have him ready in the morning for the bus that would take him home. One of his chauffeurs would accompany the boy, and bring money and instructions for the mother. Ghalib also told his valet to keep the boy downstairs; he was not to return to Ghalib's suite. It had to be a surgical amputation, Ghalib decided, even though a part of him longed to reassure Billa that he was not being rejected for another.

THE NEXT MORNING, while Ghalib slept, Billa bade a tearful farewell to the house where he'd thought he would live forever. He sat in a daze in the back seat of the car. A reunion with his mother and sisters in their small village home held no appeal. His escort pressed food upon him and tried to engage him in conversation, but Billa remained mute. Finally, an emotion did surface. But instead of the misery he had been expecting to feel, a quiet rage took hold. He understood now that the lives of the rich and the poor could never be entwined. He pressed his pocket and felt the outline of the wristwatch he had stolen. It was less than he deserved, he knew, but it had not been taken for its value alone. Despite his anger, Billa craved a sentimental token, an item that would allow him to keep a part of Ghalib close.

Billa had no way of knowing that, back in Lahore, the theft had already been discovered. By the time his four-hour journey ended, punishment was waiting for him at his mother's home in the village. The watch was a vintage Omega that Ghalib had inherited from his father. He had no intention of parting with it.

LATE THAT SAME afternoon, when Ghalib emerged from his suite for lunch, he was presented with a message from the beautiful young poetess. She had politely declined his invitation to tea. Ghalib spent the rest of his afternoon and early evening rearranging his art. He had the great tapestry removed from the downstairs living room wall. Next, he sat before a stack of paintings, deciding where to put them. His valet, armed with a hammer and a box of nails, hung each one as requested. The end result was a salon wall that was quite arresting and changed the ambience of the entire living room. So absorbed was Ghalib in the exercise that when his chauffeur returned with the stolen wristwatch in hand, he did not even inquire about Billa. The beautiful boy he had used as an amusement had been reduced in his mind to a common thief.

After completing the work in the living room, Ghalib walked through the house's long main corridor, surveying the collection of Mehrgarh artifacts displayed in the cabinets that lined the walls. If he could find the right buyer, he would sell the entire collection in minutes. With this thought in mind, he called Khalid in Barako.

"What is the news, Khalid? Have you heard from your son or anyone else?"

"I've heard nothing," Khalid said.

"I see. Well, the money is sitting in my bank, not earning any interest," Ghalib said with irritation.

"Please don't worry."

"What about Hassan?"

"His phone seems to be broken, or perhaps he has lost it. You know Hassan. But I'm confident that he will not let his father down," Khalid lied, and then changed the topic. "What is happening in your constituency? Are votes being guaranteed?"

"I am not going to run."

"Why not? If someone makes you a minister and gives you a cultural portfolio we would all benefit."

"Have you heard of this fellow who is organizing a march to Islamabad to bring the government down?"

"Tahir-ul-Qadri! Yes, his advertisements are everywhere. He is sitting on a lot of money. I like him, Ghalib. He is a brilliant man. But don't tell your people I said that."

"They are not worried, Khalid. That's the problem. They

think he is a crazy man. I am quite taken by him myself," Ghalib confessed.

"Well, plan to be in Islamabad when he arrives. Apparently, the government is not going to stop him."

"Soody is not going to like this. He thinks AK's party is going to create a new Pakistan," said Ghalib.

"Well, Qadri is not running for office. But he could be the headmaster who will show the new government how to run the country."

"They won't let him," Ghalib said bleakly. "I know the players, Khalid."

"I know you do. Stay in the game! You will win. You have owned your lands and the villagers for generations. That is the only power that counts."

"I am dying to see the sculpture, Khalid."

"It is on its way. No point in dying before it reaches you. I have to take another call," Khalid said and hung up.

Ghalib did not fall asleep easily that night. He received a long-distance call in the middle of the night from a friend who said that a book had been published by a relative of Ghalib's. The book was apparently highly critical of Ghalib's father. After he digested the news, he thought about his father, and about lost opportunities. He could have written the book himself! His father had rejected his mother and remarried a European woman. Ghalib had grown up with his mother's silent anguish, which had influenced both the poet and painter in him. A feeling of creative rivalry crept into Ghablib's heart. Not for the first time, he yearned to write a novel based upon his life as a great Punjabi landlord. But now, more than ever, he knew that this goal was out of his reach.

SIXTEEN

ADEEL JOGGED DOWN THE road, heading back to the campsite. He had found a place to charge his phone and had finished the rest of his business as well. The bus headed for Skardu would arrive at noon. He would give Norbu some money and make sure she was on it. She had to return to her father, who would probably arrange another marriage for her, Adeel thought. Divorced daughters were a liability. He was confident, though, that Norbu was strong enough to handle the next chapter of her life. All he had to do was convince her that he had no intention of taking her any farther on his journey.

Bumping into the recently promoted Zamir had been a shock, but he had recovered quickly and was already formulating a plan. His new life would not be connected to the old one. He would blend into a local community and experiment with a different way of living. For the first time in many days, there was a lightness in his heart. He finally felt he had the ability to make decisions and find clarity.

He walked under the canopy of trees and headed toward the shelter. The shock of seeing an empty car next to the road lasted only a few seconds. He swiftly moved forward, his senses on high alert, but froze at the scene before him. A man's body lay on the ground in front of the makeshift enclosure. There was no question that the man was dead. Adeel backed slowly away, then made his way to the spot where the sculpture was buried. The statue lay uncovered in the pit of earth. There was no trace of Norbu.

What had happened here? And where was Norbu? Adeel walked up to the stream to look for her but she wasn't there either. He studied the ground as he walked. There were patches of depressed wild grass. Kneeling down, he traced the outline of a man's shoeprint. Nearby, where the dirt began, he found a set of small footprints. He knew they were Norbu's. As he followed her trail back to the enclosure, he wondered why she hadn't been wearing her shoes.

Back at the campsite, Adeel knelt beside the body. Blood had congealed in spots and was pooling around the throat. The face was unrecognizable, as half of the head had been blown off on impact. But Adeel knew the man nonetheless. He had recognized the car from his trip into Chilas, and this was the same young man who had been driving it. The memory of the face he had seen at Barako when he went to collect the truck and money flashed through his mind again. But why had this man been sent to find him? Nothing about him suggested he was a with a law enforcement agency. The corpse was clad in expensive clothes and, beside it, an oversized camera lens sat on its side. The camera bag was still slung around the man's neck. Adeel knew that the bullet had come from his revolver. Stepping over the body, he crawled through the entrance of the shelter and found himself staring at the muzzle of his own gun.

Norbu sat with her legs drawn up against her body, and with both arms resting on her knees. The wavering revolver was held in a double-handed grip. Her bare feet were splattered with mud, her eyes were narrowed, and her breath emerged heavily from parted lips. The expression on her face was remote, as though she were looking at something beyond her sightline. Adeel knew she was in shock. He put his palm over the muzzle of the gun and slowly lowered it until she let go.

"I am going to take this now. It is all right," he said, placing the gun on the ground.

"The man is dead," Adeel said, gesturing at the body.

She buried her face in her hands.

"What did he do? Did he speak to you? Was he alone?" he asked, trying to determine what exactly happened.

She made a choking sound then trembled violently as tears poured down her face. He waited, letting her cry. Finally, she lifted her face to him.

"Will you kill me?"

"No," he said quietly. "I want you to tell me about everything that happened after I left."

She told Adeel that she had spent some time gathering firewood and then decided to wash herself at the stream. She hesitated when she said that she had removed her clothes. When she noticed the man behind the trees, holding a large black object, she thought it was a gun. She ran back to the shelter, but she could hear his footsteps behind her. She collided with Adeel's bag and remembered that his revolver was inside. When the man's head, and the long black object, appeared at the opening of the enclosure, she did what Adeel had taught her to do.

"It is not your fault. I taught you how to use this," he said, and put his hand on her shoulder.

She jerked her body away as though she had been singed. She wiped her feet with the end of her shawl and slipped her gym shoes back on.

"I have to go outside and take care of what has happened. I will need your help," he said, holding out his hand to help her up.

She laced her sneakers and ignored his outstretched hand.

"I will take care of this. No one will ever know. You are going on the bus to Skardu in two hours. Forget all this and never tell anyone what happened," he said.

"Do you want to kill me?" she repeated without facing him.

"Norbu, I want to set you free. Marry a better man, have children, and create your own home," he said gently.

When she still made no move to take his hand, he grabbed her arms and pulled her up to face him.

"You don't have to look at him, but I need to check his pockets. I have to search the car as well."

Norbu moaned and darted away the moment she saw the body. She collapsed on the ground nearby with her head down. Adeel ignored her and checked the pockets of the man's jacket and trousers. He found the car keys along with a wallet full of money. There were two photographs tucked behind the driving licence. One was of two little children, the other of a beautiful, scantily clad girl who pouted at the camera. The man's wristwatch was expensive.

The car—an expensive Japanese model favoured by affluent Pakistanis—was registered in the name of a business in Islamabad. The back seat was covered with bottled drinking water, soft drinks, imported potato chips, biscuits, and bags of fruit. There was a blanket lying on the passenger seat with a mobile phone sitting on top. The sound system was first class. Nothing indicated that the man was a professional photographer. He had been sent here, he reasoned, and had just explored a little off the beaten path. The man must have spied Norbu at the stream, taken a few photographs, and then followed her to the shelter.

"Come, we have to bury him," he said.

"Here?" She was stunned.

"Norbu, it was an accident, but no one will believe it. If his body is discovered then I will say that I fired the revolver."

As the words emerged from his mouth, Adeel realized that he had fallen in love. He sank to his knees, feeling as if a great rustling bird was trapped inside his chest. If the situation were discovered, Norbu's act of self-defence would lead to an arrest. And Adeel knew that he would rather sacrifice himself than allow anything to happen to her. Every skill he had learned would be harnessed to conceal the evidence and save her.

Norbu stood up, rushed to his side, and placed a hand on his chest to reassure him. He lifted the consoling hand and placed a deep kiss on its palm. She closed her eyes. A tiny smile creased her lips and grew broader until it reached her eyes. In that moment, she knew that her solitary life was over. The man bent over her hand would be a constant in her life. Adeel embraced her, then quickly released her and stood up.

He had to make a new plan. He opened the trunk of the car, rummaged through the tools he found there, and pulled out an iron wrench. He would use the hole they'd dug for the statue to bury the man's body. The grave was already half completed; all they had to do was finish it.

"I need you and both of your shawls," he said, and started walking.

It took them close to an hour to pull the statue from its spot and for Adeel to dig a deeper pit with the wrench. Adeel wrapped the body in the blanket he'd found in the car and pulled it over to the hole. After they buried the young man, Norbu collected a few wildflowers and threw them into the grave. When Adeel tried to recite the *Fateha* he found he could not utter the words. His severed faith meant he could no longer indulge in the ritual. Norbu's lips did not move either.

"I want you to listen to me very carefully, Norbu. If something happens and there is trouble, or we get separated, you are never to talk about this."

"If that happens I will say I did this," she said calmly.

"No! You must make a promise on the head of your grandmother."

"My grandmother is dead."

"It doesn't matter. We can't go any further until I have this promise."

"I will swear by this '*buth*' Buddha. Promise there will be no bus to Skardu." she added.

"There will be no bus. I am the bus." Adeel smiled.

She smiled back. Adeel grabbed her by the waist and spun her around. Her startled laughter was like a tinkling fountain that delighted his parched senses. They straightened the statue and sat in front of it, closing their eyes. No raucous fundamental exhortation intruded. The ear-splitting loudspeaker prayers of the mosque had no place here. Their mutual path was inward and intensely private. The only sound was their breathing. When Adeel opened his eyes, he turned and looked at Norbu's face, then reached out and tucked back the strands of hair that were spilling over her forehead.

"He," she said, extending her finger toward the statue, "will take care of us."

"It is just a beautiful statue," Adeel said, standing up.

"It is more than that," she replied. "It is a force that brought us together."

Adeel shifted his focus back to the situation at hand. The enormity of the accident filled his head. His adrenaline kicked in and he knew it was time for flight.

"I have to do something that might not work. I am going to try and bring the car close to here. We will put the statue in it and leave immediately."

Adeel drove the car off the path and toward the statue. The ground was bumpy and the tires churned over the uneven terrain. Adeel got as close as he could without the risk of getting stuck.

"This is going to be very difficult. Bring your shawls," he instructed.

He walked toward their shelter, collected his black nylon bag, and tossed it in the car. The ropes they had used to move the statue the first time had been lost in the truck explosion, so he doubled both shawls and knotted them around the neck of the statue.

"You have to use all your strength. We will pull together," he told her.

Norbu grasped the woollen rope. Adeel bent over and placed his hand beside hers. Together, they pulled the statue inch by inch across the wild grass and dirt. They took breaks when he saw beads of sweat descending from her forehead to her chin, or when she needed to rub her chafed palms together. The wool stretched and became as tight as a rope, but it held. Adeel felt the dull ache of strained muscles; he ignored it and continued to pull. When they finally reached the car, he picked up two bottles of water and gave one to her. She eyed the packaged chips curiously. He grinned, realizing she had probably never eaten a potato chip in her life.

Lifting the statue into the trunk of the car was the most difficult manoeuvre. Adeel bore the brunt of the weight until they were able to roll it inside the trunk, where it lay on its side. Adeel unwound one of the rope-like shawls and tried spreading it over the statue, but he needed the other one as well. Norbu stood watching without any head covering. Adeel opened his nylon bag and pulled out a black shirt.

"You can wear this like a headscarf," he said.

Norbu draped the shirt across her chest like a protective scarf.

Adeel shook his head. "No. Cover your hair with it. I don't want us to be noticed."

Reluctantly, she tied the shirt around her face like a scarf. Her appearance was comical, and Adeel turned away to hide his amusement. He knelt by the car's licence plate and scratched at it with the wrench until two of the letters were missing. He then rubbed some dirt over the numbers. When they got into the car, he leaned over, pulled the seat belt across her chest, and snapped it shut. She gave him a dark look.

"This is so you don't ever run away from me again," he teased as he snapped his own seat belt closed.

He reversed the car and raced down the path to the main road. The gas gauge indicated two-thirds of a tank. The distance to Skardu was 245 kilometres, about a five-hour drive. The prospect of turning back to Chilas to get more gas was out of the question, so Adeel pressed his foot on the accelerator and headed for Skardu.

As they drove, the waters of the Indus River churned angrily in the valley below. Norbu fell asleep, her head slumped to one side and her chapped hands lying limp on her lap. The strange and new-found intimacy of her presence enthralled him, but he could not afford to be distracted. He had to concentrate on their current predicament and all of its impending hazards. At some point, there would be a search for the dead young man and the car. Distance and time was their only advantage. In some moments, he was confident they would be safe, sure that the region's placid lakes and towering mountains would provide a refuge; in others, his self-assurance was replaced by a sense of fatalism.

When the red light of the car's temperature gauge suddenly appeared, he looked at in in disbelief. They had been driving for close to two hours. There was a Jeep travelling behind him, so he switched on his hazard lights and slowed down. The Jeep overtook him.

"What is it?" said Norbu, rubbing the sleep from her eyes.

"Stay here. I have to check the car," he said.

He opened the hood, knowing that either the engine coolant was not flowing through or the radiator was plugged. The last possibility was that the thermostat was stuck. Regardless, he would have to wait for the car to cool down before he could drive again. He closed the hood and got back into the car, deciding to risk a short drive in search of a broader stretch of road where the traffic would more easily be able to pass. Ten minutes later, Adeel stopped the car again and quickly got out to open the hood. When he heard the sound of a car approaching, he looked up. The sand-coloured Mercedes with the flag rippling from the rear-view mirror sounded its horn as it swung out to avoid his car. As it passed, it rolled to a stop.

"General sahib wants to speak to you."

Adeel walked to the parked car. He couldn't believe this was his second encounter with the man in less than two days. Surely this was not a coincidence. The call to his mother on Zamir's phone must have been tracked. Zamir would have been informed about this. The driver opened the door for him and Adeel slid inside.

"Adeel, what are you up to?" General Zamir asked, pulling out a cigarette and offering one to Adeel.

"I am fine, General," he answered, declining the offer.

"I have had a call from Army Intelligence that a call was made from my phone to a number that is under surveillance. I think you are in trouble, no?"

Adeel faced his old benefactor and said nothing.

"So, it's a secret then? Adeel, I am still your friend. I have been trying to find you! If you're in trouble I can help. Generals have a lot of power, as you know."

Adeel decided to take a leap of faith.

"Yes, sir, I'm in trouble," he finally admitted. "I need your help."

"Who is in the car with you?"

"She is my woman."

"So you are married?"

"No, but she is with me," Adeel replied, unwilling to elaborate.

The general took a few drags of his cigarette in silence, pondering how to tell Adeel that he was fully aware of his predicament, and the reason for his flight. The army could put pressure on the ISI to reveal information. The brigadier who was Adeel's control had made a private deal others in his department knew nothing about. Smuggling an antiquity did not fall in within the intelligence department's mandate. The ISI brigadier was engaged in damage control. What Zamir could not reveal were the details of the rough handling and interrogation to which Adeel's mother had been subjected. He had already made certain that it would not continue. The interrogators were simply retaining her phone in case Adeel made contact. As the general debated where to begin, Adeel spoke.

"I have something with me," he began.

"A five-thousand-year-old sculpture and a woman who is not your wife," replied the general.

If Adeel was surprised, he didn't let it show. "It's a long story, sir. I don't want her hurt. The car has a problem. The red light is on."

"Who is waiting for you in Skardu?"

"I am operating alone. I just have to stay out of sight for a while."

"Is the car yours?"

"No, sir."

"All right. Get your woman and whatever you are carrying. Your transport has been changed. We have a two-hour drive to Skardu. Enough time to discuss this situation properly."

NORBU SAT IN the front passenger seat of the general's car, while Adeel rode in the back. The sculpture rested in the Mercedes' trunk, nestled in Norbu's shawls.

"Why did you take the sculpture, Adeel?" asked the general as soon as the car started moving.

"You will not understand, sir," replied Adeel.

"I know who you are, Adeel. Something has made you step out of character."

"Perhaps I have been ready for a change for a long time. Do you really want the truth?"

"I have seen many things, Adeel. The chaotic situation in this country is beyond even the army's control. But you are a trained man; you are not a thief. Yet, at this very moment, you are being hunted."

As they drove, Adeel bared his heart, telling the general about the events of the past few days. He was aware that theft and manslaughter were both punishable offences. Still, he placed his faith in the goodwill that the general had always extended to him. The general did not say anything as Adeel talked; he only listened pensively as he chain-smoked.

When Adeel was at last finished speaking, the general leaned forward, stubbed out the remains of his cigarette, and spoke. "Faith changes over time, Adeel, as do our spiritual responses. Yes, Buddhism was the prevailing faith in Pakistan. But this situation you find yourself in is personal. Even without the sculpture it is likely you would have chosen a new path."

"The statue has a strange power, General. I cannot explain how it makes me feel. But I want to live like this for the rest of my life," said Adeel passionately.

"What about the woman?"

"She understands. Her ancestors believed in this faith."

"I see. Is she responsible for this theft?"

"No. That happened before I met her on the road."

Adeel braced himself for a reprimand.

"You have blown up a vehicle, stolen an object of value, picked up a female hitchhiker, buried the man she shot accidentally in a secret place, and stolen his car. Adeel, we need a tactical manoeuvre here!"

"It is definitely a situation, sir," replied Adeel.

"How do you want to handle it?"

"My best plan would be to shoot you and the driver and escape with the car."

The general threw back his head and roared with laughter.

"Good, very good, but my mother would never forgive you."

Adeel saw Norbu stir in the front seat. He immediately leaned forward and asked if she was all right. She turned her head and nodded. He caught a tiny smile on her face. A rumbling in his stomach served as a reminder that neither one of them had eaten a meal; all they'd had was the bottled water. The potato chips remained untouched in the other car.

"Sir? Is there any food in the car? She has not eaten all day," Adeel asked.

"Yes, we shall stop for a snack. There is also lots of food in the car. Would you like a whisky?"

Adeel had a flash of his days at the cadet college, where tales of Major Zamir travelled through the mess halls. He was a man who only observed the protocols of rank with his superiors, never with those under him.

"Did you know that my father served in the government in Skardu for many years? Part of my childhood was spent there," the general said, after asking the chauffeur to stop.

The driver brought out a hamper of food from the trunk of the car, along with plates and napkins. He piled their plates high with food and handed the first one to his superior, who took it and turned to Norbu.

"*Begum Sahiba*, please eat," he said with exquisite courtesy.

The general had addressed Norbu with the respect accorded to women of a much higher social standing, and her startled response was to lean away. Adeel took the plate from the general's hand and whispered into her ear furiously.

"Eat. We have food. We are eating together. You will not make a fuss."

"What is it?' asked the general.

"Crazy woman will not eat before the man does. She will eat this food even if I have to force-feed her," Adeel said irritably.

"Ah! She is a traditional lady. Well, let her wait then. I need a little drink first. You need one too," the general said.

The bottle of whisky that appeared was a superior imported brand. The general poured some into two army-issue enamel mugs and offered one to Adeel.

"Drink up, Adeel. We cannot let the NATO forces down," the general said, smiling at him.

"It won't be wasted on me, sir. When we served on the glacier we had access to vodka. They said it was good for the cold." Adeel peered at the vintage whisky glowing in the mug.

"Well, God bless the bootleggers of Pakistan for keeping our boys warm in the cold," said the general, clinking his mug against Adeel's.

The government of Pakistan had banned the consumption and export of alcohol, but the law was cheerfully contravened by diplomats who sold their alcohol on the side. Daring thieves also routinely stole from the numerous foreign agencies working in the country. The local Christian population, who were permitted a quota of alcohol, also did a roaring good business by selling to their Muslim friends. The top brass of the army, like the general, had no problem acquiring alcohol.

"Never undertake a long car trip without a bottle of alcohol, Adeel. It comes in handy as part of a first-aid kit," the general said, slowly sipping from his mug.

Adeel emptied his cup in two quick gulps. He felt the whisky scorch his throat and then waited for the fire to light his belly.

"Feel better now?" inquired the general. "I need to stretch my legs a little and so does the driver, so why don't you stay here and make sure the lady eats."

Adeel and Norbu found themselves alone in the luxurious car.

"This is very rich food," she said, turning around to face him.

"Eat it, Norbu. I will too. This man is my friend and he will help us. But eat quickly."

When the general returned to the car, he was holding his mobile phone in his hands. He told his driver that he wasn't interested in eating, and that he wanted the journey to resume because he had a stop to make on the way. He then turned his attention back to Adeel.

"The sculpture will be off-loaded in a suitable place. I will make some arrangements for the woman. It seems that you owe your employers another service. Your Control feels that, if you complete the assignment, it will restore your unblemished record."

Adeel digested the news in silence. All of a sudden, the stars on the general's epaulets looked sinister.

"I am taking her with me," he said.

"It is out of the question. We are staying overnight in Skardu, then you are coming back with me. She will be kept in a home there until your task is complete. Then you can return to get her."

"General, I no longer want to work on these assignments. I am very grateful for your help, but we must part ways in Skardu."

"I am the commanding officer here, Adeel."

"I respect that, but I no longer work for the army," Adeel reminded him.

"The intelligence service is a branch of both the government and the army," the general said, turning his face away.

"Pretend you have not met me, General. If you stop the car we will get out right now," Adeel pleaded.

"If we stop the car, Adeel, only one person will get out."

SEVENTEEN

KHALID SAT AT A pavement café in Kohsar Market in Islamabad. A cabinet minister had once been murdered there, and the stench of his vicious murder still hovered in the air years later. Yet, the murder did not deter the local gentry from shopping in the vacinity. Khalid had told Faisal to park the car a little distance away on the main road. It was late in the afternoon, and only one other table was occupied. Khalid ordered some green tea. The bank draft sat in his breast pocket. He was waiting for the ambassador to send someone reliable to collect it.

A row of taxis idled along one side of the market courtyard. This little shopping enclave featured several high-end stores, and very few people shopped there unnoticed. Khalid, who seldom frequented such places, felt curiously exposed. When the shabby yellow-and-black taxi pulled up, he thought the man emerging from it looked familiar. It was the same security man, Saad, who had accompanied the ambassador to the lake and rowed the boat. The man paid the cab driver, walked directly to Khalid's table, and sat down on the cane armchair next to him. He was holding a rolled-up copy of *Time* magazine.

"I believe you have something for me, sir," he said as he opened the magazine and slid it across the table toward Khalid. He placed a business card on top of the magazine.

Khalid picked up the card and studied it. He then picked up the magazine and spent a few minutes riffling through the pages.

"I have ordered some green tea. Would you like some?" Khalid asked.

"Why not? You Pakistanis make excellent tea," replied Saad.

"How long have you been posted here?"

"About two years, but I will accompany the ambassador back."

"I hope you will have good memories of your time here," said Khalid as he withdrew the envelope from his jacket pocket and slipped it between two pages of the magazine so it was no longer visible.

Saad let the magazine lie between them.

"Everybody misses their home. But our countries have a good relationship," replied Saad in his accented English.

The waiter appeared with a tray and Saad moved the magazine closer to his side of the table. They made small talk and drank their tea. When they were done, Khalid paid the bill, shook hands with Saad, and sauntered toward a bookstore. When he emerged from the bookstore a few minutes later, Khalid saw Saad, laden with two bags of shopping, walk across the courtyard and hail a taxi. Along with his groceries, Saad had walked away with two-thirds of Khalid's assets.

On the drive home to Barako, Khalid's phone rang.

"My dear Khalid, thank you. Matters are settled, but I do hope you will remember your promise of allowing me to see your collection one day," the ambassador said.

"I shall not be in town for a while," lied Khalid, deciding he would never allow the visit to happen.

"*Khuda Hafez*," said the ambassador, saying farewell in the traditional Pakistani way.

"*Allah Hafiz*," responded Khalid, using the recently adopted Arabized version.

The ambassador chuckled. "Your alphabet is Arabic, Khalid. But all of your derivatives are Persian."

WHEN KHALID RETURNED home, he glanced around at the sprawl of his property and thought of Hassan. Doubts had first entered his mind the day before, but he'ddismissed them, no doubt because he was preoccupied with plans for his meeting with the ambassador. His pampered son had grown into a young man defined by a scandalous sense of entitlement. Had Khalid been duped again? Three days had passed now without any communication. Khalid conceded that Hassan, armed with money and transportation, had probably decided to gallivant in Gilgit. There was no denying it anymore; he would finally have to lock the gates of his home to his son. Hassan's days of grace were over.

Khalid looked at Faisal, who walked beside him, and placed his hand on the young man's shoulder.

"Hassan is like a diseased limb, Faisal. And the time has come to chop this limb off," Khalid said, and stopped walking.

"Don't say that, *Chachu*. I think he really wanted to help you. But you know Hassan." Faisal shrugged.

"How are things going in the workshop?" Khalid asked, not wanting to pursue the subject any further.

"Very well. You should see the quality of the work. The man is a genius. There is a Hindu temple in Sindh that is expecting the artifacts, as well as clients across the border," Faisal replied enthusiastically.

Khalid was touched by Faisal's enthusiasm. "What do you think about the Hindu gods, Faisal?" he asked.

"They are very powerful—the work of great imagination—and they have been around for thousands of years. They are beautiful, *Chachu*, but not hard to duplicate."

"I will see the work tomorrow," said Khalid with a curt nod that told Faisal he was dismissed. The young man handed over Khalid's phone, and wished him a good evening.

Khalid stuffed the phone in his pocket and headed toward his Allah museum, though prayers were not on his mind. He opened the large door to the downstairs gallery and entered the space, feeling as if he had walked into a lifeless tomb. He realized what was missing: the energy of people who would express a sense of wonder at his collection. Somewhere along the line, ownership had become a dull affair. With a sad chuckle, he remembered an ignorant yet prophetic comment Hassan had once made: "They are huge old Korans. So what? You cannot even turn the pages in case they get soiled. You cannot even have them in the house. You should just sell them." Perhaps his son was right—or partially so. Maybe the time had come to gift his collection to a university or museum.

Khalid walked up the stairs to his sanctuary. He stood at a distance from the velvet-covered miniature *Ka'ba*, the prayer rug, and the bowl of water. Nothing induced him to take the few steps that would bring him closer to the source of his salvation. The room was cold and the ache in his shoulder returned. Just then, the telephone in his pocket vibrated. He looked at the number as it disconnected on the third ring. He waited and it rang again.

"Your property has changed hands," said Sher Khan. "It is heading to Skardu, but we will intercept it. Our special friends will take care of everyone, don't worry." He hung up before Khalid could respond.

Khalid tried dialing Sher Khan back, but his call was not returned. He raced out to his office to search for the brigadier's number. As he thumbed through a small diary, the phone rang again. He answered the call and was surprised to hear the voice of the brigadier.

"Khalid, a car whose registration papers use one of your business addresses has snarled traffic on the Gilgit–Skardu highway. Who was driving it?"

"My son Hassan," Khalid said.

"Well, he is nowhere near the car. It's the wrong time of year for tourism. What was he doing there?"

"Visiting some friends."

"Is that all? Not another kidnapping, we hope?"

"I have no idea. But I need to find my son, otherwise my wife will make all of our lives a misery," Khalid said.

"I'm sorry to say this, Khalid, but foul play is suspected. We lifted some prints off the steering wheel and found a surprise," continued the brigadier.

"What is it?" Khalid was beginning to feel alarmed.

"It seems your son met our missing agent, Adeel. And from the fingerprints on the steering wheel, it seems that Adeel has even driven the car. Tell me the truth, Khalid," said the brigadier sternly.

Khalid was stunned. Hassan had been successful in finding Adeel, but he had also broken the rules by befriend-
ing the agent enough to let him drive his car. Pain rippled
around his shoulder, almost doubling him over. He wanted
Safia and the balm of her massaging fingers.

"Oh my God!" Khalid shouted into the phone.

"Khalid, a search for Adeel will be conducted. Please
don't engage in any other plans without consulting me."

"Just keep me in the loop. This is my son we are talking
about."

"This is quite serious, Khalid. A general may also be
involved, so it has become a highly sensitive issue. I will let
you know as soon as we have any news," the brigadier said
and hung up.

"Was it Hassan? Is he all right?" Safia said, appearing at
his office door.

"Yes. He is fine. He'll be home in a couple of days. His
phone broke," Khalid said, looking up at her.

"I told you. He's becoming more responsible. Oh, Khalid,
I wonder what he is eating."

"He'll be all right," Khalid said, rubbing his shoulder.

"You have to see the doctor about your shoulder. Let us
go now," Safia pleaded.

"I don't have time for physiotherapy unless the person
comes here. I will take care of my shoulder this week. I will
see you in the bedroom in half an hour."

Khalid walked out of his office and headed toward the
main gate. The guard who sat nearby was a man from the
region of Hazara. He was familiar with firearms and had
been with Khalid for five years. Although he generally
maintained an aloof distance from his employees, Khalid
knew that once in a while the guard smoked *charas*, the

local marijuana. Khalid greeted the man and he sprang to attention.

"Khan sahib. Can you let me have one of your special cigarettes? I'm hoping it will help the pain in my shoulder."

"It is rough, sir. Not a very good variety. They mix dried grass with it as well," replied the guard.

Khalid just smiled at him and waited. The guard pulled out a little package from his pocket. He fished out a hand-rolled cigarette that contained both tobacco and *charas*. He lit it and passed it to Khalid, who took three short puffs then handed it back.

"Where do you get it locally?" asked Khalid.

"Some of the farmers in Simly Dam area grow it, sir. But the prime *charas* comes from Afghanistan."

"I hope you are not smoking it on your night duty."

"No, sir, I have a few puffs only in the day when I need to catch up on some sleep."

Khalid headed back toward his living area. He felt a slight buzz and hoped that the smoking would not trigger another spell of labyrinthitis. The pain in his shoulder seemed to have dulled, he noticed.

Khalid lay on his stomach in his bed and felt as though he was floating. Safia's fingers brushed heated oil into his shoulder. Despite his dislike of drugs, Khalid felt that the pain management properties of the locally grown cannabis were formidable. He understood why so many people who frequented religious shrines relied on drugs of one kind or another. On the one hand, they lessened the pain of existence; on the other, they allowed one to grab at the gossamer strands that connected mere mortals to the divine. The way humans were designed contained a flaw of sorts, thought Khalid, because the divine connection could only be experienced in an altered state. Khalid felt that divinity was not related to any sacred text, ritual, or house of worship but to the collective human spirit. In his case, divinity was manifested through art. This form of human expression moved him more completely than any other. He felt his desperate exhortations and daily prayers were fraudulent. What was truly worthy of worship were the dreams of artists. This was the reason that museums existed. Museums, he decided, were the only houses of worship that mattered.

In this moment, Khalid even began to understand his friend Ghalib a bit better. Ghalib never observed any ritual of faith. His insatiable appetite for and custodianship of art was his primary response to life. Now Khalid viewed Ghalib not just as a prominent client but as a comrade. In the past two decades, the Arabization of Pakistan had proceeded apace. Mosques and religious centres — manned by bearded zealots posing as the clergy in a faith that had no history of a clergy — influenced even the politicians. A false piety blossomed, spreading throughout the country like a toxic virus. The secular state had vanished. Mosques as large as emporiums mushroomed around the country. The Buddhist sculpture smuggled from Bamiyan — this remarkable artefact that seemed to thwart every attempt at ownership — had created a collision of unrelated events in his life, he realized. Khalid began to wonder what price both he and Ghalib would eventually pay for it.

Safia was murmuring something. He turned over and watched her wipe her fingers on a towel. The way she rubbed each slim, long figure before slipping her massive emerald ring back on reminded him of a miniature Mughal painting entitled *In the Bath*. When she smiled at him, he found himself staring into their son Hassan's eyes. A tremor rippled through his entire body.

"There might have been an accident," he heard himself saying.

Safia's smile vanished.

"Where is my son?"

"I don't know."

"Bring my son home," said Safia as she began to cry.

"Have I ever denied you anything?" Khalid slowly sat up.

"Yes! When I wanted you to spend more time with Hassan and less on your business," Safia said, repeating an ancient reproach.

"I was building the family's future. All of this," he said, spreading his arms expansively.

"No, you were indulging in your passion for art, which came before all of us. You are my life, Khalid, but I want to go back to a time when we had very little," she said as she stepped away from the bed.

Khalid watched her retreating.

"There is something you need to know," he shouted.

Safia stopped, but did not walk back to him.

"I have never told you about my dream," he said.

"Is it a new one?"

"No. It is a political dream. I want to take all the Kashmiri art I have collected in a procession across the border to Kashmir. I want to display my treasures for people who are being mistreated by that government. I want to show them who they really are."

"You are mad! The government will never allow it, and the Indians will probably destroy everything," Safia said.

"I want to take a caravan of treasures from Pakistan to

India. It would be a gift of art, not an act of war. Who could refuse such an offer?"

Safia imagined a long procession of men wrapped in shawls who would carry the items for Khalid. He had two special salons that housed the treasures of Kashmir. Even Ghalib was not allowed to purchase them. She knew they were priceless, and that her husband's dream was admirable, but at this moment, she didn't care. All she wanted was for her son to be at home, playing computer games with his three-year-old son.

"Let us all go to Gilgit and bring Hassan home. Let's bring everyone, including the children," she said.

"Let me take you for a Chinese dinner tonight in Islamabad, Safia," Khalid said.

"I have set things out to cook," replied Safia.

"Cook them another time. I will bring Hassan home. I have already sent someone," he said as he walked over to embrace her.

"Well, let's take everyone to dinner. Even the children and also Faisal," said Safia.

"Yes, the whole family," Khalid agreed, knowing she did not want to spend time with him alone.

A FEW HOURS later, the car left Barako carrying the entire family, including Hassan's wife. In the Barako bazaar, huge posters of Dr. Qadri were plastered everywhere.

"Who is he, Faisal?" asked Khalid.

"Dr. Tahir-ul Qadri. He is returning soon from Canada. He is going to march up to Parliament with his followers. There's been lots of advertising on television. He has a great deal of money," Faisal said, sounding excited.

"They won't let him. He sounds like the same sort as

the leader of the new party Ghalib is supporting. Perhaps they will join together and frighten the government." Khalid chuckled.

"Hassan listens to his speeches," his wife added.

"Hassan?"

"Yes. He said the man is brilliant and has centres all across the world. He is arriving tomorrow."

"Well, I'll call Ghalib and ask him about this. He is running in the election. He knows a lot of important people in his party."

The Chinese restaurant was located behind a huge shopping complex. It was packed, but the manager knew Khalid and immediately secured a table. Khalid gazed at his family and indulged his rambunctious grandchildren while Safia ordered from the ten-page menu. As a tureen of soup arrived, Faisal flashed Khalid a look.

"Just check it," Khalid said, knowing his phone was vibrating in Faisal's pocket.

Safia stopped filling the soup bowl held in her hand. Khalid's comment brought silence to the table. He ignored Safia and held out his hand for the phone. He looked at it, rose from his chair, and walked toward the men's washroom. He entered a stall, shut the door, and dialed Sher Khan's number. Within two minutes, his call was returned.

"You should not have sent your son, Khalid sahib." Sher Khan's voice was cold.

"Give me your news, Sher Khan."

"We have a big fish in our hands, and our special friends will send him where he belongs."

"What does this have to do with finding the agent and my property?" Khalid said, fighting the panic that was rising in his chest.

"Your son, the agent, and your property are all together. The man helping them is a general—a sworn enemy of our special friends," replied Sher Khan.

"Has this become a Taliban operation?" Khalid whispered. "Don't involve me in this, Sher Khan."

"They are the only soldiers of this land, Khalid. Your *kafir* statue has delivered prey into our hands. Your son will be kept safe."

The phone disconnected. Khalid resisted the urge to throw it into the toilet. He had accidentally landed in the eye of a storm. His promise to Safia resounded in his head. This could well be the costliest mistake he had ever made. Khalid rushed out of the washroom.

"I have ordered steamed fish for you, Khalid," Safia said, staring at him.

"Baba, Baba! Why can't Daddy eat with us," lisped his four-year-old granddaughter.

Hassan's wife sat with an untouched plate of food in front of her. Khalid glanced at the steaming dishes arranged on the table and realized that he, too, had no appetite.

"Give me a little piece of fish, please," he said, turning to Safia.

"The children love the noodles. I think this was a good idea." She paused for a moment before speaking again. "What's bothering you, Khalid?"

Khalid knew she had sensed his agitation, and he had no wish to further worry her. "Safia, I want to bring Hassan home myself," he said. "I am going to fly to Gilgit in the morning."

"Fine. This time I want to go with you."

"You cannot. There are some complications. Don't worry, I will find him. I know all of his ways," Khalid said, lifting his fork and swallowing some fish to reassure her.

"Then take Faisal with you so I don't worry." Safia offered him a brave smile.

"No, Faisal will stay here with all of you. Hassan and I will return home together and everything will be just as it always was."

KHALID ARRIVED AT the airport the next morning for an 11 a.m. flight. Benazir Bhutto International Airport had introduced more security checks than he remembered. His small carry-on luggage went through three X-ray machines. Only passengers with airline tickets were allowed to enter the large central hall. He waited in the lounge with a handful of people. Tourism had declined drastically in the entire country, particularly in the remote northern areas. Khalid had booked a rental car and driver. Beyond that, he had made no other arrangements.

In his breast pocket he carried an envelope with a large amount of money. He was dressed in the local *shalwar kameez* with a black Western-style jacket over it. He wore highly polished black loafers with socks. He looked like the well-dressed local businessman that he was.

The two men who sat next to him on the plane were army officers. Khalid had the window seat and barely glanced at them. They were in uniform and appeared to be quite senior. As they took off their caps and placed them on the overhead racks, he was struck by their sombre expressions.

"Posted in Gilgit?" he inquired.

"Yes. On special duty," said the one next to him.

"I didn't know we had much of a military presence in Gilgit. I thought the military would be closer to Skardu," said Khalid, feeling an acute sense of discomfort.

"There are many situations in the country, sir. What about you?" asked the one sitting in the aisle seat.

"I'm going to join my son for a day or so in Gilgit," replied Khalid.

"Ah! What does your son do there?"

"He has gone to do some photography for a tourist brochure."

"I hope he has stayed clear of the unrest."

Khalid took a newspaper from the flight attendant. The entire front page was dedicated to the goateed cleric who was arriving from Canada to lead the protest march in the nations's capital.

"What is your opinion of this man?" Khalid asked.

"He is popular. The march is a publicity stunt," said the officer next to him. "The Americans might be behind him."

"But he is not running for office. He runs educational centres," said Khalid.

"Nothing is going to happen, sir. It is just a pre-election game."

Over the speakers in the cabin, the pilot announced the preparation for landing and informed his passengers that the weather in Gilgit was clear. The short flight was at an end. Khalid disembarked with urgency. He spotted a man carrying a placard emblazoned with his name standing near the cordoned-off zone and walked toward him.

"Thank you," he said.

The man reached for Khalid's small carry-on and led the way out.

"Would you like to check into the hotel, sir," he asked.

Khalid just stood for a minute, breathing in the air.

"No. I want you to take me to the local bazaar. I am

looking for someone," he said as he climbed into the front seat with the driver.

"There are a lot of army checkpoints, sir. There has been some trouble," said the driver.

"What sort of trouble?"

"First, there was the sectarian killings, and then a truck blew up. There is trouble on the Gilgit–Skardu road."

"What happened?"

"The Taliban, sir. There has been an attack. A suicide attack," the driver said.

"Are there any handicraft or antique stores around here? People who sell old stuff?" asked Khalid.

"There is a co-operative store. I know the man who runs it."

"Take me to him."

Twenty minutes later, they arrived at a modest structure that seemed to be a tourist office of sorts. A man with yellowing teeth and a drooping moustache greeted Khalid.

"Do you have any Gandharan antiquities here?" asked Khalid.

"Strange. Another man was in here yesterday asking the same thing," said the man.

"Can you describe him?"

"What do you want to know?" asked the man, trying to look stern.

Khalid withdrew his cash envelope and pulled out two five-thousand-rupee notes and placed them on the table.

The man looked around nervously, then quickly slid both notes into the opened drawer of a wooden table.

"It was a young man. He was fashionably dressed with a big camera. He wanted to know if there were any Gandharan pieces here. But he left quickly."

"Did he tell you where he was going?" Khalid asked.

"No. He just got into his car and drove away."

"Do any of the old Buddhist sculptures ever come your way?"

"No. You find those in Swat. We just have some handi-crafts. Wools, shawls, baskets, and local jewellery. But no tourists." He shrugged his shoulders.

Khalid left. He planned to set out for the local bazaar in Chilas. His driver was standing outside the car talking to a local. When he saw Khalid, he rushed over. "Terrible news, sir! There has been a Taliban attack near Skardu. A car and the people in it were blown up. No one survived."

Khalid's veins turned to ice.

"What sort of a car?"

"An expensive one. Where do you want to go next?"

EIGHTEEN

GHALIB HAD BECOME MORE reclusive. He ate sparingly and spent hours reading fitfully. He felt there was very little to look forward to, so when he was informed that his gem dealer had arrived he decided to end his self-imposed withdrawal. In the past, the man's spontaneous visits had always managed to amuse him. Ghalib served drinks in the first-floor living room and had the meal catered from the club. Chafing under his strict vegetarian regimen, Ghalib allowed himself a few small treats: he nibbled on beef kebabs and even smoked two joints that the gem dealer had brought with him.

"How is the politics going?" inquired the man.

"Well, it seems I have been persuaded very strongly to switch my party," said Ghalib in a burst of recklessness.

"Well, nobody in the Punjab wants this AK and his two recycled running mates," replied the gem dealer peevishly.

"I want to serve the nation, but I have to be clever," Ghalib continued as the dealer pulled a paper bundle from his case.

"Let me show you the pick of my collection," he said.

The brown-paper cone was opened and about ninety karats of brilliant aquamarines were spread out in front of Ghalib. There were easily fifty flawless cut stones in various shapes. Ghalib leaned forward, mesmerized by the colour. His imagination fashioned a choker that cascaded down the throat of a beautiful young woman, descending like a waterfall in the cleft of her breasts. Unfortunately, he could not summon any candidate for this treasure he felt he could so easily design. He was still in the midst of a sexual drought.

"Put them away, please." He drew back. "There is no one whom I could pamper with these."

"The price will be excellent for you. Buy them and put them away for later," the dealer encouraged.

"I want someone to tell me about this Dr. Qadri. Is it true that he will take a large caravan of people to Islamabad?" Ghalib asked, ignoring the dealer.

"He is an army stooge. He appeared so suddenly! Maybe even the president is behind this," said the gem dealer, leaving the stones on the coffee table.

"No, the president is hiding in his bunker in Karachi," said Ghalib.

"Well, change can be very dangerous. What if they take your land away?"

"Then I will have to become like you, my friend, running around selling smuggled gems from Afghanistan," said Ghalib, suddenly irritated by the turn in the conversation.

Ghalib rose abruptly, signalling that the revelry, if it could be called that, was over. He told his valet to make a bed for the gem dealer and retreated upstairs. For a moment, he missed the footsteps that used to scamper up behind him. The news he had received about Billa was not good. The boy had become violent at school, and had almost sent his victim to the hospital. His mother had responded by keeping him home so an elder brother could use him as an apprentice in a local trade. Ghalib knew he had failed to understand what deprivation did to people in rural Pakistan. He dismissed his failure swiftly so it would not prey on his conscience.

THE NEXT DAY, Ghalib decided to go to the country. Somehow, his constituency would have to be definitively told that he was not running for the party with which he had been affiliated. He would decline, due to ill health, at a community meeting Nur Hyat would organize. He cancelled his appointment with his psychiatrist and ordered that his paints, canvas, and easel be packed. Ghalib's two-car convoy sailed out from the front gate in the evening.

When he arrived on the outskirts of the sleeping country village his spirits lightened considerably. The large door to his home was open and the front courtyard was lit. His night watchman stood at attention with a broad smile on his face. The hustle and bustle that accompanied his arrival made the great country estate come alive. Ghalib got out of the car and inhaled the pure country air, redolent with the scent of flowers and rich, fertile soil. He had planned to have his easel set up in the pre-dawn light so that he could paint, but instead, he climbed up to the terrace and watched the stars disappear one by one.

A few hours later, Nur Hyat arrived. A meeting of the local constituency was scheduled for the early evening. Ghalib thought Nur Hyat did not seem like himself. Even his typical sartorial splendour appeared to be a little diminished. His shirt was wrinkled and his heavily pomaded hair was flatter than usual.

"What is wrong, Nur Hyat?" Ghalib asked.

"Terrible things will happen and many people will be involved," Nur Hyat replied cryptically.

"What are you talking about?" pressed Ghalib.

"I have just heard that no real elections will take place in two months' time. The results have already been fixed," he said, avoiding Ghalib's eyes. "The vote boxes will appear and disappear."

"Rubbish! The Election Commission has returning officers who are in charge of those boxes," Ghalib snapped.

"This is a small community. Everybody knows everything," Nur Hyat replied.

Ghalib knew a certain amount of rigging and coercion always took place, but the prospect of exchanging entire ballot boxes required a certain degree of organization. He digested the information slowly, and pondered calling Soody to ask if he'd heard the same thing. Then he began to wonder if he really did need to meet with his largely illiterate constituency members, who might also be privy to this information.

"Bring the constituency members here. Tea will be served. I have an announcement to make," Ghalib said.

When the local constituents arrived, they sat in a semicircle on the front patio. From their subdued manner, Ghalib sensed that Nur Hyat might have said something to them about the ballot boxes before he arrived. The locals drank tea, ignored the biscuits, and fixed their reproachful eyes on him. As Ghalib announced that he was withdrawing his candidacy, they saw the possibility of future rewards vanish before their eyes. Their departing handshakes were much less effusive than their greetings had been. When they were gone, Ghalib told Nur Hyat that his services were no longer needed, and that his estate manager would pay him. Ghalib added that if he ever had any concrete information about the ballot boxes being removed, an extra payment would find its way to him. Nur Hyat just nodded.

"The crazy cleric, Qadri, who wants to march on the government, is the only man in the country who knows it will happen," Nur Hyat said as he walked away.

Ghalib mused over Nur Hyat's comment as he strolled through his gigantic front garden, which was larger than a cricket pitch. Would this truly happen? he wondered. Would the goateed cleric take on the might of the entrenched politicians and win? Why wasn't the government taking him seriously as a threat? As Ghalib reached the end of the garden, next to the encircling wall, he heard a sound behind him. He swung around. Standing in front of him was Saqib, dressed in dirt-stained clothing.

"How did you get past the guard at the front door?"

"I have come from the back. I jumped the wall," said Saqib.

Ghalib surveyed the boy who had run away with the drummer from the Sufi shrine. He was almost skeletal.

"How was life with the drummer?"

"He lied about everything. He told me he would teach me how to play music and I could make money at the shrines," Saqib said.

"You know, Saqib, when someone whom I have taken care of runs away, he is no longer welcome here."

"I heard in the village that you are sick and not running in the election, so I came to see you."

Ghalib roared with laughter. Saqib had not lost his ability to think expediently. He saw a familiar smile play across Saqib's gaunt face.

"Do you remember your English?"

"Yes. I will never forget anything that you have taught me," replied Saqib in perfect English.

"I should have been a schoolteacher," Ghalib replied.

"Yes! You should build a school right here in this garden."

"And have hooligans like you running around and not studying?" Ghalib replied. He was beginning to enjoy himself.

"It is better than politics, and it would make everyone happy," Saqib said.

"What do you know about politics? You are fifteen — too young to even vote."

"I hate politicians. They come in big cars and are all fat, old, and ugly," the boy added viciously.

"When you grow up you could become a revolutionary."

"What is a revolutionary?" asked Saqib.

Ghalib sighed. He wanted to grab the boy by the scruff of his neck, march him inside to the study, and show him books. How would it feel to open the realm of possibilities to this bright vagrant? It would be like planting a seed, and waiting for it to blossom into a flower. Yet Saqib's own father was a teacher, and he had given up on the runaway. Suddenly, Ghalib felt that the privilege of his vaunted life was a dark and ugly thing. A wave of depression descended on him.

"Go home, Saqib," he said, turning away.

"No. I will live in the garden. I won't bother you. But you can call me to press you," he added desperately.

"That is over, Saqib. Forever. I am lonely but you will not be. Everything will be all right," Ghalib reassured him.

Saqib flashed him a disbelieving look, then nimbly scaled the wall and disappeared as quickly as he had appeared.

Ghalib walked back to the house and instructed the watchmen to make sure no one was lurking in the garden at night. When he entered his room, his valet told him that Khalid had called him twice, so he called him back.

"Khalid, my friend. How are you? The countryside is becoming as dangerous as the cities. I miss you. You should come and see me."

"Ghalib, everything has gone wrong. I am in Gilgit."

"Where is the sculpture, Khalid? I dream about it."

"Ghalib, my son is missing, but he made contact with the man who stole the sculpture. There may have been some trouble."

"What is it? Tell me. You don't sound like yourself."

"I seem to have lost control of the situation. These blasted Taliban are everywhere and the army cannot control them. I fear we may lose the sculpture."

"Does this have to do with money, Khalid? Does someone want to make a side deal for more money? I will not pay more than the agreed sum," Ghalib said with irritation.

"To hell with your money, Ghalib! You are not listening to me. Come out of your damn country paradise. My son is missing. Where is your sympathy?" Khalid shouted.

"Khalid, I have sold valuable land that is jointly owned by my relatives. They don't know about this. Make sure I do not have a reason to regret this. Find your son. You never should have sent him. Goodbye."

Ghalib hung up, realizing that this was the first time he had acknowledged yet another serious breach of trust. He had two sisters who were also entitled to a share of the vast land holdings that he managed. Relations with both were frosty at best, and Ghalib felt that he had greater power than either of them, even thought they were quite affluent in their own right. Even his estate manager knew nothing about his transaction. Litigation over land rights in Pakistan was notoriously long and difficult. The courts took an average of ten years to settle disputes.

Ghalib switched on the television and once again found the cleric from Canada being interviewed. Ghalib was glued to the screen, unable to shake off the hypnotic power of the man's oratory. He called Soody at once.

"Why is this man, Qadri, not being taken seriously?" he asked.

"I have told you. He has Koranic centres. He is a kook. A few years ago he immigrated to Canada. He has been duping people over there. Now he returns and wants to create a diversion. It's all rubbish," Soody calmly explained.

"I think you are wrong. He is a very compelling man," Ghalib replied.

"We have only two months to go and then we will be in power," replied Soody.

"I think you are too smug," Ghalib said in frustration. "You have an inexperienced leader and a lot of unemployed youth. Hardly the foundation for an ascent to power."

"You just keep your end of the bargain and get elected. We will take care of the rest."

"I am no longer your party's candidate."

"When the hell did this happen?"

"Today. Doctor's orders," Ghalib said.

"I won't forgive this," Soody said, his voice menacing.

"I know. But it will work out in the end. The rival candidate is going to win anyway."

"This was an opportunity for you to serve this great nation of ours," Soody said.

"I am not the man for the job, Soody. I am just a doddering

old fool. You carry on. I hope you win back a cabinet position."

"This is an absurd conversation. I am ending it," Soody said and hung up.

There was no sleep for Ghalib that night. The ambience of the country house had changed. Everything seemed lifeless. He riffled through his music CDs aimlessly, then ordered a late-night snack from the kitchen, which he barely touched. Finally, he returned to the main house and prowled though the various bedrooms, switching lights on and off as he went. Ghalib felt like the vitality of his life was ebbing away. When he returned to his bedroom, he swallowed a sleeping pill and went to sleep.

WHEN HE AWOKE the next afternoon, Ghalib called Khalid, but there was no answer. Ghalib had made a decision. The sculpture that had so obsessed him had slipped out of his hands, but there were other opportunities to be explored. He wanted to buy Khalid's fine art collection. In the past, Khalid had brushed away Ghalib's interest, but the missing statue now gave him an advantage. Khalid wasn't answering his phone, but Ghalib kept dialing until he heard his valet's discreet cough behind him.

"What is it? I am busy," he snapped.

"Nur Hyat is here and says he has to see you at once."

Ghalib didn't want to see him, but he relented and asked for him to be shown in. A few minutes later, Nur Hyat was standing in the bedroom suite.

"A man has been killed on your land."

Ghalib shot up from the edge of the bed. "Have the police been notified? Is the person connected to my household?"

"People are scared," replied Nur Hyat. "The body is lying in your mango orchard."

"Did you find the body?" he said, slipping on his shoes. "Take me there. I am not scared of anything."

Ghalib called his most trusted chauffeur to drive them to the area. Nur Hyat sat in the front seat, providing directions. The car headed toward the main road and stopped just at the edge of the mango orchard. Nur Hyat sprang out and held the door open for Ghalib.

"Stay here," he told the chauffeur. "Nur Hyat has to show me something that the manager has missed."

"Sir, your shoes will get ruined in the mud," the chauffeur pointed out.

"Damn the shoes!" roared Ghalib. "Wait here till we come back."

Ghalib followed Nur Hyat into the orchard. The large spreading trees were covered with small green mangoes that would ripen in another three months. Ghulam wondered if a farmhand had committed suicide. There had never been an incident of this sort before. The moist, fertile soil squelched under his feet and the mud rose close to the tops of his shoes. He continued following Nur Hyat, who circled a large tree ahead and pointed a finger to one side. Ghalib drew closer. The man's throat had been cut and rigor mortis had set in. The man's eyes — terror-stricken — were wide open. Ghalib felt his breakfast rise in his stomach before he turned his face away.

"Who is he?"

"The story is very interesting, sir. This is the man who was involved with the people of the rival political party. He is the one who told me about the fake ballot boxes."

"Why is he here in my orchard?" asked Ghalib.

"He worked for you."

"Do you think that he worked for both sides and was

found out?" Ghalib asked, genuinely shocked.

"The country is not full of simple people. People will sell their daughters only if they have to," Nur Hyat said cynically.

"Still, this is a police matter. What am I supposed to do? I'll give some money to his family, but that is all."

"I am frightened," Nur Hyat said in a low voice. "I told you what this man told me and I'm scared they will find out."

"It is just part of a political game. Killing him in my orchard is what bothers me the most. Perhaps it is intended as a message for me. Anyway, we need to call the estate manager. He will handle this," replied Ghalib, wondering if he should report the situation to Soody.

Then he realized something.

"How did you know this man's body was here?"

"I was told by someone in the village," Nur Hyat said.

"I want you to leave the village immediately. You have been paid for your services. Your employment is over," Ghalib said, heading back to his car. "Do not mention a word of this to my driver. I don't want any talk in my household."

When he got into the car, Ghalib instructed his chauffeur to drop Nur Hyat off at the bus station in the neighbouring village. During the ride, Ghalib called his farm manager and told him about the body. He also asked him to deliver extra food provisions to the man's house, and to check that his family had enough money to bury him. He couldn't shake the feeling that the murder in the orchard was a bad omen.

GHALIB PAINTED THAT evening, working on a large canvas. He painted throngs of bodies with glowing eyes. His cook was standing by his side, observing him keenly. The man longed to hold a paintbrush instead of a paring knife, and sometimes Ghalib would let him paint the background.

"It is a violent image," the cook said softly.

"Death is violent and so is life," replied Ghalib, mixing ochre for the eyes.

"You should go abroad, sir. You should marry again," said the cook.

"I am not a traveller. I live like a king in my own country. Why should I leave it?"

"Go for a short while, sir. It will help your mood."

"There are many ways to change your mood. Marriage and travel are not among them," Ghalib replied with a wan smile.

"Dinner is ready, sir. Would you like to eat?"

"No. Let the staff eat. Perhaps later," Ghalib said, continuing to paint.

When the cook left, Ghalib contemplated other possibilities for his life. Saqib's words from earlier in the day echoed in his head. Could his ancestral home be converted to a school? The grounds of his estate were large enough to include a pool as well as a cricket pitch. He could do this in the loving memory of his ancestors.

Ghalib thought he could dedicate the school to the children in the village that bordered his great estate. It would be his final act of redemption. Ghalib longed for forgiveness for his many transgressions. He felt that this one act had the potential to wipe the slate clean. Pleased with his decision, Ghalib worked steadily and calmly on the painting until his valet burst into the billiard room, interrupting his work.

"You must call Khalid sahib, please," he said, and handed him the phone.

"I'll call in the morning. I don't want to stop."

"Please call him now. There was a call from his number and when I answered I heard him crying and then the phone was disconnected."

Ghalib stared at the phone in his valet's hand but did not extend his own hand to take it. He could sense catastrophe. He looked at his canvas and then back at the phone as another wave of darkness overcame him. The weight of his body exhausted him. All at once, he realized he had neglected to eat for most of the day. He wondered if he was on the verge of a diabetic collapse.

"Enough!" he whispered, and slowly sank to his knees.

NINETEEN

THE SIGNPOST THAT FLEW by indicated that Skardu was only sixty kilometres way. The ride was no longer pleasant as a new tension had entered the car. General Zamir seemed to be lost in thought, and Adeel was having difficulty accepting that he was no longer in charge of his own destiny. He also knew he would have no opportunity to tell Norbu, who sat bundled up in the front seat, that she was going to be left in Skardu alone.

"She will be very frightened, if I leave her alone, General," Adeel said quietly.

"I have given you my word that both the sculpture and the woman will be safe, but I have to bring you back with me," the general replied.

"I have another suggestion, sir. Take the sculpture, but let me go with her," Adeel suggested slowly.

"You would part with what you stole, at such great cost, for this woman?"

Adeel closed his eyes and saw the face of the Buddha

sculpture. He did this to centre himself. He saw the marble lips part, uttering words he could not hear. He could feel moisture gathering in his closed eyes.

".Yes," he replied, brushing his eyes with the back of his hand.

"Are you in love with her, Adeel?" the general asked, smiling.

"I am connected to her soul. She is my soul. I never thought it was possible."

"Then I will make sure she is well taken care of until you return," Zamir said.

Adeel knew he had failed. He placed his hand on the revolver concealed by his wool waistcoat. In order to change the general's decision, one person in this car would have to die. Adeel glanced at the driver. He knew he had to create a situation that would make the car stop, even if it meant putting them all at risk.

"Don't even think of it, Adeel," the general said, as if he could read his thoughts.

Adeel looked straight ahead.

"If you take the driver out, I will go for your woman. At such close range it would be quite unfortunate," he continued in a deceptively mild tone.

"Are you armed, sir?" asked Adeel, wondering if the man's words were simply a bluff.

"What do you think?"

Adeel knew that army protocol called for the driver of the car to be accompanied by a security officer. General Zamir had disregarded this rule, so the driver himself must be armed, although it was hard to gauge where his weapon was. It was probably under the front seat. The general was a slim man, and his army tunic fit snugly. All that had come out of his trouser pockets was a pack of cigarettes. Yet, like Adeel, the general was also a trained soldier.

"Why are you going to Skardu, sir," Adeel asked.

"For purely sentimental reasons. I am going to visit the beautiful Satpara Lake, where my father used to take me for picnics. It is just an overnight break. It is a private visit, so no army fuss."

"What are the arrangements for Norbu?"

"I know a family. They will take care of her. Can she cook?"

Adeel thought of the chicken she had cooked on the rooftop in Chilas and shook his head.

"They have a small child. She can help with that," said the general.

"She is frightened of people. She has been living in the forests alone."

"They are very kind. I shall leave some money for expenses and—"

"I have the money. I can take care of her," Adeel said, interrupting him.

"Pride is a useful thing, but not when you are talking about stolen money, Adeel."

"I can take care of her," Adeel said gruffly.

"Not at this moment."

The general's phone rang twice. He answered and listened more than he talked. Finally, he turned to Adeel.

"We are going to town first to settle her with the family. Then we will store the sculpture before heading to the lake."

Adeel knew all he could do was to wait for an opportunity to change the general's plan. Sitting in the back seat, he focused on Norbu's shawl-covered head, conscious of his great desire to pull the shawl away and run his fingers through her hair. The fact that he was about to betray her devastated him.

When they arrived in Skardu, the town appeared deserted. The car headed to a small neighbourhood of sturdy brick and cement homes and eventually stopped before a gate. The general got out.

"Please explain the arrangements to her while I go in to talk to the family."

Adeel got out of the car and motioned for the driver to do the same. He slid into the driver's seat, watching as General Zamir was greeted at the door of the house by a tall burly man and led inside.

"I have to go with the general. There is a family here who will take care of you until I get back," he said.

"No," replied Norbu.

"I have to do some work and it will take a few days. I will come back for you. These people will keep you; they need some help with their child." He smiled with encouragement.

"I will come with you," Norbu insisted.

"No, you cannot. But you are mine. Put this around your neck," Adeel said and untied the amulet his mother had given to him.

Norbu leaned away from him, her body rigid with anger and fear. Adeel reached over and tried to put the amulet around her neck, but she pushed his hands away.

"Stop it," Adeel shouted. "My mother gave this to me. I am giving it to you to wear. You are mine. I will come back for you." He pried her fingers open and placed the amulet in her hand.

"You promise?" she said, and stopped struggling.

"Yes!"

"You swear in front of the *buth*, then I will believe you," she said.

"It is not necessary. I will always be with you." He took the amulet from her fingers and draped it around her neck.

"I have nothing to give you," she said as she knotted the strings of the amulet tightly around her neck.

He lifted her hand and placed a kiss at the centre of her palm to reassure her. She brought her other hand up and pressed it against his mouth. He could feel the rough skin of her chapped fingers as they grazed his lips. This brief physical contact felt like the tingling of a mild electric shock. Then the car door opened and the general's eyes flickered over their faces.

"Let me take her in. She will be treated like a family member and not a servant."

"Norbu, they are waiting for you. Please go and wait for me," Adeel said with great reluctance.

Norbu pulled her shawl tight around herself as she got out of the car. Adeel watched General Zamir bend down to say something to her as he escorted her to the door, where a woman stood with a smile on her face. She put her arm around Norbu's shoulders before drawing her inside. A second before she cleared the doorway, Norbu turned around to look at Adeel one last time. He saw the curve of her high cheekbones gleaming brightly, as if her entire face was lit by a lamp. When the door shut, he felt like he had been shot in the heart.

He returned to the back seat and rested his head in his hands. He hardly noticed as the general slid in next to him and the driver pulled back out onto the road. As they neared the main street, near the bazaar, the driver asked permission to stop briefly so he could go to the toilet. He parked hastily at a local restaurant and got out.

"What about you, Adeel?" asked the general.

"I am fine, sir," Adeel replied.

"Would you like a cigarette?"

After about ten minutes, when the chauffeur did not return, General Zamir got out of the car and went into the shabby restaurant. The keys were still in the ignition. Adeel quickly got behind the driver's seat, but he was too late. Before he could start the car, Zamir had returned.

"The driver has disappeared and is not answering his phone," the general said, peering down at him.

"Impossible," said Adeel, shocked.

"Well, we are not going to wait. I will drive and you will be my security guard. Move over," the general commanded.

"I can drive, sir," said Adeel.

"I know Skardu like the back of my hand, Adeel. Your Buddha is expected in Hussainabad and we need to get there before we head to the lake," the general said as he opened Adeel's door.

"Please! Let me drive for you," Adeel protested.

"I think a general seen driving his own car is good for morale."

"What's in Hussainabad?" asked Adeel.

"There is a Balti museum there."

Adeel changed seats. He was relieved to know a museum would be the Bamiyan sculpture's new home. His thoughts returned to Norbu.

"The man who opened the museum is a scholar. He owns it, not the government."

"What will he do with the statue?" asked Adeel.

"It will rest there until I have more information about the person who brought it out of Afghanistan. Also another assignment has been arranged for you to make up for stealing the statue. After we drop off the sculpture, we will head for the lake, spend a pleasant night there, and head to Rawalpindi in the morning. I will secure a replacement for the driver, and your mess will have been cleaned up," replied the general.

"As I said, sir, I am finished with this line of work. I want to lead a different life now," Adeel said.

"We will sort out your life when we get to Rawalpindi," the general replied.

"I want to talk to my mother. I am worried about her."

"She is fine now," said the general.

"I hope so," said Adeel. "Is she in her own house?"

The general did not respond. His telephone rang and he pulled it out of his pocket with one hand, glanced at it, then answered. The car swerved and Adeel grasped the steering wheel to keep them on course.

"Impossible! Are you sure? I have a trained man with me. I will be in touch. Find that runaway driver! Get the military police on it."

"What is it, sir?"

"A message has been delivered. It appears to be a Taliban threat of some sort. My name was used. They don't operate in this area, but these days you never know."

"I think the Taliban may be looking for me," Adeel said.

"It's too early to know. I'm not here in any official capacity. Have you been seen by anyone?"

Adeel scanned the road ahead. The snow-capped peaks of the mighty Karakoram mountains surrounded the small valley of Skardu. There were no hiding places here. He pulled out his revolver and checked it.

"There is an automatic rifle under the seat as well. Relax,

Adeel, just breathe in the air of this miraculous place. Ever been to the Khaplu valley?"

Adeel searched for the rifle and found nothing. Something was wrong, he thought.

"There's nothing here, sir. This is very dangerous."

"The driver has been careless. It might be in the trunk with your Buddha."

Adeel caught sight of two men behind them, riding on a beaten-up motorcycle. Their faces were masked by scarves.

"Stop the car, sir. I am worried about these men behind us," Adeel said.

The general slowed down, stopping the car. The motorcycle also slowed, as if it too were going to stop. Without waiting for instructions, Adeel jumped out of the car and charged toward the men on the bike, revolver drawn. He was within four hundred metres of them when a thunderous explosion knocked the air of out of his lungs, instantly deafening him and hurling his body across the road.

Adeel tasted the metallic flavour of his own blood. He turned his head and saw that his revolver had been knocked out of his hands and was lying on the road nearby. The motorcycle and its two drivers were gone. A powerful and familiar odour assailed his nostrils. A bomb had exploded. He rose slowly on his hands and knees. Fighting dizziness, he stood up. He wanted to turn around, but he could not bring himself to do it. He stood with his arms curved around his chest and his head tucked down. He knew that the smoke and flames would continue for a while, and that the general's body had in all likelihood been ripped into fragments and charred beyond recognition. As shock gave way to rage, Adeel finally turned to view the destruction.

As he walked toward the wreckage, he raised his right arm in a military salute. The Mercedes had been reduced to a metal frame. The first object that caught his eye was a severed hand with a cigarette still gripped between two fingers. The entire back of the car was missing. He raised his hand again, gave two salutes, and backed away, stumbling as he did on some rubble. He looked down at the dust-covered shards of the marble statue. He bent down and picked up a small chunk. The curving marble lips of the shattered sculpture lay in the palm of his hand.

As his hearing slowly returned, he began to hear voices. Two men ran down the side of the road toward him. They were local Balti men. One of them reached him and placed his hands on his shoulders.

"Are you all right?" he asked.

"Yes. Do you have a bicycle or something I could use to go to town?" Adeel asked.

"Don't worry, the explosion will be heard in town. They will send people with the ambulance. Who was killed?"

"An army general," replied Adeel

The man shuddered. "Who will stop these killers? Skardu is a clean place! We live simple lives here, but the tourists have stopped coming. These are bad times, brother."

Three vehicles raced toward them from down the road. Two were army Jeeps and the third was a makeshift local ambulance. The latter stopped in front of the bombed car and men in uniform got out. Adeel walked toward them.

"Oh no! Not General Zamir's vehicle!" a man shouted. "Bring a body bag and a stretcher!"

Adeel stopped. He did not want to see the remains of the general's body being gathered and placed on the stretcher. He looked up at the mountains and wished he could simply levitate to a peaceful spot far away. He had been trained to view death as disposal, but now that it was someone he knew, it was a blow from which recovery seemed impossible. Although he had not seen the general for years, Adeel nevertheless felt as if he had lost a father. He was still holding the marble chunk of the statue in his hand; he transferred it to his pocket as an army official approached him.

"What can you tell me? Are you Adeel?" he snapped.

Adeel hesitated, knowing it would be easy to lie, or deny everything, thus seizing his freedom. But he could not.

"Yes, sir. We were headed to Hussainabad for a short while en route to Satpara Lake."

"We know. We were going to send a replacement driver for the general. How is it that you were not in the car?"

Adeel gave a full account of the events leading up to the bombing, including the appearance of the motorcycle. The bomb had to have been placed on the car much earlier, and detonated by the men on the motorcycle via a mobile phone. The missing chauffeur must have been involved, Adeel told them, because he had vanished just before it happened.

"Would you recognize the chauffeur?" asked the officer.

"Yes, I would. The owner of the restaurant he disappeared into must know something as well. I will help in the investigation,"Adeel said.

"To hell with your help! This scum has killed one of ours. It should have been you who was killed, and not him," the man said, expressing his grief.

"We can find them," replied Adeel calmly. "The motorcycle can not have gotten very far."

"By now they will be walking around the bazaar like all the other men. The motorcycle is probably already hidden. They will slip away, as they always do."

"I am not in the army anymore, but I can help you. I have been trained," Adeel offered again.

"Yes, we know what you do and for whom. Why were you with the general?"

"I had some car trouble so I was hitchhiking. Luckily, he came along. He was my commanding officer years ago. I know him well."

"Go to the second Jeep and wait. We will determine if we need to put you under arrest." The officer walked toward a cluster of men standing around the bombed-out remains of the general's car.

Adeel climbed into the empty Jeep. He would never know what plans the general had made for him. The sculpture no longer existed. The memento in his pocket was for Norbu. He only hoped he would have a chance to give it to her.

After a little while, the little convoy began the short trip back to Skardu. Adeel was surprised when, after just one kilometre, they slowed to a halt. There was a car parked on the side of the road, and a man standing next to it. Adeel recognized the brigadier—the man who had been his original contact for this assignment. The brigadier had a brief exchange with one of the officers travelling with Adeel, and then walked over to Adeel himself.

"Get out. You have to transfer to that car."

Adeel climbed out of the Jeep, relieved to see a familiar face.

"Was the sculpture in the car?" the brigadier asked as Adeel climbed into the new vehicle.

"Yes. It was destroyed in the explosion."

"Did you check?"

"Yes. It was all rubble. Beyond repair."

"What a waste of time and money. You are not fit to work with us anymore. But you will do one last thing. A few men have been rounded up, and I want you to see if the general's driver is one of them," explained the brigadier.

They travelled the rest of the way to a small police station in silence. A small cluster of people stood outside. The brigadier parked his car and they both walked up the short flight of steps. Inside, two constables stood near a crude wooden table. Five men wearing handcuffs stood against the wall. The driver was third from left. He flashed a look of hatred at Adeel.

"That is him, sir," Adeel said, pointing to the man.

"I was sick. I had diarrhea and my clothes got soiled. So I went through the back to find some fresh clothes in the bazaar. I did not want General sahib to see me like that. But you had left when I returned," he said fiercely.

"You are wearing the same clothes," said Adeel.

"Are you sure?" the brigadier asked Adeel.

"He is a liar! He is an abductor. He stole that woman until the general dropped her off where she would be safe from him," shouted the driver.

"What woman?" the brigadier asked, turning to Adeel.

"He is crazy. He was the assigned driver. Nobody could have placed two bombs in the car without his knowledge," Adeel said coldly, ignoring the officer's question.

"I would never do this. You are with the Taliban. You must have done this," continued the desperate driver.

"Keep him in jail. He needs to be interrogated. Come with me, Adeel," said the brigadier, leading him out the door.

Adeel was driven to a small government rest house, led inside, and taken to a private room.

"I need facts. I need details, Adeel. But I think you need to clean yourself up first. We will get you a set of fresh clothes. Shower, change, and then join me in the lounge," the brigadier said.

As soon as he left, Adeel emptied his pockets. He still had a roll of money, a revolver, a phone, and a chunk of the statue. There was a knock on the door, and Adeel turned to find an employee of the guesthouse standing in the doorway with a pile of clothing. When he left, Adeel locked his door and entered the bathroom. He dropped his soiled clothing on the floor, wondering if Norbu still had his shirt. His black nylon bag must have been incinerated in the car. He realized then that the brigadier's appearance meant that he had no intention of letting Adeel go.

The offer to wash and the provision of clean clothing were nothing more than attempts to lull Adeel into a false sense of security. He had double-crossed his employer, and nothing was all right when an assignment went all wrong. When something unravelled as completely as this assignment had, sorting out the mess was part of the intelligence office's job. Every detail would have to be verified, and at some opportune moment, the information gathered would be used to condemn him. His protector no longer existed, and his rogue status ensured that the measures taken against him would be serious. His failure could result in his identity being buried in a locked, secret file. He could be imprisoned somewhere without anyone knowing about it, or he could even be killed.

Adeel entered the shower with a bar of soap. The hot water felt like a healing balm. As he cleaned himself, he felt his life was being washed away. His thoughts flew to the patch of land that belonged to his mother. Both the soil and climate of the location made it a suitable place for growing vegetables, but it had been left unattended over the years as he executed his assignments for the intelligence agency. Now he imagined planting neat rows of vegetables that would bear a rich harvest throughout the year. He pictured a large wheelbarrow carrying fresh vegetables for sale. He saw Norbu working with him on the land. He envisioned his mother dressing Norbu as a bride. If he had to beg the brigadier for his life, he would get down on his hands and knees and do it. Then he wavered. He considered climbing out of the bathroom window and hiding until he could return and collect Norbu.

The same thoughts must have also crossed the brigadier's mind; the window opened to a set of iron bars. A knock on the door interrupted Adeel's thoughts. He walked over and opened it.

"Good, you've cleaned up. Let us eat something and talk."

Neither man was truly prepared for the conversation that followed. The brigadier asked about Adeel's reasons for stealing the sculpture.

"What do you mean it had a power over you? Are we talking about local magic?"

"Yes, it is a kind of magic. The brain is encased by the skull, so a special light is needed to illuminate it," Adeel said, being deliberately cryptic.

"Don't be absurd. We have medicine for that. You know, X-rays."

"No, that's not what I mean. Technology is not needed for this. The Buddhist civilizations had none of that. They choose a path for life," Adeel said, stumbling on his words.

"If you are a religious man, Adeel, you can get into

your own faith and see the light as well," said the brigadier dismissively.

Adeel did not respond. The brigadier studied him closely.

"What will your family say about all of this religious mumbo-jumbo? It is not fashionable, or safe, to be a Buddhist hippie in Pakistan these days."

"It is my life." Adeel shrugged.

"Keep these thoughts to yourself then. Where is the woman?" he said abruptly.

"There is no woman."

"I see. There is also a twenty-four-year-old man missing, Adeel. You were driving his car. Where is he now?"

A month ago, Adeel would have covered his tracks brilliantly and admitted nothing. But now, he took his biggest gamble.

"I can take you to where he is buried."

The brigadier's eyebrows shot up. He took a deep breath.

"So, Khalid's prince has died. Good God! Did you kill him?"

"No," replied Adeel, looking directly into his eyes.

"Let's start at the beginning again. At the point when you removed the sculpture from the half-truck before it blew up."

"I have already told you everything."

"So you drag this sculpture, which weighs about seventy kilograms, all by yourself up a steep incline?"

"I am quite strong, as you well know," Adeel said.

"I don't believe you, Adeel. I know there's a woman involved. The driver gave the exact address of the house where she was dropped off, and I have had her picked up. She has not been interrogated yet."

Adeel restrained his impulse to leap from the chair. He

willed his unspoken anguish not to express itself in any outward gesture. Police interrogations were notorious in Pakistan. Everyone broke down and confessed. It was only a matter of time before Norbu confessed to the killing.

"You are a trained agent, Adeel. You would not take a life unless it was a matter of a personal threat or an obstruction of some sort. Was Hassan a threat?" the brigadier asked, folding his hands together.

"I did not kill him," repeated Adeel.

"This illiterate Balti woman is the key to all of this. If you do not tell me yourself then I guarantee that she will be made to talk."

A tea tray arrived. The brigadier poured tea into both cups and then offered the sugar bowl to Adeel. Adeel shook his head and watched the brigadier's spoon rotating in his cup. This was a test. Perhaps Norbu had already confessed.

"Are you in the middle of a breakdown of some sort? You know, we have good army psychiatrists who deal with this sort of thing," the brigadier said in a more sympathetic tone.

"It was an accident. I was shooting an animal that he was photographing. He stepped into my line of fire," said Adeel.

"Ah! So now we have a confession?"

Adeel did not respond.

"The father will never buy it, but I will. We have to locate the body and change the story. I want to attend to this immediately," the brigadier said, springing up from his chair. "We will travel back to Gilgit and you will lead me to the body."

"Fine," Adeel said as he stood up, "but my assistance is conditional."

"I know what you are going to ask. We are going to bring her with us."

"Let her go."

"Unthinkable. When you have been cleared in this matter, then I will clear her as well. I don't want loose ends. We will wrap things up and then you will be dismissed."

When they walked out together to the parked car, they found two men with fearful expressions standing next to it.

The car was empty.

"Where is she?" the brigadier asked furiously.

"She went inside to drink some water, but she never came back. We have searched the entire rest house and she has disappeared," stammered the security guard.

Adeel concealed his relief from the brigadier. Norbu had the ability to hide. She must have found the perfect spot; perhaps she was even watching the car now. He wondered if she was still wearing the gym shoes he had bought for her. The image of her bloodstained feet on the day they met came to his mind. Once again she would have to fend for herself, Adeel realized. He consoled himself with the knowledge that he had taught her many survival and defensive tactics. He hoped that she knew he would find her.

As THE CAR carrying Adeel raced away from Skardu, forces stronger than both of them were directing Norbu's fate. She found shelter at a shabby government school, where the teacher recognized that the oddly dignified woman who had stumbled into the compound was both starving and abandoned. The teacher hired her as a sweeper and permitted her to sleep in the canteen, where a small wooden bed was put in one corner for her. The three other teachers who taught in the rundown school treated Norbu harshly, but the one who had taken her in continued to watch her with a protective eye. After Norbu completed her chores, she was allowed to sit in on the teacher's class. She sat on a wooden stool at the back of the room, enraptured by the words and sentences that appeared on the blackboard. One day, she thought, she might even write something, and create a whole new life for Adeel and herself.

THE BRIGADIER KNEW that if Khalid had not lost faith in him, Hassan would be alive today. Adeel led him to the spot where Hassan was buried. The two-day-old corpse was immediately prepared, encased in a shroud, and placed in a coffin. The brigadier chose to accept Adeel's story because it gave him leverage. The marker on Adeel's debt could be called in at any time. Adeel had never failed at an assignment before. Time and money had been invested in his training, and the return on that investment had not yet been earned. He also sensed that the woman who had run away was linked to this killing. Any kill shot made by Adeel— whether it was aimed at a human or an animal—would not have made such a mess. Most operatives avoided close-range kill shots. Still, he chose not to press Adeel any further on the subject. He had to deal with Khalid first, although the man's financial loss was of little consequence in the larger scheme of things.

The brigadier sat with Adeel and carefully instructed him. He would have to disappear for a while, along with any knowledge of his ride in the general's car.

"I want you to go underground for a while. If it is necessary, you may be given the opportunity to clear this great debt you owe to the agency."

"I cannot do this work anymore," Adeel said.

"I will transfer some funds to you so you can survive."

"I can manage on my own. I shall go home to my mother

and find something to do locally."

"Don't worry about the woman. We can find her for you."

"There is no need. She was travelling to Skardu. I just gave her a ride," replied Adeel.

"Keep the phone we gave you. Take it easy for a while," the brigadier said and held out his hand to say goodbye.

Adeel left the phone in the car and, taking only his revolver, walked away.

TWENTY

Khalid had returned from his overnight trip to Gilgit empty-handed. No sculpture had appeared in the Gilgit ba-zaar. No further leads about Hassan's whereabouts came his way. The brigadier was incommunicado, as was Sher Khan. Safia's distress was unbearable. Hassan's disappearance had driven a wedge between him and his wife. These days, Safia spent most of her time with her grandchildren, often sleep-ing with them at night.

Khalid was seated on a chair in the marble Mughal pavilion. He could not sleep without Safia in the bed. He watched the sun rising above the hills of Barako, immune to its beauty due to the well of emptiness that had now opened up inside of him. He was utterly defeated. His pic-turesque estate felt like an amusement park that had lost all of its rides. He realized now that his lifelong romance with history and antiquities had imprisoned him. The depth of his greed, which had led to his insatiable acquisitive-ness, astounded him. His father's acquisitions could have filled nothing more than a small, horse-drawn cart; his own required more than three thousand square metres of buildings, with more in planning. He acknowledged that his behaviour had wounded Safia, and no longer bothered to hide his grief. Safia's joy lay in simple pleasures, yet he had mistakenly heaped treasures at her feet as an apology for his absences. His elder son preferred to to live abroad, and Hassan's betrayals, disappointments, and absences had pushed him further away from his youngest. The frugal simplicity of his own childhood had motivated him to take giant steps to raise himself above his underprivileged childhood. He thought of himself as the captain of a pirate ship, a man who seized all the bounty that crossed his path and then voyaged to other countries for more. His large circle of acquaintances included lawbreakers, thieves, corrupt officials, and master forgers. The totality of his life had become a bitter pill that he was now forced to swallow.

Khalid heard footsteps on the patio and saw Safia outside. He went to her.

"There is news of Hassan," he said, not bothering to explain the doubts that the brigadier's early phone call had raised in his own mind. "I am going to bring him back this time. I am going to bring our son home."

"Are you sure? Where is he?" she asked.

"Gilgit. I have to go back again, so I need to change quickly. Faisal will take me to the airport," Khalid said.

As he turned to walk away, Safia's hand shot out and grabbed Khalid's arm.

"Did you eat the breakfast I sent for you?"

"Yes, I ate it because you prepared it," he said and gave her a weak smile.

"Not because it's good?" asked Safia.

"Everything prepared by your hands is good. But I must change, Safia. This is one flight I don't want to miss," Khalid said and slid her hand from his forearm.

"Don't fight with him, Khalid," she called after him, "just allow him to come home. He can provide explanations later."

ON THE FLIGHT, Khalid wondered what all the secrecy was about. The brigadier had called before dawn to say that Hassan had been located and that Khalid must fly to Gilgit immediately. When Khalid had demanded to speak to Hassan, however, the brigadier said it was not possible. Khalid was tempted not to go—after all, he had been there just two days ago—but he sensed trouble. He consoled himself by thinking that this would be the end of Hassan's escapades. He wanted his wife's smiles to return; he wanted peace in his house. He riffled through the paper handed to him by a flight attendant and read about a prominent man who had been placed under house arrest. Perhaps that was a solution for his wayward son.

There was a chill in the Gilgit air. Khalid shivered under his light jacket as he walked through the terminal. He spotted the brigadier immediately.

"Where is my son?" Khalid asked as he approached.

"Follow me, Khalid," the brigadier said, steering him into a small corridor that led away from the baggage carousel.

Khalid followed him until they reached a brown wooden door. The brigadier opened it and ushered him inside. The room was empty, save for an upholstered couch and two armchairs. The brigadier shut the door behind them and led Khalid to the couch.

"More surprises?" asked Khalid as he sat down. "Did he

get himself arrested? I am prepared for it all. I am travelling with my chequebook, Brigadier." He gave a dry laugh.

"Khalid, the news is not good."

"I expected that. Let's get on with it. Where are you hiding him?"

The brigadier placed his hands on Khalid's shoulders. "There was an accident, Khalid. Your son has died. The coffin is prepared and will be flown back with you."

An unearthly cry escaped from Khalid as he pushed the brigadier with both of his hands and stood up. The sudden movement triggered the labyrinthitis that had lay dormant for the past few days. The room spun at a dizzying speed and Khalid knew he was falling. He braced himself against a chair but it seemed to drop away. Khalid slid to the floor. He shut his eyes tightly, which only heightened his dizziness, so he reopened them and saw the brigadier's face looming over his.

"Khalid! Khalid! My dear friend, I know this is horrible news. Are you all right? Do I need to call a doctor?"

Khalid looked at the face peering at him and watched as it rotated away, then came back. As the rotations slowed, he leaned back against the sofa and asked one question.

"Is my son really dead?"

"It was an unfortunate accident. He had climbed on a steep hill to take a photograph. He slipped and broke his neck. Death was instantaneous. Khalid, he did not suffer." The brigadier helped him to get up and sit back on the couch.

"I won't believe it until I see his face. Where is his body?" Khalid asked.

"Here. I have had the coffin sealed, Khalid. It had to be done. There is a terrible injury to one side of the head."

"You will take me to Hassan now," he demanded.

"It's not a good idea. The embalming techniques here are not very good. I will have the coffin opened, Khalid, but you will not see his face," the brigadier said. "Are you able to walk?"

"Something happens to the fluid in my inner ear and I lose my balance. My son has the same problem. I'm fine now."

They walked together to a section of the terminal where cargo was stored. An unadorned pine casket lay on the floor. Khalid stopped, grappling with his disbelief. The wild, beautiful creature whose wings he had planned to clip had found another escape. Khalid felt as though he was struggling to breathe. He felt the pressure of the brigadier's arm around his back and stepped forward. *Safia*, he thought, *look at our son lying in this box.*

The padlock on the side of the coffin was opened. The lid was lifted. The scent of attar of roses wafted out and assaulted Khalid's nostrils. The white shroud was long and narrow, the head slightly depressed. The brigadier unwound the linen from the bottom. Hassan's lips and nostrils appeared in front of Khalid's eyes. He wept and then turned away from the face. The brigadier drew the cloth back quickly, then slowly brought the lid of the coffin down.

Khalid wept uncontrollably — for Safia more than for himself. He also wept for Hassan's wife and children. He wanted to remove Hassan from the coffin and cradle him in his arms. He backed away and faced the brigadier.

"What happened to the upper part of his face?"

"You don't want to know," said the brigadier.

"The worst is over. Tell me."

"There must have been an animal nearby. The face was damaged by the creature before the body was discovered," the brigadier said solemnly.

Safia, look what has happened to your prince, Khalid thought. "I can never tell my wife about this," he said.

"Khalid, the return flight to Islamabad leaves at two in the afternoon. I want you to come back and rest. I shall order some coffee for you. Or would you prefer something stronger?"

"No," replied Khalid. "I shall sit here with my son until it is time to go."

"It is a loading area, Khalid. You won't be comfortable," protested the brigadier.

"Just have a chair brought here for me."

"I will have two sent. I shall sit with you."

"No, I prefer to be alone," replied Khalid, walking back toward the coffin.

When the chair was brought, Khalid had it placed close to the head of the coffin. He ignored the small table that was set up with coffee a little farther away. For two hours, Khalid held a vigil for his son. It was not a silent one. He told stories — the narratives of great ancient kings from many civilizations. He closed his eyes and told wondrous tales, describing the treasures that existed and the ones that had come his way. In the face of his son's death, he did what he had failed to do during his life.

THE SMALL AIRCRAFT that rose from the Gilgit runway took Khalid and his son home. Three hours after seeing Hassan's body, Khalid had regrouped. With a cool head and a fixed resolve, he planned a funeral. He contacted his siblings in Lahore and asked them to immediately come to Barako. They would need to be with Safia when he returned. The gates to his hidden estate would be flung wide open. He would give his son a funeral fit for a prince. Hassan would be the first person to be buried in the family tomb he had been constructing for months. His elder son would be arriving from Bangkok later that night. A shattered Faisal helped to make the arrangements for Khalid to be met at the Islamabad airport. Only Safia had been kept completely in the dark.

When Khalid walked into the terminal, he was folded into Faisal's wordless embrace. Special permission had been arranged for Faisal to be at the gate. Khalid felt not only the weight of Faisal's slumped head but also his tears on his shoulder. He drew back, giving consolation before receiving it.

"It will be all right, Faisal," he murmured.

Outside, Khalid watched Faisal and two other people lift the coffin and place it into a waiting van. Faisal stayed inside the van for several minutes, saying goodbye to Hassan. When he emerged, Khalid saw a heap of roses, rising in an oblong mound, covering the entire coffin. The back door to the van was carefully fastened, but the fragrance still lingered outside.

"The van will follow us home, *Chachu*," Faisal said, his eyes red from crying. "Let's go to the car."

Khalid did not follow him.

"I shall ride with the coffin. My son deserves that," he said, walking to the side of the van.

The drive took an hour. Khalid knew he would face his biggest challenge upon arriving home. He knew that many funeral rites specific to the Muslim faith had been violated. The burial would not take place within twenty-four hours, and before sunset. It would take him another day to make some adjustments to Hassan's final resting place. He kept himself engaged in these thoughts to avoid thinking about Safia.

When he arrived home, Khalid directed the van away from the bricked driveway where cars were normally parked and toward the side of the raised hill where it would remain concealed. His brother-in-law's face appeared at the side of his window. Khalid disembarked and found the condolences offered too painful to accept.

"Where is Safia?" he asked.

"She is upstairs with your sister. All she knows is that you are both coming home."

"Please remove your wife from Safia's side. I have to do this alone."

Khalid slowly climbed the staircase to the bedroom with steps that felt leaden. He knew Safia would have spent the day preparing food. She was probably watching television to pass the time while she waited for him to arrive. But once he walked into the room, her life would be altered. He could hear the sounds of singing from the television. A husky drone pulled him into the room. He walked in a trance toward his wife, who was curled up on the small chaise.

"Turn the television off," he said, hearing his own voice as if from a distance and wondering if someone else had spoken.

Safia sat up and looked at Khalid without moving. Her hair had escaped from her braid and her gauzy scarf tumbled from her shoulders but she made no move to adjust it.

"Where is my son?" she asked.

"Our son has been taken from us. I have brought his body home."

The scream that filled the space between them entered Khalid's body and exploded in his heart. Although his strength had utterly deserted him, he knew he had to cover the distance that separated him from his wife. But as he walked toward Safia, he was instantly pushed backwards. She had launched herself like a torpedo at him. With her fists curled, she hammered his chest with blows.

"No! No! Where is my son! What have you done to my Hassan!"

Khalid wrapped his arms around her to stop her fury as she struggled and continued to strike him. On her face was nothing but loathing. She screamed at him with words of hate and pent-up fury. She did not ask a single question because she knew it was pointless. Her son was dead.

"Where is his body? I want to kiss my son. I made his favourite food." She slipped from his grasp and sank to the floor.

He knelt down on the floor with her, but she lashed out at him again with her feet. He kept repeating "I am sorry, I am sorry," over and over again.

"It was an accident, Safia. He fell off a mountain in Gilgit," he finally said.

Two relatives entered the room, along with Faisal. If Safia noticed, Khalid couldn't tell. She remained on the floor, rocking back and forth. For hours, she continued, unabated. It was only once Hamza arrived following his late-night flight from Bangkok that she agreed to take a sedative and go to sleep. The drugged Safia was placed on her bed, and two relatives kept watch over her for the night. Khalid, bludgeoned by his wife's grief, allowed Hamza to lead him away from the room. Once they were alone, his son pried the details of his brother's death from his father.

"What a horrible, stupid accident, Father. I am here, I am with you," moaned Hamza.

Khalid gazed at his "good son" and began weeping again.

"I need a drink. Where do you keep the alcohol in this house," Hamza asked.

"It is in the dining room cabinet. I don't drink anymore. You go ahead."

"I am going to bring you a whisky. It's good for shock."

"When this is all over, I think you should take your mother back with you to Bangkok," Khalid said.

Hamza stopped and gave his father a curious look.

"She would never leave you."

"She will never forgive me," replied Khalid.

AT MID-MORNING KHALID ventured alone to the bedroom to see Safia. She sat in an armchair, holding a framed photograph of Hassan in her hands. She looked up at Khalid.

"Is he really dead?"

"Yes. We will bury him tomorrow," replied Khalid softly.

"Why not today?"

"I am having his grave prepared in a special way," Khalid said, and knelt by the side of her chair.

"It's all right. I could never see his dead face anyway. That is not how I want to remember my son. This is," she said, lifting the picture for him to see.

"You are a brave mother, and he loved you more than anyone," said Khalid.

"He was very much like you." Safia put the photograph down.

"Me?"

"He had his own ideas and dreams. He didn't want anyone else's. You have been like that all your life, Khalid."

JUST BEFORE DAWN, two workmen had peered into the concrete chamber they had created the day before. The cement would take another half a day to dry. The bricked walkway was complete, as were two-thirds of the calligraphic verses chiselled into the stone borders over the columns.

In another part of the grounds, the whine of a saw could be heard. In a workroom, two men toiled over a large wooden box. They cut out a stencilled scroll onto the lid. They sanded the box by hand, and applied a varnish. The box was made of dark rosewood, and had gleaming brass handles fastened along the sides. Hassan's unadorned casket would be placed in this ornate box and be transported to his final resting place.

Khalid had centred himself by supervising these arrangements while the gathering family members sat with Safia and Hassan's wife. Piety was expressed by simplicity in the Muslim faith, yet Khalid's natural affinity for sumptuous artistry gained the upper hand. He knew that the greatest architecture in the world had been produced as a way to show reverence to death. If he had time, he would have studied the art of mummification and built a pyramid to house his son's remains.

By the evening, when the cement was dry in the burial chamber, Khalid had resolved to break another religious tradition. He wanted to place some objects in Hassan's grave. The objects would be covered with a platform of wood and the coffin would rest on top. The objects came from the far corners of the world, and were a selection of Khalid's favourite treasures. At Khalid's request, Faisal placed a small stepladder at the burial spot.

"Lower this ladder along one side and hold it for me, Faisal," Khalid said. "Also, make sure no one wanders over here."

Khalid descended into the square concrete burial

chamber. He instructed Faisal to take the objects from the box one by one. He placed them on the floor and stroked each one for the last time. Then he climbed out. Together, they lowered a length of wood that would cover the treasures.

A LINE OF cars filed in through the front gates the next day at noon. Khalid moved from one solemn embrace to another along the line of mourners waiting for the funeral prayer. Safia's tears had dried completely, but she remained silent and remote. Khalid did not intrude on her grief, but remained close.

The shining casket was carried by six men. Ghalib, who had flown in from Lahore for the funeral, was one of them. The casket was draped in garlands of wild roses and local jasmine and was lowered until it settled on the wooden platform. Safia walked to the edge of the grave and released a bouquet of long-stemmed white gladiolas that cascaded down onto the casket. She sighed deeply, blew a kiss to her son on three fingers, and retreated.

Hours later, Khalid acknowledged to himself that he had buried not only his son but also his vanity. He was ready to make the best deal of his life. He was going to sell his private collection to the highest bidder, but with the stipulation that it remain in the country. With a new government on its way to power, Khalid thought, the cabinet would be changed. Perhaps the new powers that be would be interested in helping to preserve his collection. His catalogue was nearly complete, and its publication would be his finest calling card. He would send it to the department of archaeology and museums at the Ministry of Culture.

THE DAY AFTER the funeral, Faisal knocked on Khalid's office door. He stood with a laptop in his hands.

"I have to show you something on Hassan's computer."

"What is it?" Khalid asked wearily.

A gift from beyond the grave appeared before Khalid's eyes on the screen of the computer. Unbeknownst to Khalid, his son had created a website called Barako. It was an inter-active virtual museum, designed for the education of chil-dren. Hassan had applied his formidable gift for technology, which Khalid had always dismissed, to showcase his father's collection. Khalid felt a belly laugh welling up from deep inside his body. He let it loose, and began to laugh until his pain released itself and vaporized. He clasped the computer to his chest and rose to search for Safia. He wanted to show her how their son's talents had been so richly entwined with his own.

TWENTY-ONE

GHALIB STAYED FOR THE meal following Hassan's funeral. He viewed the tureens of meat curries and mountains of rice with distaste. For some perplexing reason, food was always served at funerals, as though grief could only be assuaged by gluttony. He was shocked when he learned of the events that led to Hassan's death. He was at a loss for words, so he kept his distance from everyone. He had booked a room for one night at the Serena Hotel in Islamabad and would take a flight back to Lahore the next day. When he sought Khalid out to say goodbye, his host pulled him aside.

"Ghalib, the sculpture was destroyed in an explosion. I have lost a son. And you have lost some land. I am sorry. Perhaps at some later date there may be something good I can offer you in return."

"What do you mean by an explosion?" Ghalib was shocked.

"The Taliban. They killed the general whose car it was travelling in. But you will not read about it in the news,"

Khalid said and looked away.

"What a waste! So even the army is powerless against the Taliban," Ghalib said angrily.

Ghalib rode back to Islamabad in a rented car. As they reached the outskirts of the city, he noticed that new security barriers had been erected. Ghalib's driver told the policeman that they were headed to the Serena Hotel. They were told to take an alternative route as a political rally was taking place. The man suggested that they prepare for delays.

"What is happening?" asked Ghalib, leaning forward.

"The Canadian cleric, Qadri, is leading a revolutionary march from Lahore to Parliament. I have never seen anything like it. People have come from all over Pakistan," the policeman said excitedly.

"I forgot about the march! I have to see this," said Ghalib to the driver.

As the driver proceeded on an alternative route to the hotel, Ghalib called Soody.

"The man you regard as a nobody is marching to Parliament with his supporters today."

"So I hear. Don't worry; they will use the army if there is a problem. They are ready for him."

"They army cannot assault civilians just for marching. I am heading over there later."

"You are mad, Ghalib. There could be crowd-control issues. If you are determined to see this cleric, then head for the press enclosure. It's always the safest place."

Ghalib's evening would be enshrined in his memory for a long time. He found a place to sit on a concrete ledge that flanked the open-air press enclosure. He had made a few calls and secured a contact with a leading television station. Barbed wire separated the press space from the unending ribbon of people who marched down the length of Jinnah Avenue. There were people everywhere. There were men seated on the ground. There were women and children flanked by teenagers with painted faces. Nobody jostled or shouted. The calm discipline on display was completely alien to the Pakistani temperament. The cleric, who would address the crowds from a podium protected by bulletproof glass, was due to arrive soon. It was not possible, Ghalib found, to be unaffected by the anticipation. Even the press, with its silent cameras and strolling journalists, was thoroughly moved. Depending on what television or radio station you were listening to, the crowd was estimated at between fifty thousand and a hundred thousand people. It was the biggest protest march the country had seen.

While Ghalib waited for Dr. Qadri to arrive, Soody called him back.

"He will not appear. Metal containers have been placed as a barricade in front of the Parliament buildings so he cannot speak," he informed Ghalib.

"I hate to tell you this, Soody, but the people will move them for him. There is real people power assembled here."

"If that's the case, Ghalib, leave before it happens. "

"The reporters tell me that members of your party are here as well."

"Impossible!" replied Soody.

"Actually, why is your chairman not here? His pre-election promises are based on the same principles."

"We don't want to cripple the Election Commission so elections are delayed. "

"Or perhaps the chairman is a coward," Ghalib said, unable to resist the jibe.

"This man is a Canadian import. He has no credibility in this country," Soody replied.

"What about the Argentinian doctor Che who helped Castro win his revolution?" Ghalib shot back.

"Our party is going to have a landslide victory. And we don't want anyone raining on our parade. Stay safe," Soody said, and hung up.

To the left of the press enclosure a wall of canvas was spread out, blocking the crowd's view of the road. Quite unobtrusively, a few people started pushing the fabric aside. All of a sudden, Ghalib saw the reporters surge forward, with cameras aimed directly at the opening. Ghalib got off the ledge and briskly marched up to the line of cameras. The first sign of movement was the arrival of a black SUV heaped with flowers. It was travelling slowly toward the steps that led up to the podium. From behind Ghalib, an enormous cheer erupted. The man they had all been waiting for had arrived. His journey, which should have taken four hours, had taken eighteen because of the various government-installed obstacles along the route.

The flower-bedecked vehicle stopped, but no one emerged. Ghalib kept his eyes on the staircase leading up to the podium that led up to a small glass-enclosed booth. He saw a line of men pass a dark brown blanket from the bottom of the step to the top. Then the lights came on in the booth and seated in it was Tahir-ul-Qadri. He had appeared like a wizard, thought Ghalib as the chatter around him gave way to applause. In a country where political assassinations and Taliban killings were all too common, no protection had been spared. Qadri was wrapped in a bulletproof blanket so no trace of his body was visible before he was lifted up into the booth.

Ghalib was hypnotized by the sheer brilliance of Qadri's speech. His oratory was filled with a radiant new authority. It was a call to arms for those tired of the moral decay and misuse of power that plagued the country. Ghalib was so moved that he caught a glimpse of his own mortality. He left before the crowds disbanded and returned to his hotel.

WHEN GHALIB BOARDED his flight back to Lahore the next day, he clung to the euphoria induced by his experience at the march. Upon his arrival home, he found the gates of his estate open and a small group of people waiting on his front lawn. Three of them were the lawyers of his family members, whom he had avoided in the weeks since selling his land. Despite a growing sense of apprehension, he got out of the car and walked toward them.

"I have just returned from a trip. I am going to rest. Is there anything pressing?" he asked.

"We have been waiting. This is a matter of urgency about the land that was recently sold," one of them replied angrily.

"Come inside to the library," Ghalib said.

Ghalib studied the papers spread in front of him on the coffee table. Each one indicated that a war had begun. It was as he had expected: the wrath of his fellow land inheritors would be unrelenting. Litigation would tie up his property for years. Ghalib didn't want to argue, so he scooped up the papers and told the men that he would deal with it immediately.

Ghalib sat alone in the vast living room downstairs. He did not call his lawyers or even his estate manager. He had simply asked that a portable music player be brought to him. Then he inserted disc after disc of classical music and listened, as though he were attending a concert. He refused to let any stray thought enter his mind. Although his mood was contemplative, in truth, he contemplated nothing. Finally, he said to himself, "I am going to go broke." He repeated the word *broke* aloud. He knew that large sums of income would be taken away from him, but the full extent of his loss was abstract. Perhaps, he thought, he would liquidate his assets, disband his staff, and go live abroad for a spell. Suddenly, he felt that the real excitement of his life was just beginning.

He made his way to his bedroom with these thoughts in mind. Before he turned out his light, he realized that he needed to hear another voice. He telephoned Khalid.

"How are you, my friend?"

"Life is full of miracles, Ghalib." Khalid's voice boomed out.

"I am listening."

"We are gatekeepers. It is time to let in the people. And you need to take care of your health. Get rid of your bad habits."

Ghalib laughed. "My bad habits have all departed without my permission."

"Go abroad for a while. Live overseas. You can afford it. Paint and write. It will be better for your health."

"Pakistan is my home, Khalid, I could never leave it."

"Then get out of the Punjab and build a house in Islamabad. You still have that land in Margalla Hills?"

"That land is close to Buddhist caves, Khalid. Permission to build has not been given as yet. I don't need another headache. Give my regards to Safia. We will talk again soon."

"Wait! Ghalib, I want to share something with you. Hassan has taught me that life continues. What are your plans for your art collection?"

"When I die someone else will make that decision. I have no plans."

"I have leveraged my assets for a loan, Ghalib, or I would take it all off your hands," said Khalid.

"Yes, I've always feared that, Khalid." Ghalib laughed.

"I have sent you something on the computer. Tell your secretary to show it to you. Then we will talk."

"What is it?"

"This is a new way of doing business, Ghalib. You can make a lot of money without lifting a finger."

Ghalib knew that Khalid was unaware of the ongoing work on the catalogues for his various art collections. Although he had never been in a rush, he had made good progress over the previous year. His secretary was a gifted photographer and had assembled a huge collection of images that were just waiting for appropriate text. Ghalib was the only one who could supply these details, but he attended to it only once in a while. Recently, he had initiated correspondence with many international art experts whose opinions he sought. Ghalib knew that cataloguing a collection was a life's work. Perhaps Khalid had begun similar work, he thought.

GHALIB PASSED A fitful night. The large house was silent. The only person awake was the solicitous valet, who had received calls from the village where Ghalib's country home was located. A sixteen-year-old girl had been strangled to death by her father. Both the girl and the father were known to the valet, and to Ghalib himself, but the valet did not wish to wake his employer in the middle of the night to tell him the news. Horrified and anxious, the man waited through the night. It was after dawn when the intercom from the master bedroom finally sounded.

Over breakfast, Ghalib sipped fresh orange juice and digested the shocking news. He left his breakfast untouched, got dressed, and woke his driver. Ghalib then headed out on the three-hour drive to the village. He had to attend yet another funeral. He arrived at a small house that was surrounded by people preparing to leave for the burial. They looked at Ghalib in silence. He walked past them and entered the little courtyard, where a shroud-covered body was lying on a wooden pallet. A woman wailed loudly and clutched his arm. It was her mother.

"I made a mistake. If I had given you my daughter she would be alive." She beat her head with both of her hands.

Sixteen-year-old Shehla had been killed by Nilu, her father. The mother who had thwarted his desire weeks ago was bereft, yet her grief-laden logic seared him. He murmured a funeral prayer and walked away. Outside, he instructed his chauffeur to go back and give money to the mother for the funeral expenses. When they left, a few clods of dirt were hurled at the car as it cleared the small laneway. The habitually welcoming villagers were now expressing hostility toward him. Ghalib was certain that they were aware of his unreciprocated interest in the girl. He suspected her death would be justified as an "honour killing," although farming communities tended to prize their offspring as a supplementary labour force, and Shehla had worked with her parents in his fields.

Nilu had been taken to Central Jail in Sahiwal, where he would stay until he was sentenced. Ghalib travelled to the jail and asked to see him.

"There is no need, Mian sahib," said the policeman. "He has made a full confession."

"This man has worked for me for years. I have come from

Lahore to speak to him," Ghalib said, refusing to budge.

"You have to get permission from the superintendent to see him."

"I will do that. Where is he?" asked Ghalib.

"Who should I say is here?"

Ghalib eyed the man irritably and then announced his three given names. The policeman dashed off, leaving Ghalib in the stark entrance room. He returned almost immediately.

"The superintendent wants to know if you would like to have tea with him before you see the prisoner."

"No. But thank him, please. I only want to see the man."

Ghalib was escorted down a dimly lit passage that led to rows of cells. The guard took him to Nilu's cell and then walked away. Nilu sat with his back to the bars.

"Nilu, why have you done this terrible thing?" Ghalib asked quietly.

Nilu swung around and his eyes widened. He instantly dashed to the bars.

"Can you get me out? They will listen to you. You are the biggest landlord in the area."

"Nilu, you have murdered your daughter. They will hang you. Why did you do it?" Ghalib repeated.

Nilu did not answer. The expression on his face shifted from elation to sullen despair.

"Tell me. Maybe a lesser punishment can be arranged," coaxed Ghalib.

"I did it for you," said Nilu.

"You are insane!"

"I caught her with a boy near the water tank. I knew she had been seeing him for days. She had become unclean. I knew you would never take her into your house, so I got rid of her."

"That was never going to happen, Nilu. Your wife was against her coming to the house for work," said Ghalib sadly.

"No. I had made my wife change her mind. We were waiting for the next time you came to the village," replied Nilu.

"This is terrible, Nilu! You have killed your daughter. The boy would probably have married her."

"She was going to secure our future with you, and she destroyed that. Let them hang me," said Nilu.

Ghalib backed away from the bars. "You have done a horrible thing. Do not use my name in this, Nilu. She was a child. I came to deliver some gifts for the family. That is all," Ghalib lied.

"You go to hell!" Nilu screamed at him.

Ghalib turned and walked out as two guards rushed toward Nilu's cell.

"It is all right. He is mad with grief," said Ghalib, walking away.

AFTER HIS VISIT to the prison, Ghalib travelled to the Sufi shrine, where people came to find the path to heaven. The shrine was crowded. Ghalib walked up the long flight of marble steps and headed to the tomb, where he confessed silently and prayed for absolution. A life had been taken because of his cavalier sexuality.

When Ghalib returned to the car, he instructed his driver to turn the car around. "I have to go back to Nilu's house."

"They must have buried her by now, sir. They do it very fast in the villages."

There was no longer a crowd outside the house. The men had gone to bury Shehla, but the women had stayed behind. He heard the sounds of wailing as he entered the courtyard. Shehla's mother sat on the same wooden pallet that had recently held her daughter's corpse. She saw him and struck her chest repeatedly.

Without any ceremony, Ghalib walked up to her and spoke. "Where did your daughter sleep in this house?"

"We sleep in one room," she said, refusing to meet his gaze.

"What is the other room used for?"

"It is where we store the bedding, trunks, and food."

"When did you find out your daughter had died?" asked Ghalib.

"When I woke up and heard Nilu crying outside. She was in her bed, but I could not wake her." Tears flowed down her face.

Ghalib jerked away in revulsion. The woman's lie was preposterous. She would have heard her daughter struggling and making noise. When she saw his expression change, she sprang up and stood in front of him.

"He told me that if I told anyone he would kill me."

"He killed your daughter and you did not stop him."

"He is a strong man, Mian sahib. She was a slender little thing," she sobbed.

Ghalib tore out of the courtyard and got into the car.

"Drive back to the jail," Ghalib commanded. He needed to ensure there was nothing to connect him to Shehla's death.

THE SUPERINTENDENT PREPARED tea and sat down with Ghalib to discuss the murder.

"Do you think the mother was involved?" he asked Ghalib.

"No, she would've protected her daughter."

"Then the father's confession stands. He said his wife was sleeping. What is your connection to the family?" the superintendent asked casually.

"They worked on my lands at harvest. I was looking for a new maid so I visited them," replied Ghalib.

"She was a beautiful creature. It's a shame the death penalty has been revoked; he deserves to be hanged."

"Well, I must be off, Superintendent. I have a long journey back to Lahore," said Ghalib. "You're not staying at your beautiful estate?"

"I have decided to convert it into a school," Ghalib said, marvelling at the ease with which the words came out of his mouth.

"Oh, I think ancestral homes should be preserved," said the superintendent, shocked by this disclosure.

"I think people need to be educated in this country if we are to prevent crimes like this," replied Ghalib.

"Noble thought, Mian sahib. But this is the agricultural heart of the Punjab, and the young people will leave the classroom for the fields," the superintendent said as he walked Ghalib to the door.

"Your prison could do with a school too," Ghalib suggested.

"The men are trained to make blankets and other useful crafts," said the superintendent defensively.

"Well, you have a new government coming in. Perhaps they will lift the ban on the death penalty and you will have the pleasure of hanging the man who killed his daughter," replied Ghalib.

"Nothing will ever change," said the superintendent.

"We are all in for a surprise, I think," Ghalib said as he headed for his car.

"Are your referring to that mad Qadri?" the superintendent asked, following him out.

"Yes, I was at his rally."

"They will drive him and his ideas out of the country. Just wait and see."

"Yes, but people like you and I still live here," Ghalib said, walking faster to create more distance between them. "And things need to change."

TWENTY-TWO

THE WHITE UNMARKED VAN pulled up beside Adeel as
he made his way to the bus stop in Gilgit. He thrust the
ticket to Skardu into his pocket as four men surrounded
him. The brigadier had collected his marker with lightning
speed, it seemed. As he was led to the van, the men assured
him that this last assignment would buy his freedom. Adeel
knew there was no use protesting. Until the job was done,
a reunion with Norbu would be out of reach.

Many hours later, Adeel gazed out of the window of the
van and wondered how the parched wasteland flying by had
become such a hotbed of terror. They had just entered South
Waziristan in Pakistan's Federally Administered Tribal Belt.
The well-known Taliban hideout bordered Afghanistan.
Ground information about Taliban movements helped the
government to make decisive strikes. The head of the operation—a member of a special army force—explained that
a high-value target was expected in the area. A man with
Adeel's skills could help both Pakistan and its Western allies.

There was an envelope that contained photographs of the target as well as some of his close companions. Adeel's mission was to penetrate the hideout and confirm the identification of the man there. He was to be used as an informant in one of the most dangerous places in Pakistan.

The men who hid in the region's caves and mud homes used a garbled version of their faith as a political weapon. They launched regular assaults on the local army unit, whose job was to slowly chip away at the terrorist stronghold and prevent casualties. And they did not spare civilian targets either. Schools, places of worship, theatres, and markets were all blown up, leaving innocent people dead. None of it mattered to the men who considered themselves God's warriors. When they took a life, they shouted *"Allah-o Akbar,"* convinced that God had blessed the barrels of their guns, the sightlines of their rocket launchers, and the wires of the bombs they detonated.

Adeel pulled out his ticket to Skardu and looked at it. He thought he could see the outline of Norbu's face on the slip of paper. He had already convinced himself that her resilience and his thirst for her would eventually reunite them. The ability to compartmentalize his thoughts was an effective part of his training. In his backpack he carried the marble lips of the Buddha. He regarded the small piece of stone as his new protective amulet. When he took Norbu home to his mother, he would have to explain why her amulet was around Norbu's throat and not his own.

When they reached the army unit's living quarters, Adeel did not shower like the others. The men he would be infiltrating viewed personal hygiene as a sign of weakness, and he wanted to do everything possible to blend in. He was led to a large basement room where the head of the operation waited for him. The room was filled with computers, and maps were tacked on every available wall space.

"We think they are in these three homes." The major's finger tapped at an aerial photograph. "The target is expected today. They are not going to move for a few days."

"I need to see the houses," replied Adeel.

"You need a shower first."

"Sorry, sir. I may have to mingle and I want to be just like them."

The major chuckled. "All right. You are going in an armoured vehicle. A quick check is all we need."

"I would prefer to do it on foot," Adeel replied.

"This is Waziristan. Your request is absurd. You are a stranger here. You cannot just stroll into their community. Leave it to us."

"No, sir, I cannot. I am on assignment and have my own ways. I can mingle with them. I need a pair of Pathan sandals. I will take the ride, but only up to a point," Adeel said, standing his ground.

Adeel was dropped off half a kilometre from the settlement. He wore a bulletproof vest under his flowing tunic and carried nothing. It did not take him long to identify the house. The low-lying concrete home featured a hastily added extension. Smoke rose from the front, and Adeel could smell meat being grilled. A dust-laden, dented white van was parked nearby. Adeel pushed open a wooden gate and entered the front courtyard. The man who stood over the cooking grill looked at him.

"What do you want?"

"I'm looking for some water for ablutions. I want to pray," said Adeel, moving closer to him.

"There," the man pointed to an outdoor faucet. "Don't waste the water."

"Can I pray here?"

"This is somebody's house. Why are you here? Who has sent you?" the man said, suddenly suspicious.

"My brother is opening a shop near here. He was supposed to pick me up, but his car broke down. He will be here tomorrow. It is time to pray. Don't make me go out on the road for that," begged Adeel.

The man scrutinized him silently. Adeel could see him struggling with his decision before he finally gave in. Ablutions before prayers were obligatory in the Muslim religion. To deny a man the opportunity to say his prayers was a sin in itself.

"All right. Say your prayers and then get out."

Adeel knelt near the faucet. He turned on the tap and noticed the loose assembly and the crumbling mortar around it. The water poured out fitfully.

"Your tap has a problem. I can fix it for you. I know this kind of work. But let me pray first."

The man did not respond. He was bent over the grill, threading chunks of meat onto a skewer.

Adeel folded his hands on his chest and prayed. When the time came to prostrate himself, he stayed down longer than necessary and scanned the house. He knew that he was being watched by the man cooking the leathery strips of meat, so he completed his observations carefully. Finally, Adeel rose.

"I will fix your tap before I go to thank you for letting me pray."

"I know it is broken," said the man, keeping an eye on the cooking meat.

"All I need is a wrench and pliers," Adeel replied. "It will take five minutes."

The man studied him again, taking in Adeel's shabby appearance.

"Do it quickly. My guests will be here any minute. Keep an eye on the meat for me while I get the tools," he said and walked inside.

Adeel moved closer to the grill and rearranged the skewers. The man reappeared, looked at the grill, and flashed him a smile.

"You know how to cook?"

"Many trades, brother," Adeel murmured before taking the wrench and pliers.

"That tap gives me a headache every day. I'm glad to have it fixed."

Adeel squatted on the ground next to the tap. He removed the tap and then did what he had intended to do all along. He dislodged the mortar further and, with the pliers, broke the inner bush assembly. A spray of water shot out, drenching him. He shouted and jumped up.

"Everything was rotting inside. It has just broken!"

The man cursed loudly and advanced toward him, furious.

"You fool! Look what you have done. Stop this water at once!"

A telephone rang from beside the grill. The man grabbed the phone, listened, and then struck his forehead with his palm in misery.

"Can you stop the water gushing out like this? My guests are here. They are coming. You have to fix this and get out! No one is allowed in here."

"Do you have a hose?" replied Adeel. "I need a plastic pipe. I can direct the water farther along until there is a solution."

"I give you one minute for this. Stay here. Don't move!"

the man said and dashed toward the side of the house.

Adeel stayed where he was. He knew the house was empty; there hadn't been a sound or sign of movement the entire time he had been in the courtyard. The man appeared again with a long length of rubber hose. He flung it toward Adeel and went back to check on his meat.

"I need a rag to tie this with," Adeel said.

But it was too late. An SUV roared into the courtyard and almost collided with the grill. Adeel sprang up. The man jumped aside and slammed his wool cap on his head. Four men got out of the SUV. The man swung around and gestured furiously at Adeel, telling him that he should go. Adeel shuffled toward him, keeping his gaze lowered. Someone shouted at him, so Adeel pasted a bewildered expression on his face. The diversion worked. The next man who stepped out of the car was the target. The photographs that had been handed to Adeel in the brown envelope suddenly came to life. His muscles tensed involuntarily as he was grabbed roughly by the shoulder and pushed forward.

"Wait! Who is he?" asked the target, stopping to examine him.

"A fool who was trying to fix the tap, but he has done more harm than good. He just came off the road to pray."

Four pairs of eyes looked at Adeel. Despite the excitement of seeing the target and his companions, Adeel maintained his confused, humble demeanour.

"Why did you come to this house?"

"It was time for prayer and I could not find water for the ablutions. I thought this house would not mind giving me some," he said slowly.

"You are not Pakhtun?"

"My brother's wife is from here. She has some family

land and we thought we would open a shop. I am here to help."

"Get him out," said the target.

"I am sorry, brother. I can come back tomorrow to fix this. Just close the water at night," said Adeel, moving quickly toward the gate.

"Don't come back," shouted the target, extending two forefingers in the shape of a gun and pointing them at Adeel.

THE PAVED ROAD built by the army sent bone-jarring shocks through the soles of Adeel's crude leather sandals. He had first started walking fast and then broke into a run. Any change of heart with the men would result in a search for him. His army rendezvous vehicle was waiting half a kilometre away, in the same spot where it had dropped him off. The buckle on one of his sandals broke, making him stumble. He cursed, kicked off both sandals, and tossed them into a ditch by the side of the road. He shortened his stride and sprinted in his socks. When he reached the military vehicle, Adeel collapsed by its side. His socks were red with the blood from his torn heels. Back at the army compound, a doctor checked his feet.

"I am going to clean this by freezing you a little," he said. "You won't be able to wear shoes for a day."

When the doctor was done, Adeel was taken to a basement room that served as the communication heart of the base. Screens flashed and phone signals hummed. As four pictures flashed across one of the screens, Adeel made a positive identification of the target. All three people in the room let out a raucous cheer and thumped Adeel on the back. He was then handed a phone.

"So you walked into a hornet's nest and lived to tell the tale," said the brigadier.

"I have done it, sir. I have completed your assignment. I am now going to pick up the pieces of my life."

"It will take another day to arrange your transportation, as I gather you have hurt your feet?"

"I'll be able to walk by tomorrow."

"No rush. I think your woman was spotted in Skardu. Besides, you have to see the show tonight. It could be an all-nighter," he said before he hung up.

Later that evening, at an elevation of eighteen thousand feet, an aircraft received a message from the Afghan border adjoining North Waziristan. The screen in the cockpit lit up with the data collected by sensors somewhere in the United States. The images showed the concrete structure with its two adjoining mud-thatched rooms. Images moved constantly across the screen, indicating human activity. The pilot gave a thumbs-up to the slender young soldier peering intently at the screen. The soldier checked the figures on dials. He coded in the time and other logistical data. His fingers were long and steady. The only sign of tension that could be seen was in his index finger, which he used to occasionally reach up and scratch his ear. He was relaxed because he had done this countless times before. In fact, all he had to do was picture his best friend, Buzz, who had been decapitated by the Taliban, and then the blood would rush to his steady hands as he released the drone with superb precision.

Death on the ground was swift. If there was collateral damage, the governments involved would sort it out. This war would never be won, but taking out significant leaders could inflict a lot of damage. Although he had just killed four people, and reduced the surrounding area to rubble, the young soldier's thoughts were on his cabin in Vermont, where the front porch was in need of repair.

The drone hovered in the evening sky. In the Pakhtun language, it was called *darinda* — "bird of death." The locals trembled in fear, confused by how people seemed to simply disappear whenever the drone was spotted. The concept of vaporization was unimaginable to them. The underground mess, where the army officers were drinking tea, was quiet as they waited for the mission to end. Adeel was lost in his own thoughts. At the moment of the drone strike, all of the young army officers shouted *"Allah-o Akbar"* in jubilation. *I am part of this*, thought Adeel, *but only until tomorrow*. Two of the officers walked up to him and patted him on his shoulder.

"You know how long we have waited to get this guy? You will get a commendation for this one."

"I am not in the army," Adeel said.

The other officers watched him silently. They knew Adeel was a special-operations man, which could mean that he worked for both intelligences. He was a seasoned professional and a mystery, so they watched him uneasily and did not try to stop him from going to his room. Privately, they marvelled at his courage and knew they would never be able to do what he had done.

As Adeel limped to his room, he bumped into the soldier who was in charge of the spartan accommodations.

"Do you have a phone?" he asked.

"Yes, sir," the man said, pulling a mobile phone from his breast pocket.

"I just have to make one call. In my room," Adeel said.

"No problem. It is fully charged."

He dialed the number and the phone was answered.

"Mother?"

"Adeel?" she whispered.

He could hear her whisper break into a sob.

"I have been waiting. Are you safe, my son?"

"I will be home in three days. Wait for me."

He returned the phone to the soldier and asked for a tray of food to be sent to his room. When it arrived, he ate ravenously. An hour later, as he fell asleep, he gripped the small piece of the statue in one of his hands. He had stroked the marble lips as he murmured to himself, hoping his words of comfort would fly from Waziristan all the way to Norbu in Skardu.

THE MILITARY TRANSPORT took Adeel north to Miran Shah and from there proceeded east to Bannu and Kohat. He was dropped off in Peshawar, at which point he headed north by bus to Gilgit. A profound sense of déjà vu accompanied him during the trip. He had travelled this route with Norbu and General Zamir, and, finally, with the brigadier; each trip had been different in tone, and each had ended at a different destination. This would be the final trek—and this time, he would return with Norbu. There was talk on the bus that the route to Skardu was blocked, as an unseasonably early snowfall had descended on the mountains. Adeel slept in his uncomfortable seat until the bus slowed down and eventually came to a halt.

When the driver announced that there would be a delay because a section of the road ahead was not clear, the passengers disembarked to stretch their legs. Adeel was in no mood to be patient. He knew he had to find some way to continue his journey, perhaps with a vehicle that would be able to travel through the obstruction. That vehicle appeared half an hour later in the form of an electric-blue Willys Jeep with chains wrapped around the tires. As the Jeep skirted past the bus, Adeel waved at the driver and ran over.

"Can you make it to Skardu?" he asked.

"I can take you to the top of the Himalayas," said the cocky young man, smiling broadly.

"It is an emergency. I can pay you anything you want."

"Of course you will pay me," the driver said as Adeel climbed into the back.

It took the Jeep half an hour to reach the snow-covered section of the road, where an ancient snowplow was making slow progress. The driver of the Jeep laughed, saying that his vehicle could also act as a plough. He made about half a dozen drive-and-reverse manoeuvres, and, on the last try, cleared a path large enough to get through.

"If we fall into the ravine, my mother will kill me. She has arranged my marriage next week," the driver said, smiling.

"I have a lot of experience with snow," Adeel replied, thinking about his time on the glacier.

By the time the Jeep roared victoriously into Skardu, Adeel had struck up his first friendship in years. The driver, whose name was Rashid, had curly hair, a lanky frame, and a penchant for laughing through danger. He told Adeel that he had been driving this route, without a licence, since he was eighteen years old. His expertise and humour won Adeel's admiration. Adeel paid him generously and asked if he would take him back to Gilgit the following day.

"I will find a place to spend the night," said Rashid. "I will see you tomorrow."

"I hope so. I have to find someone," replied Adeel.

"Who is it?"

"She is my woman. She is somewhere here."

"Do you have an address?"

"No. It's all right; I am a tracker. I will find her," replied Adeel.

"I will help you," said Rashid, further cementing the camaraderie that had formed between the two men.

They searched for three days. Rashid did not leave Adeel's side. They roamed through the bazaars and knocked on doors. Adeel was convinced that Norbu must have found refuge indoors; the weather did not permit an outdoor existence. He knew she would not have returned to the home from which the brigadier had removed her. Above all, he hoped she did not think he had abandoned her. If that were the case, he would never find her. Fear gnawed at him. He had finally found someone to love; he could not bear the thought of losing her.

"I know she is here somewhere," he said aloud.

"Then we will find her," said Rashid. "You are a strong man and so am I." He swung an arm around Adeel.

They headed to a part of the town where a shabby government school was located. The building had a scruffy front yard strewn with mud and pebbles and two rickety wooden swings that stood motionless in the still air. A wooden fence with a gate encircled the compound. Adeel stopped and looked at the swings, thinking that, one day, a child would be injured playing on them. As he stood, taking in the front yard, a figure emerged from the entrance, carrying a short-handled broom. The woman knelt over and started to sweep the floor with fast strokes. At one point, her head covering slipped and settled around her shoulders. Adeel saw the straight black hair and knew, in an instant, that he was looking at Norbu; he would recognize her from the other end of the world. He leapt over the fence. She looked up, tossed the broom away, and ran toward him. He reached her first and closed his arms around her like an iron band. He pivoted on his heel and swung her around, lifting her clear off the ground. She laughed and kept repeating his name.

"I found a job. I clean the school. I sleep here," she said proudly.

"I have come to take you home," he said, burying his face in her shoulder.

"Yes!" She cradled his face in the palms of her hands.

He grabbed her hand and pulled her toward the fence.

"No. This way." She led him to the gate and opened it with a key. Then she placed the key on top of the gate. Together, they raced back to Rashid and the Jeep.

THE BATTERED TAXI that had driven them from the bus station stopped in front of a sturdy brick home. Adeel glanced at Norbu; two of her fingers were hooked into the amulet around her throat. She was coming to the home of strangers, and she was apprehensive and frightened.

"Nothing bad will ever happen to you here. This is my mother's home," he said as he helped her out of the taxi.

"It is a fine house," she replied.

"This is our family home. My father built it years ago but it needs some repairs." He looked at the cracked concrete of the front stoop.

The front door opened and his mother stepped out. He held Norbu's hand and walked up to her. Kisses rained on his forehead as his mother eyes filled with tears. Norbu stepped away to give the mother's and son a chance to reunite. Adeel turned to her and pulled her forward.

"Mother, this is my life. She is my heart and my destiny. Her name is Norbu."

His mother put her arm around Norbu and examined her. She noticed her son's amulet around Norbu's throat and nodded. And with that gesture, Adeel knew she understood; he would only part with it for someone special, someone who belonged to him.

"Come inside. You need to eat, rest, and wash. Your journey must have been long."

They entered the modest front room that led to a dining room. Beyond this were the two bedrooms. There were no other rooms. Adeel's sister-in-law was placing plates on the dining table.

"Ah, Adeel! You have not called your mother for weeks! Your brother is very angry with you," was her petulant greeting.

Then she noticed Norbu.

"Oh! Have you brought a maid for the house?"

"When you came into this house, we made the same mistake. I thought my son had brought a maid," replied Adeel's mother, instantly reassuring Norbu about her place in the family.

After the meal, Adeel's mother took Norbu to her room and arranged for her to bathe and rest. She pressed one of her own outfits upon her. She admired the rare beauty of the young woman who shyly consented to wear her clothes, and when she noticed Norbu's fearful body language, she was flooded with tenderness for her. She waited until Norbu fell asleep, then turned to shut the door. She almost collided with Adeel, who had been watching from the doorway.

Mother and son walked to the kitchen door and stepped out into the little back garden for privacy.

"I want the story from the beginning to the end," his mother said.

After listening for a few minutes, she interrupted Adeel.

"Are these thoughts you have about religion new?"

Adeel remained silent.

"Do you believe in God, Adeel?"

"Not in the way the religion is practised. I have seen too much violence and bloodshed from the so-called believers of the faith. I can do without it," he said.

"An old statue did this to you?"

"I think it just released something inside of me that was always there. No one has to know, Mother. I will not bring either shame or harm your way."

"People who do not believe in Islam are targeted here now. You know what happens! Christians and Shias do not feel safe. How will you protect yourself?" she said, distressed.

"I want to marry her, Mother, but I don't want a bearded mullah to perform the marriage. Will you help me?"

"What about Norbu? She is a Muslim."

"Yes and no. Her ancestors were Tibetan. They were Buddhists many years ago."

"So you intend to worship a different God?"

"I am sick of all of it, Mother!" Adeel said, raising his voice. "My beliefs are just an attribute, a way of leading the life I want. You will see in the coming days."

"I have lived in this town all my life. I will find a way for you to marry," she said, accepting Adeel's decision grace-fully. "Your father's best friend is still alive. He is a respected lawyer and he will help you."

Adeel was filled with gratitude. He knew that most of his strength had come from this woman. The love that his father had expressed for his mother had always been evident during his childhood. His mother had the grace of a woman who had experienced love and was able, in turn, to accept his love for Norbu.

"Would you like to grow something on the land and make a life here? Your brother has no interest in it," she asked him.

"Yes," he said, gratefully.

SPRING CAME EARLY in the small town. It was time to plant seedlings and to get a head start for the season. On a half-acre stretch of land, Adeel and Norbu worked side by side. They planted vegetables and worked harmoniously for most of the morning, until a row erupted. Their raised voices could be heard nearby.

"You cannot plant flowers between the vegetables! Flowers are expensive and nobody buys them here," Adeel said, trying to control his exasperation.

"We will see," declared Norbu, flinging her trowel on the ground.

"We are going home," said Adeel.

"No! I am going to dig a small pond. There is a flower that grows in water," she said as she backed away with a mischievous smile on her face.

"That flower is a lotus," Adeel said, amused.

"It is a sacred flower."

Just then, the call to prayer boomed out from the mosque. It was Friday, the day when the most important prayer of the week was recited. All of the men from town would attend the mosque for this prayer and listen to the accompanying sermon. But Adeel had no interest. The peace and harmony he sought came through the fruits of his and Norbu's labour in their field. His father's lawyer had conducted their marriage privately at home. The certificate crafted was genuine. However, the lawyer had also registered it at the local municipal office; Adeel kept another copy at home. He knew that he still had to be vigilant in his newly erected paradise.

"You can never talk about our beliefs outside of this house, not to anyone," Adeel had told Norbu after they were married.

She'd looked at him thoughtfully. "It is okay. It is here," she said, and tapped her head. "There has never been language, only feelings."

Adeel smiled at her now, grateful for the life they had built together and all it entailed.

"I have a gift for you. Do you want it?" Adeel said as he grabbed her hand.

He walked back with her to their motorcycle, which was equipped with a sidecar that they used to carry their tools and fertilizer. He lifted a small cloth pouch that he had placed there and grinned at her as she hopped up and down like an excited child. Then he drew out the small chunk of marble that was the fragment of the sculpture's mouth. He thought he saw the lips moving, but the voice he heard was Norbu's, telling him that she was expecting a child.

ACKNOWLEDGEMENTS

I thank Anwar Saif-ullah Khan for arranging "a room of one's own" in Islamabad and the use of a vintage home in the snow-capped mountains of northern Pakistan for writing the first section of the book. I salute my cousin, a retired General in the Pakistani Army, for selecting routes on a map of Pakistan. My dear friend Margaret Atwood for her customary generosity and for gamely playing the role of literary *consigliere*. Khalid Usman, Barbara Adhiya, David Dyment, Brian Fawcett, Helen Richardson Scroggie, Elizabeth Melanoir Scroggie, Carrie Flaherty, Bruce Walsh, George Gianopolous, and Deepa Mehta for simply being there at crazy times. To my wonderful editor Janice Zawerbny, who understood the book and rattled the cage. Bravo! Also deep appreciation for the hard-pressed copy editor. I thank my wonderful agent, Chris Bucci, who knows how to hold my hand and sell a book. Also *merci* to my French agent, Anne Confuron, in Paris, France. The Writers' Reserve Program at the Ontario Arts Council also assisted in the completion of the book. Finally, bravo to Sarah MacLachlan, publisher at House of Anansi, for taking a wild ride.

NAZNEEN SHEIKH has written several fiction and nonfiction titles for adult and young adult audiences, including *Moon Over Marrakech: A Memoir of Loving Too Deeply in a Foreign Land, Chopin People,* and *Ice Bangles.* Her culinary memoir, *Tea and Pomegranates: A Memoir of Food, Family and Kashmir* was a critically acclaimed success. Nazneen was born in Kashmir and went to school in Pakistan and Texas. She lives in Toronto.